SEA

CHANGE SERIES

RICHTER'S CROSSINGS

BY: S.M. DONALDSON

FORGIVENESS OF SUMMER

FALLING FOR AUTUMN

HOLIDAY WITH HOLLI

CAMELLIA IN BLOOM

SEASONS OF CHANGE SERIES

RICHTER'S CROSSINGS

BY: S.M. DONALDSON

FORGIVENESS OF SUMMER

FALLING FOR AUTUMN

HOLIDAY WITH HOLLI

CAMELLIA IN BLOOM

Forgiveness of Summer

A Richter's Crossing Seasons of Change Novella

By: S.M. Donaldson

For anyone who needed a do-over in life.

Introduction

• Due to mature subject matter this book is for readers 17+.

•This book is written in a true southern dialect, from a true southern person. Therefore, it is NOT going to have proper grammar.

Cover by: SM Donaldson
Images: Shutterstock
Editing by Chelly Peeler

Seasons of Change Novella Series

Forgiveness of Summer

A Richter's Crossing Seasons of Change Novella

Editing by Chelly Peeler

Silas

Why in the fuck do I feel like there is a mariachi band playing in my head? My damn tongue is stuck to the roof of my mouth. I finally open my eyes looking around and remember, I'm home for the summer, in Richter's Crossing. Well, possibly forever now.

I should really back off of the drinking, my body is going to go to shit. I guess it really doesn't matter since my football days are over. Getting out of bed, I trudge to the bathroom and brush my teeth praying that it gets rid of the dead taste in my mouth. I reach over and turn on the shower. Maybe, just maybe, I can wash some of the whiskey smell off of me because I know it's going to sweat out later.

Thirty minutes later, I'm in the kitchen attempting to find something edible in this house. My mom walks in the kitchen. "Hey, Silas, you look like shit."

I roll my eyes. "Well, that's real sweet of you to say, mom."

"What the fuck crawled up your ass?"

"Nothing, I'm just hung over." I say shaking my head.

She reaches in the fridge. "Here, drink some of this. A little of the hair of the dog that bit you should do the trick." I take the pitcher of Bloody Mary and pour myself a glass.

I shake my head thinking about the fact that she always keeps a damn pitcher of Bloody Marys in the fridge but she can't manage to keep some fucking food in the house.

"Mom, I need some money. I need to go buy some groceries today."

"Ugh, fine, go take a hundred out of my stash. Damien gave me some money to buy myself something nice, but I guess I'll have to buy fucking food for you."

"Well, mom, that's what most people do. Don't worry though, after today I'm going to talk to Mr. Whitman about working at the lake for the summer."

"Oh, you think they're gonna hire you when you are letting them down next season?"

"Mom, no one knows about all of that yet, and as far as I'm concerned right now, they don't need to know. No final ruling has come down yet, and if you don't want to support me totally for the summer then you'll keep your mouth shut."

She lights her cigarette and exhales. "Yeah, I guess you're right. Just go find you a damn job today. Football was supposed to be your ticket out of here and to the NFL so you could help me for a change, instead of me having to raise you."

Really, she thinks she raised me? My grandmother raised me, mom was always too busy whoring around town with old men, rich men, married men. It didn't matter as long as she made some money.

To her, I was always a scam that went completely wrong. She had a pro football player all lined up to marry her after he knocked her up with me. That all ended when he crashed his car on the interstate and died on impact, leaving his drug abusing sister with everything.

Grabbing her money out of the coffee can on top of the fridge, I head out to go talk to Mr. Whitman and shop for some groceries.

I left here at the end of my senior year a freakin' hero and now, because of some shit scandal with our athletic program that hasn't hit the media yet, I may be the biggest fucking joke in town.

Simone

Rolling over and seeing the out of town douchebag I decided to fuck last night laying on my arm is a total *Coyote Ugly* moment. To top that off, looking around I see that I not only hooked up with a tourist, but a tourist staying in one of my dad's rental cabins on the lake.

Great, just fucking great.

I try to slide my arm out from under Mr. Tourist without waking him. Luckily, he groans and rolls over and I quickly grab my clothes, sliding my panties and bra on. Quietly, I step outside the cabin door.

I hear a deep chuckle from behind me and turn around to see Silas Manning. Shit, I forgot it was summer and I might be running into him.

"What's so funny, Silas?" I roll my eyes.

"Take your pick. You trying to sneak out on your latest one night stand. You standing out here almost as naked as the damn day you were born, holding your clothes in your hand."

I roll my eyes and sit my clothes on the patio chair, turning my back to him. "Shut up, don't act like you don't sneak out of some poor *college Barbie's* room in your boxers." I say as I snatch my shirt over my head and slide my shorts on. I turn back around and smirk. "Or is it still those super hero whitey tighties?" I throw my hands up before he can speak anymore. "My life is none of your business and hasn't been for a long time."

With that said, I storm past him and down the path to my house. Silas and I had been best friends growing up. We both knew what it was like to grow up with only one parent. Don't get me wrong, my daddy is a good man, he just wasn't prepared for raising me by himself. He would have been better off raising a boy. My mom took off and was always chasing her latest man. This week, she's in New Orleans, probably methed out and on the arm of someone old enough to be her great granddaddy. She really is a whore.

Silas's momma is a piece of work, she's a lot like my mom minus the drugs, but add alcohol. He and I pretty much raised ourselves. We grew up spending our summer's hanging out on this lake, doing odd jobs for my daddy to make money. Once we were in high school and he started playing football, he started hanging out with the jocks and cheerleaders. That wasn't my crew, I was more of a loner.

Let's just say him parading twatty cheerleaders in front of me constantly didn't make me join his fan club. He practically left here at the end of our senior year in a parade down Main Street on a fucking toilet paper float. He was gonna be Mr. College Football and then Mr. NFL Football. He forgot me and everything he promised.

Opening the back door to my daddy's house, I'm hoping he's not here. I'd rather not do the walk of shame in front of him many more times. I've got to get my own fucking place. I know I smell like whiskey, cigarettes, sweat and sex.

I manage to slip into my bathroom and get in the shower before he hears me. Twenty minutes later, I'm standing in my bedroom and the only thing I have on is the towel around my head when my door opens.

"Shit!" We say at the same time. I grab my robe quickly off the bed and hold it in front of me.

"Sorry, Tom said I could use the bathroom back here. I guessed the wrong door."

"Really, Silas? What the fuck are you doing here?" I manage to slip in my robe and tie it.

He throws his hands out in frustration. "I came to talk to your dad about a job."

"Mr. Football needs a job?" I say with my hands on my hips.

"Yes, if I would like to eat this summer." He turns to walk off.

"So, Dee Dee still doesn't grocery shop, huh?"

He starts walking away from the door. "Nope. Nice tat, by the way."

I walk over and slam my door. He fucking pisses me off so bad. Plus, I can't believe he saw my tattoo just above my pubic hairline.

It hurts, we used to do everything together. We worked together, skinny dipped together (until Daddy caught us), drank together, tried pot for the first time together and hell, we were even each other's first kiss. Then, he just dropped me. At first he acted like he wanted me to come to the games with him. I could only hear the cheerleaders refer to me as his lesbian friend so many times, though, before I just didn't want to go.

So, it started that summer and just never ended. I find random guys whenever I feel the need, guys I know I'll have no attachment to, and screw their brains out. I'm not a whore, I don't have sex to see what I can get from someone like my mom does, and it's not every single night or anything. I've just been let down my entire life. If I don't let anybody in, I can't be let down anymore. I'm in charge this way.

Silas

Fuck!!!! I did not expect to see her naked. I knew that was her room, hell I've known which room was hers since we were seven. I was just going to fuck with her, I didn't expect to see her the way I did. I know I kinda saw her this morning coming out of the cabin, but not full frontal and still a little wet from her shower. That damn tattoo, I didn't get a great look at it, but fuck, it was sexy. She's still so hot. Man, I'm fucked.

I walk into the living room where Tom walks back in. "You find the bathroom's in the same place it's always been?"

I chuckle. "Yes, sir." I can't let on that I just saw his daughter fucking hot, wet and naked.

"Okay, well I'm glad your back. I really need some help this summer. I know the past couple you've stayed at college, so it's a blessing you are here. Simone is great with some stuff, but I'm getting too old to do all of the maintenance by myself anymore. So, let's go walk and make a list." He slaps me on the shoulder and looks at me seriously. "I'm really glad you're home this summer, son."

"Thanks, Tom." Even though I really didn't want to be here this summer. We were all sent home until they figure out who was and wasn't involved in the scandal.

Tom and I walk around making a list of all the things that need attention around the lake. It's funny how much older he looks from just being gone a couple of years.

I remember him being a big man, he seemed larger than life to a boy.

Simone and I met in kindergarten, she and I would share snacks. She asked me over one day to play and I never wanted to leave. I love this lake, and so many times growing up I had wished that Tom was my dad. My grandma did a really good job raising me, but I wanted a guy around. When my grandma died the summer before my freshman year in high school everything changed.

All my grandma had asked me to do was find true love and be successful, so I played my heart out playing football. I knew football was my only ticket out of this town, so I had to be the best. Sometime during the chase for my dreams, I lost Simone.

I wanted her there for all of my games and everything, but after a while it was like she just slipped away. We didn't even really see each other at the lake much anymore. I couldn't work as much as I always had because of football, but Tom always understood. He kept pushing me to achieve.

Little by little, the Simone I knew slipped further and further away. Then, I heard all the cheerleaders talking about how she was hooking up with random guys and my heart broke a little. I mean, when she didn't seem interested in me I started dating different girls, but I never wanted her to be like that. She's never had a serious boyfriend, I don't think. I heard her tell a guy one night down by the lake that she doesn't do commitment. That trusting someone hurts too much.

"Silas, did you get all of that?"

I nod. "Yes, sir. I'm gonna head down to Tackett's and grab some supplies. Do I need to take a check or do you still have an account down there?"

"I still have an account. You don't have to get started today, I know you just got home. If you've got some things you need to do today, I understand."

"No, it's cool, I'd rather get started than go back to Dee Dee's. Some things don't change, you know?"

He nods sympathetically and shakes my hand. “Fine then, go get started.” He turns to walk away and turns back. “Silas, how about soon you tell me why you’re home this summer?”

I shake my head. “You could always tell when I had something else in my head.”

He nods. “Yep.”

I lean against a tree. “There is a scandal going on at the college. There were some tests stolen. When they dug deeper, they figured out there’s been a lot more than that going on with some of the athletic departments, football included. I wasn’t involved, but enough of our guys were that we were all sent home for the summer while they investigate. We aren’t supposed to talk about it. The college is in deep shit.”

He nods his head. “Okay. I understand why you didn’t want to talk. Just know sometimes the good Lord closes a door to open a window. Well, head on down to Tackett’s, I’ll be here when you get back.”

“See you in a bit.” I run out to my truck and hop in. My truck is old and as a matter of fact, I bought it from Tom a few years ago, but it’s mine.

It’s weird. Here I was this great guy, a star. Everyone’s hopes and dreams hung on me. At college, I’m just the poor kid on a scholarship that drives a fifteen year old truck. I’m the kid that is supposed take a corrupt football team to a national championship. Now, I’m probably not any of those things. I’m probably the shithead kid that’s going to be stuck in this town with nothing and no one.

Simone

Walking down to the rental office, I see Daddy and Silas making a list. I guess it is a good thing he's here. Dad really does need some help with some stuff around here, and Silas does know what to do. I would help but it's shit I can't do.

Unlocking the office door, it's the same routine every morning - turn on the computer, turn on the lights, check the email and check the voicemails. During the regular school year, I take some classes at the local college, but the summer time is too busy here for me to do that now.

I sit down to check the voicemails and it's pretty much the usual people wanting to make last minute reservations that we can't accommodate because we're fully booked. *Daddy really needs to build about six more cabins.* Wait, he has a doctor's appointment this week? He had one last week, what the hell? I write it down and remind myself I need to ask him what's going on.

The day is going pretty busy and before I know it lunch time is already here. *Man, I wish we had like a snack shack here or something.* I warm a cup of Ramen Noodles and sit back down at my desk when I hear the bell go off on the door. Great, I can't even get a minute to eat.

Suddenly, he rounds the corner and runs right into me. "Shit, I'm sorry, Mone."

"Don't call me that."

He puts up his hands defensively. "Sorry."

"I thought you were another customer."

"Oh, sorry. I just came in to get a bottle of water. I had a few in my cooler but I ran out. I swear it's already over a hundred out there." He says as he strips his sweaty t-shirt off. Fuck, he still looks edible.

"Put your damn shirt back on. This is an office, not a locker room."

He tugs it back on. "Sorry. When did you get so bitchy?"

I sit back down to my lunch. "About the time you got so fucking conceited."

Oh, I've pissed him off now, I see the steam rolling off of him. "Fuck you, Simone!" He grabs a six pack of water and goes out the door slamming it.

My daddy walks in a few minutes later. "Well, it looks like you and Silas are already off to a great start."

"Yeah, well, he's so charming and all." I say with sarcasm dripping off my tongue.

"Just try to get along with him, he'll be a great help to me this summer. I don't know what happened between you and him. You guys were best friends for the longest time."

I shake my head. "It's complicated, Daddy. Anyway, enough about him. Dr. Spark called, you have an appointment this week. Didn't you just have one last week? What's going on?"

He shrugs. "I'm getting old, they like to do blood work all the damn time. They should just put in a valve."

"So it's just blood work?"

"Yes, honey, they are just doing more blood work." He quickly turns and heads back out of the room.

He's hiding something. I bet Dr. Spark is getting on to him about his blood pressure again.

I don't get much time to think about it because the phone starts ringing off the hook. On the plus side, it makes my afternoon go faster.

Next thing I know, it's after five when my dad walks back in the office. "So, honey, what are you going to do tonight?"

"I'm just going to head into town for some food. I promise I'll be home at a decent hour tonight."

He hugs me. "Please do. I worry when you stay out so late."

I nod. "Okay, Daddy."

An hour later, I'm walking into the Tavern Inn, a local bar and grill. I sit down at the bar and Tuck, the bartender, looks at me. "What can I get for you tonight, Simone? The usual?"

"Yeah, just make sure that asshole cook puts some hot peppers in it tonight and extra hot sauce. Last time that shit was weak."

He nods, walking off laughing to get my beer and put in my order for a nuclear hot buffalo chicken wrap.

I notice someone sit down beside me. "So, you still trying to blow holes in your stomach with all the spicy stuff?"

I roll my eyes and look at Silas. "Yeah, and?"

"Look, I'm just trying to make conversation. We are going to be working together this summer so maybe we, you know, should be able to speak to each other. Just a little."

"Fine. Yes, I still like spicy food." I turn as Tuck sits my beer and wrap down. "Look, I'm leaving as soon as I finish my food, so you'll have the run of the bar."

He goes to say something and then he stops. He stands up. "Nice talking with you, Mone." He walks away.

ASSHOLE!

Silas

Fuck, she is going to drive me insane. I'll never know what I did to her. She's the one who dropped me. The best thing I can do is walk away for the time being. I see a couple of the guys I went to high school with sitting in the corner and I walk over.

"Hey, guys."

Jake stands up. "Hey, man. Great to see you." He gives me a back slapping guy hug.

Zack stands up next doing the same thing.

I motion to the table. "Mind if I join you guys?"

Jake smiles. "Nah man, grab a chair. We need to catch up."

I look at them. "So, how's it going at State?"

They both nod. "Pretty good, man. How's it going for you? You guys think you got a shot at the Championship this year?"

I shrug. "I don't know, man. It's different every year." I signed a contract that said I wouldn't say anything until the investigation is over.

"So, you working for Tom this summer while you're home?"

I nod and take a swig of my beer. "Yeah. Need to make some cash and he could use the help."

Jake nods. "So I saw you talking to Simone. She still her usual bitchy self?"

I laugh and nod. "I don't know what I ever did to her, she used to be my best friend."

Zack smiles. "Well, I think you're the only person in town she never slept with, aside from me and Jake here." Jake rolls his eyes at Zack.

I put my hand up. "Hey, she isn't that bad."

Zack shrugs. "No, she's into out of towners. Never wants to be with someone she might see again, I guess."

I see Jake motion behind us. I look back and see Simone take a few shots and then get her check to leave. Then, I see Claire, a girl we went to school with. She was a cheerleader and always had a thing for me. I had sex with her one time before I knew what she was really like and she practically tried to act like we were engaged or something.

She struts over to me. "Well, look who blew into town for the summer." She practically purrs.

"Hey, Claire. Nice to see you." I say trying to make a general conversation. Then she takes it upon herself to sit in my lap.

I look up to see Simone notice. She slams some money on the counter and stands up to leave.

I try to push Claire off my lap but she won't budge. "So, you home for the whole summer?"

"Yes. I'm working out at the lake. Claire, can you move to your own chair, please?"

She huffs, moving to the empty chair next to me. "So you are working with the town slut again?"

"Okay, she isn't the town slut and yes, I'm working for her father."

I stand up. "Now if you'll excuse me, I have a long day tomorrow." I nod to Zack and Jake. "Thanks for the seat guys, I'll see you around."

Jake nods and Zack nods. "See you, man."

I have to get away from Claire and her grabby hands. Plus, I still need to go to the grocery store and I need to check on Simone.

I walk out into the parking lot and see Simone pulling out in her jeep. I climb in my truck and drive down the street to the Piggly Wiggly. I get out of the truck and see that Simone is actually here, too. Shit, she's gonna swear I followed her or something.

I walk in and grab a buggy. I make my way around the store, grabbing whatever a hundred dollars will get me. Some fruit, a couple of packages of meat, some stuff to make for lunch, a case of water, and stuff for breakfast.

I walk up on Simone on the aisle with canned goods.

"Hey." I throw my hand up.

"Hey, done at the bar so soon?"

"Yeah. I needed to get some groceries and head home. You know, long day tomorrow."

She nods. "Yeah. Just grabbing a few things for the office myself." She throws some canned chicken, ramen noodles and canned meals in her buggy.

I smile. "I still wish Tom would do like a sandwich cart or something out there."

She laughs. "I was just thinking that today."

I nod. "Okay, well I'll see you in the morning." Man, it's great to see her smile.

She nods and starts walking to the check out. “Yeah, see you in the morning.”

I grab a few things of noodles and canned soup, then make my own way up to the front of the store to check out. The cashier is another girl I went to school with, but she was always kind of a quiet girl.

“Hey, Silas. You home for the summer?”

“Yeah, I am. How are you doing, Mary?”

She smiles. “I’m doing good. I work here and go to school at State, I’m almost finished.”

She hands me my change. “Great, well I’ll see you around. Have a good night.”

She smiles. “You, too.”

Simone

Okay, so we had a half way normal conversation in the Pig. I'm still not going to put too much thought into it.

When I get home, I see my daddy sitting in his desk chair in his home office. I stick my head in the door. "Hey, Daddy. What are you doing up so late?"

"Ah, just going over some papers and stuff. Writing out some bills so you don't have to."

"Good, well I picked up some groceries. I'm gonna get them put away and then I'm going to get to bed."

"Okay. Did you have a good wrap down at the bar?"

I laugh because my daddy knows me better than anyone. "Yeah. Tuck made sure they got enough peppers and hot sauce in it this time."

He laughs. "My momma was like that, she had a damn cast iron stomach, I swear."

I walk over and give him a kiss on his temple. "Night, Daddy."

"Night, baby."

I get the groceries put away, except for the few dry items I'm taking to the office. I put all the cold stuff I'm taking to the office in one of the shopping bags and sit them in the fridge to grab in the morning.

~*~*~

Silas and I did our best today to be pleasant to each other. I will say, though, I'm relieved that the day is over. I'm ready for a drink, something spicy and maybe something of the male gender. I have so many thoughts going through my mind, I need to escape for a little while.

I run home and throw on my jean skirt, boots and a red tank top. Checking my make-up and running a brush through my hair, I head down to the Tavern.

Walking through the door, I see that Tuck must be off tonight. That bitch Claire is working. Great. Just fucking great.

I don't take my normal seat at the bar, I take a seat at a booth in the corner. At least this way she and I can ignore each other. We've never gotten along, especially after we got to high school. She was dead set on getting Silas and I'm sure she did a few times. She reminds me so much of his damn mom it's a shame.

She's the one who told everyone that I was Silas's lesbian friend. That is the reason none of the other guys ever talked to me. I'm sure of it. I spent my high school years a lot like I do now. Alone, with out of town strangers.

Sitting in a corner in the library, no one could tell I was here. I hear the cheerleaders come in, but I always try to ignore them.

"So, Claire, I see you've set your sights on Silas."

"Yep." She says, popping the p.

"Well isn't he with that girl from the lake? Simone?"

"Oh, they aren't like that. Didn't you know? She's not into guys, if you get my meaning. Why else would Silas be hanging out with her? She's not pretty."

"Oh God, I have Bio with her! I hope she doesn't hit on me."

"What can I get for you?" One of the waitresses has come over to take my order.

"Ah, yeah. I'll have some nuclear hot buffalo wings, beer and a shot of whiskey."

I hear Claire let out a squeal. "Silas! Sweetie, come on over here and have a seat."

Great, Silas is here. I don't know if I can handle seeing her rub all over him again tonight. I can't watch it. I try to catch the waitress's attention and tell her just to cancel my order, but I can't.

Great. I try to concentrate on the table and play a game on my phone.

Maybe if I don't look up no one will notice I'm here.

The waitress brings me my beer and shot. I know if I'm staying here I'm gonna need more. I look up at her. "Hey, go ahead and bring me another shot. Actually, two."

"Sure." She scoots off back to the bar.

Thirty minutes later, I've had my three shots and I'm on my second beer. Finally, they bring my wings out and I eat them. I've managed to stay pretty well under the radar while I've been here. This back corner is my friend most definitely.

After coming back out of the bathroom, I see that some guys have taken over my booth. When I make my way back over to the booth, one of the guys look up at me. "Hey, sorry, did we take your table?"

I shake my head. "No, I was leaving anyway."

The spokesman looks up. "Why don't you join us?"

"No thanks, I was really just going." I start toward the door.

The spokesman stops me. "Hey, my name is Clint. Will you at least dance with me?" He holds up his finger. "Just one dance and I promise I'll leave you alone."

I shrug. “Fine.”

The DJ is playing a slow country song, he looks at me. “What’s your name, beautiful?”

“Simone.”

“You really are beautiful, you know.”

I look down. “Um, thanks.”

“Hey, don’t look down when someone compliments you.”

“Sorry, it’s just that most people don’t call me beautiful.”

He shakes his head. “Then that’s their loss. If they don’t see you as beautiful, they must be blind.”

I smile. “Thanks. Where are you from?”

“Just north of Atlanta.”

“How long are you here for?”

He motions back to the table. “Well, my buddies are here for a week, but I’m possibly moving here. I’m here looking at a job.”

Nope, can’t burn off stress with him, as pretty as he is. “Well, this is a nice place to live.”

“Good to know.”

The song ends and I step back. “Thanks for the dance, but I’m gonna go now.”

“Hey, wait, let me at least get you one more drink before you go.”

I shake my head. "No thanks, I've had my limit for the night." I walk to the front door. I reach in my pocket and realize I must've left my keys in the bathroom.

I breeze back in without being noticed. Thank God my keys are still on the vanity. I grab them up to rush back out.

As I walk back through, I see Silas giving Clint a horrible stare down. It must be because Clint is in a pretty intense conversation with Claire.

As I try to sneak back by the bar without being seen, Clint raises his voice. "What the hell, Claire? You told me she was going to be a sure thing. I had the guys all lined up to come back to the room a few minutes after I closed the deal."

I stop in my tracks and look back to the three other guys sitting in the booth. Then, I hear Claire speak up. "Normally she is. It's probably just the fact that she's still hung up on someone she'll never have."

I try to quietly ease my way out, but before I can, there is a commotion at the bar. I see Silas punching Clint in the face. Shit.

The bouncer breaks them up and Silas says he'll leave. I quickly scurry toward the door, not paying attention, and I run into a waitress. A tray full of drinks falls to the ground.

I look down at her. "I'm so sorry." I step over her and run out to my jeep. Once I'm in the safety of my jeep, I spin gravel all over the place leaving. I've got to get out of here and go to my happy place.

Silas

Claire all over me like some sort of skank was not the way I had planned tonight. I just wanted to come in, grab a drink from Tuck, and hopefully get to have a nice conversation with Simone. When I came in the bar, though, I didn't see her so I sat at the bar. After Claire made such a fool of herself about me, I noticed Simone in the corner, trying not to make eye contact with anyone.

I seem to get a little relief from Claire when a group of guys walk in. She starts chatting them up and being her obnoxious self.

Ugh, I wish Claire would shut up. I'm about to go sit with Simone when I see her get up and go to the restroom.

I see Claire and one of the guys nod at each other knowingly. The guys make their way over to Simone's booth. When she comes back out they say something to her, but I see her motion that she was leaving. Good. Those guys seem a little weird.

As she's walking for the door, the guy that was talking so much to Claire stops her and asks her to dance. They dance and then I can tell he's trying to get her to join him for a drink, but she declines.

Good girl. I really can't stand the thought of her being with other men. It's always made me mad that I wasn't her one. I wish the two of us could've been each other's only ones, and I thought we would be, but I don't know what happened.

As Simone slips out the door, I see that guy make a beeline for Claire. They are having words and then he raises his voice.

"What the hell, Claire? You told me she was going to be a sure thing. I had the guys all lined up to come back to the room a few minutes after I closed the deal." My blood boils.

I'm about to say something when I notice that Simone didn't leave, she's still standing there. She's heard everything.

Claire's damn voice breaks my concentration. "Normally she is. It's probably just the fact that she's still hung up on someone she'll never have."

That guy says something else about his friends and the gangbang scenario they had in mind for Simone. I can't take it. I lunge at the guy, punching him in the face.

The bouncer, Pat, who I've known since high school, breaks us up. I glare at Claire knowing she set this up. Why on earth would you do that to someone?

I put my hands up at Pat. "I'll go, I was leaving anyway."

I notice movement and hear a commotion near the door. I see that a waitress got knocked over, I'm guessing by Simone, who I see bolting for the door.

I reach the parking lot just in time to see her tail lights and her spinning gravel everywhere.

I shake my head. I need to talk to her. I have to know she's okay. I know we are just getting our friendship back but I need to know she's okay.

I pull up at her house but her jeep's not there. I drive to the office, but no luck there either.

Then, it hits me. I wonder if she still goes to that old boat house? It used to be our hiding spot.

I see fresh tire tracks ahead of me on the two-trail road leading in to the boat house. I drive slowly down, this path seemed so much bigger when we were growing up.

I can see the oil lamp is lit through the old cracked window when I pull up. I walk over to the door and push it open. She's sitting there staring out at lake.

I hear her sniff. "Congratulations, you found me."

"It wasn't real hard. You always come here when you're running."

She looks over at me and her eyes are red from crying. "Why in the fuck do you pretend to know anything about me? Why don't you go back and let Claire fuck your brains out? You don't know me, you haven't for a long time! Why can't you just go away?"

I don't know why but how she acts is pissing me off. I'm tired of not knowing what I've done to her. She dropped me as her friend, not the other way around.

I storm over to her, getting practically in her face. "What in the fuck is your problem with me? I've never done anything to you."

"Right!"

"I was always your friend, Simone. You dropped me."

"Sorry if I couldn't handle being called your lesbian friend and watching you parade a new skank in front of me every day!"

"I never called you a lesbian."

"No, you didn't, but your girlfriend did."

"What girlfriend?"

"Claire. She told everyone in school that I was a lesbian and you never said anything."

"Claire wasn't my girlfriend."

"Fuck buddy, whatever. Look, why don't you just leave me alone. I can handle my own life, I've been doing it for a long time now."

"Oh yeah, you handled it tonight all right. You almost went off with some guy planning to bring his friends in and gangbang you in a motel room!"

"Fuck you. I didn't plan on going anywhere near his room."

"Oh, but you do normally. Only strangers, right? Never the same guy twice."

She slaps me across the face. "Just because you and the fuck heads of this town never wanted me doesn't me that no one else does."

I grab her shoulder and slam her into the wall. I press my mouth into hers. "I never wanted you? Does this feel like I never wanted you?"

She tries to shove me back. "I'm not your pity fuck."

"Pity fuck? Seriously?" I grab her around the waist and sit her up on an old cleaning table. I slam my mouth back on her, tugging her shirt over her head. "Don't ever fucking say that again."

I unclasp her bra and drop my mouth to her nipple. She cries out. "Ah. Shit."

I work my mouth back up to hers. She fists my shirt, pulling it over my head. I reach under her skirt and snatch her panties so hard they break.

She fumbles with my belt and pants, getting them open, and I shove them down a little. I slam into her warm wet sex.

"Does this feel like pity?" I growl at her.

"No. Oh. God. Fuck me. Harder."

I slam into her harder and harder until we are both screaming out as we come.

I pull out, pulling my pants back up, and turn to walk out. “Don’t ever say that I didn’t want you. I’ve always wanted you.”

I walk out before she can say anything else and before I can fuck anything else up.

Simone

It feels like this week has almost flown by. The night in the boat house confused me about Silas and me even more than I was already. I haven't been back to the Tavern since that night either. I don't think I've ever been that embarrassed in my life.

Neither of us have spoken about what happened between us. I will say that no sex I've ever had could compare to that. The way he just grabbed me and took charge in the moment pissed me off. Now, it just fucking turns me on.

He and I have both tried to stay pleasant toward each other this week for my daddy's sake. He pretty much stays out of my office as much as possible, and I try to be nice when I see him in town.

I know him being here helping Dad is a good thing. We need him. He's already repaired the dock, some of the decks around the property and some issues inside some of the cabins. I could never do all of that.

Speaking of Daddy, he should be in from his appointment soon. It was first thing this morning.

As if he's reading my thoughts, he comes through the door. "Hey, baby girl. How's it going today?"

I shrug. "Okay. We really gotta look into adding a couple of more cabins at some point. We are booked out all the way through Labor day and then some."

He nods. "Yeah. Can you handle things here today? I need to meet with some of the local businesses." He waves his hands around. "Some kind of local business chamber crap."

I nod. "Yeah, sure."

"Hey, how about we grill some steaks tonight for supper? I'm hankering some red meat."

I laugh. "Sure, Daddy. I'll run to the Pig and grab a couple. Then I'll go home and lay them in to marinate."

He nods. "Good. Radio Silas and ask him to watch the office for ya." He turns to walk out. "Oh, and invite him over."

Fuck. "O-kay." No way am I going to try and explain to Daddy why Silas and I don't need to be in the same room.

"You know he could use a good home cooked meal." I nod and he smiles. "Good, see you in a little bit."

As he walks out the door, I take in how strange that conversation was.

I pick up our little work radio. "Silas."

"Yeah."

"Can you come up and cover the office in a little bit? Dad is out in town and I need to do something for him."

"Yeah. I can come right now. That okay?"

"Yeah."

A few minutes later, he walks into the office. "Hey, you leaving now?"

"Yeah. I gotta go grab some steaks and put them in to marinate. We are grilling this afternoon and he wants you to join us."

He shrugs. "Okay. What time?"

"Um, maybe around 7."

He nods. "Didn't he have a doctor's appointment today?"

"Yeah, he went this morning. Then he had some local business bull crap in town."

He sits down at the office counter. "Oh, okay then. Has he been feeling okay?"

I turn around to him. "Yeah, why?"

He shrugs. "I just never remember him going to the doctor, and well, he just seems to be acting a little different."

Who does he think he is trying to tell me something is wrong with my dad? "Sorry, I'm sure he's changed a little since you flew out of town a couple of years ago like your ass was on fire."

"Simone, don't be so bitchy about it. I was just simply stating what I've noticed."

I storm for the door. "I'm going to take care of this, don't fuck up a bunch of my stuff while I'm gone."

I slam the door going out to my jeep. When I finally get in the safety of my jeep, I fall apart. I can't stop crying and I'm not sure why. Maybe it's because I know he's right about something being wrong with my dad.

I dry up my face and make my way down to the Piggly Wiggly to get the steaks, I grab some salad mix and baking potatoes while I'm there.

I go to check out and Mary from school is my cashier. "Hey, Simone. How's it going?"

I smile. "You know, it's going, we're busy out at the lake."

"I was at the bar the other night. What Claire did was really ugly. Well, that's not unusual from her, she's still so hung up on Silas."

"Well, she can have him and he can have her. I don't know what her problem ever was with me."

She laughs. "You're kidding, right? She always knew Silas was in love with you. She was jealous."

I start laughing. "Silas was never in love with me."

She hands me my change. "That's what it looked like to everyone else."

Taking my groceries out to the car, I wonder why she thinks Silas was in love with me. Well, that's for me to figure out another day, I need to get back to the office. I run home, set the steaks in marinade and go back to take over for Silas.

I open the door and see Silas on the phone. "Yes, ma'am. I'll be right there to check things out."

I nod. "Hey, what's going on?"

"Cabin 4 has a pipe leaking, I'm gonna go take a look."

"Thanks. Anything else I need to know?"

He shakes his head walking to the door. "Nope, you seem to have it all figured out. Everything and everybody." He slams the door behind him.

I flop down in my chair, then open up the plans I've been drawing up on my computer for some new cabins and a snack shack. I always pull them up and tinker with them when I get depressed. When I need to dream about my future. My future, here, just me, alone like I've always been.

Silas

How does she do this to me every fucking time? All I did was ask a question about her dad. He's been looking pale and going to the doctor, I'm just concerned. Does she really feel like I just forgot everything and everyone in this town?

She keeps my head a screwed up mess. Like the other night in the boat house. I don't know what came over me, I just had this need to make her mine and make her know it.

I think it all failed, though. She started spouting off that shit about me never wanting her and her being a pity fuck. How could she not see?

The reason the guys we went to school with never talked to her is because they all knew. The guys knew she was mine.

Sure, I dated other girls. In my defense I was young and stupid. I got to high school and got attention I'd never gotten from anyone. By the time I realized I was in love with Simone, she'd faded into the back ground like an old memory. Zack made an attempt one time to ask her out and after I nearly beat his ass, I made my point known. After that, guys our age pretty much steered clear of her.

I tried getting her to come to my games again or just to hang out but she always had plans.

Then, the guys starting giving me shit when she started the whole sleeping with strangers thing. So, I just kind of gave up. I backed away. I looked like some love sick douche.

I spend the rest of the day working on things around the lake, trying to keep her out of my head. It isn't working too well. I've hit my head numerous times, hit my thumb with the hammer and I just dropped a board on my toe.

I glance at my watch and see it's almost time to be at Tom's for supper. No shower for me, I guess. Good thing I always keep an extra set of clothes in the truck.

When I pull up to Tom's house, I see that he's already grilling. I step out of the truck and he smiles.

"Hey, son. You just finish working?"

"Yes, sir. One of the cabins had a leak and then I just got busy. I'm gonna run in and change clothes. I didn't have time to run home and shower."

He waves his hand. "Go on in and take a shower. It'll be a few minutes before the food is ready."

I nod. "Okay, thanks."

Making my way in the house that I practically grew up in is nerve racking. I need to shower but I'm not sure if I'm ready to run into Simone yet this afternoon.

I hear her in the kitchen so I decide just to slip down the hall and take a quick shower.

I strip down and glance in the mirror, seeing some dried blood on my forehead. I lean closer to the mirror to inspect it.

Abruptly, the bathroom door opens and Simone is standing there. "What are you doing in my bathroom?"

I reach over, shoving the door closed behind her since I'm standing here butt ass naked. "Tom told me I could take a shower in here. I was just about to jump in."

"Oh. Look, we need to try and get through this dinner for my Dad's benefit, okay?"

I prop against the vanity, acting like it doesn't bother me at all that I'm naked and she's fully clothed. "I can get through a dinner with you. You seem to be the one that has a problem with me."

"Are you even going to attempt to be a little modest in front of me?"

I let out a small laugh as I'm turning on the shower. "Oh honey, let's not pretend like we haven't seen each other in all of our naked glory several times growing up." I lean down to her ear and whisper. "Especially the other night when I had you screaming my name and coming like a fountain all over my dick." I run my hand down over her breast while still having my lips on her ear. "You do remember that, don't you?"

She shudders. "Yes." Finding her balance, she backs away and stares at me defiantly like when we were kids. "I just remember someone coming at me like a mad man and tearing my fucking clothes off." That spite she has, it's just one of the reasons I've always known I loved her. As much as she knows she loved the other night, it wasn't on her terms so she's going to fight about it. She wants control. Well, I'm not giving it to her.

"Oh baby, if you wanna go again right here, just let me know." Looking down at myself and the stiff erection that's now sticking glamorously out there. "We are already half way there."

She lets out an angry growl. "Just shut the fuck up. Supper will be ready in about fifteen minutes." She turns to grab the door knob.

I grab her hand and spin her around, pinning her to the door, and slam my mouth into hers. "Just so you know, the other night was no accident, and it will be happening again." Without another word, I step back and open the door to the shower and climb in.

Twenty minutes later, we are sitting down to the supper table. Tom grilled steaks and Simone made some baked potato casserole and a big salad.

I look up to both of them. “Thanks for inviting me to supper. I don’t get too many home cooked meals.”

Tom nods. “Well, we are happy to have you helping us this summer. In all honesty, I would probably have to hire a crew of workers to do what you’ve done. I just want you to know how much I appreciate it.”

I nod. “Thanks. I’m glad to have a job here.” I glance over at Simone, catching her eye. “It’s starting to feel like old times.”

Simone doesn’t say much through supper, she mainly listens to Tom and I talk about work around the lake, football and any other kind of sport.

Once we finish eating, she stands up and starts to gather our plates. Tom excuses himself to the living room. I start helping clear the table and carry things back into the kitchen.

Once we are in the kitchen, I take every chance I can to touch her.

By the time we are finished, I see all of the pent up frustration and lust built up in her eyes.

My cock is pressing so hard against my fly, it’s going to have my zipper print tattooed into it.

Adjusting myself, I walk through the living room to tell Tom good night, as Simone walks in behind me.

“Well, Tom, thanks again for dinner.”

“Don’t leave just yet. I need to talk to you two.”

Shit, he knows about the bathroom. Fuck. No, he would have killed me earlier.

Fuck, one of the customers complained about us, maybe they saw our fight earlier.

"Both of you get those guilty looks off your faces. This isn't anything you've done."

We both sit down. I look up at him. "Okay."

"I know you've both been concerned about how much I've been going to the doctor lately. I didn't want to talk about it until I was sure what was what."

Simone looks like she may cry. "Daddy, what's going on?" I touch her hand.

"Tom, you're freaking us out a little."

"I have stage four pancreatic cancer. Even with treatments, they only give me three to four months at best."

I sit there, not sure if I'm even still breathing. I feel Simone's hand tighten on mine.

Simone

I'm sitting here. I don't know if I'm in shock or dying. I can hear words coming from my daddy's mouth, but I don't know what he's saying. It sounds like I'm underwater. After he said cancer my ears went boggled.

I know I'm holding Silas's hand. He's trying to say things to me, too, but I can't make them out either.

Finally, I decide just to close my eyes.

The next thing I know, water is hitting me.

"What the fuck!"

"Simone, baby, are you coming around?" I hear my Daddy with worry in his voice.

I shake my face. "Yeah." I look up at Silas, who has obviously been flicking water in my face and using a wet cloth on me. "Are you trying to water board me now as a new form of torture?"

"Simone, don't give him a hard time. I didn't know what to do. I've never seen someone go into shock."

Silas looks at me and hugs me. Then, he whispers in my ear. "As much as I'd love to torture you, we have things to take care of, and I like to leave my torture for the bedroom."

I nod and squeeze his leg to the point I know it's hurting. "Yes. I'm sorry, Daddy. I didn't mean to worry you."

"It's okay, that was a lot to take in. If you're up to it, we do need to talk."

I nod. "Yes, sir. Just give me a minute to go to the bathroom. Okay?"

I stand up a little unsteady. Silas grabs my arm and walks me down the hall to the bathroom. I make my way inside and he shuts the door behind us.

He pulls me into his chest and I fall apart. I can feel him crying, too. Once we both have a good cry without a word being said, we clean up and walk back out to talk to my dad.

We sit down holding hands. He's my comfort zone. I take a deep breath. "Dad, how long has this been going on?"

He sits back in his chair. "Well, I started getting tired and I was having some stomach trouble back around Christmas. I thought I'd just over done it with the big dinners. After the first of the year, I went to see Jack. He first treated me for what we thought was a stomach virus."

I nod. "Yeah, you were on bland liquids for a few days."

"Yes. We thought it was either a virus or maybe my gallbladder starting to act up."

"Well, it seemed to get a little better, but then everything started hurting again. So Jack started doing some more blood work and we hoped it wasn't what he was thinking. Unfortunately, it was. They say this type of cancer is the most sneaky and aggressive. For almost everyone, by the time they figure out what it is, it's too late."

"So what is the plan, Tom?" Silas asks.

"Well, I'm not rolling over and playing dead. I told Jack I want to try something, so I'm doing an aggressive round of chemo and radiation. That is not saying anything will work, but I'm gonna try."

I nod. "Okay, so what do I need to do? What can I do?"

"Well, I fibbed a little today. I went to my lawyer's after my appointment this morning. I'm going ahead and giving you power of attorney. That way the business, the house, the property is where you can maintain and run it. I also went ahead and did my will. All of that is taken care of. I just need you to run this place."

He looks over at Silas. "I said before son, I'm so glad you're here this summer. I don't know what I would do if you weren't here. I just need you to help Simone. Help her keep everything going around here, repair stuff as it needs it."

He looks back to both of us. "They say when I do that chemo, it's gonna have me down for a few days at the time, so you two will be in charge of things around here. I'm sure I'll need Simone to help me back and forth, so Silas, you may have to be in the office some more. Just please, you two try to get along. I don't know what happened but whatever it was, it was past yesterday so don't worry about it anymore."

We both nod and I try to smile. "Yes, sir."

He stands up from his recliner. "I'm gonna hit the hay. I'm a little tuckered out."

I stand up and give him a kiss on the cheek before he goes down the hall to bed.

After he goes down the hall, I walk in the kitchen and grab my bottle of whiskey from the cabinet and two glasses. I look over at Silas. "Care to join me?"

He nods. "Yeah. Where do you wanna go?"

I sigh. "Down to the dock."

~*~*~

We sit down on the dock and I pour us both some whiskey. He looks over at me. "I think we need to clear the air. We need to get everything out in the open, so there aren't any more misunderstandings. We are going to have to depend on each other too much here soon."

I nod. "I agree."

He lets out a cleansing breath. "I was in love with you."

"Huh? What?"

"In high school. I was in love with you."

"You really had a funny way of showing it."

He leans back against the post. "When my grandma died, you were there for me. You were my best friend. Then, when I got so busy with football and trying to be the success she wanted me to be, I guess you got left behind. I was getting off on all of the attention from everyone. Teachers, coaches, girls and other players, no one had ever made a big deal about me. No one but you and my grandma."

I nod. "I guess I get that. I mean, I tried to support you, but when Claire started her attacks and you never defended me, it hurt."

"I never knew she was telling people you were my lesbian friend. I'd have corrected that quickly. I went out with her a couple of times and had sex with her once. She's like a leach, though."

"I was hurt, and then when the other guys avoided me, I was all alone."

"I'm so sorry. The guys knew I liked you. I threatened to kick Zack's ass when he wanted to ask you out."

"Oh, so that explains why he's always acted so weird to me."

"Yeah, but then when the stranger thing started for you, well, they all gave me a hard time. I felt stupid for wanting you, so I tried to let it go."

We sit there just sipping our whiskey and I lean back against him.

Silas

She looks up at the sky. “The stranger thing started when no guy around here would ask me out. I thought for some reason you hated me. I was insecure and didn’t feel attractive. A guy was staying here for the weekend, he was a couple of years older. He told me how beautiful I was and couldn’t believe I didn’t have a boyfriend. I pretty much called him a bullshit liar. Somehow, he talked me out of my pants and into his bed.”

She shakes her head continuing. “When I woke up the next morning, I was heartbroken because he wasn’t you. So, I got up and left. The good thing about out of town people is I never had to look them in the eye after I was finished. Everyone acted like I hooked up all the time, but I only hooked up when I needed to blow off steam. Like when I saw you parading around the latest cheerleader, or when you took one of them to prom and no one asked me. I’m not proud of it, but I never had to worry about one of them developing feelings for me when I would never emotionally be available. After you left, it became like a once or twice a month thing. The morning you saw me, that was the last time. I always had to get super drunk and most of the guys were your shape or build. Something about them would make me be able to pretend somewhere in my head that it was you.”

I pull her tight to my chest. “Wow. We must be two of the biggest idiots on the planet. We were both so damn crazy for each other but neither one of us thought to bring it up to the other one. We could’ve saved us both a lot of time and heartache, huh?”

“Yeah, I guess.”

“So, are we finished with this now? No more screwing around and hating each other?”

She shakes her head. “I don’t know. I know I don’t hate you, but I don’t know if us being together is the smart thing right now.”

"What do you mean?"

She lets out a sigh. "Well, I've got a lot coming up. I've got to run this place, take care of Dad and deal with whatever comes from that. I'll need to postpone my classes. I'm sure I'll have several more breakdowns between now and whenever."

I grab the side of her face and turn it up to look at me. "Hey, you aren't going through this by yourself. I'm here."

"You have to leave at the end of summer to go back to school. Actually, I know you'll have to go back sooner for practice."

I shake my head. "I'm not so sure about that."

"What do you mean? You have to go back for football, it's part of your scholarship."

I take a deep breath. "Look, I'm not supposed to discuss this, but our entire athletics program may be suspended. There is a big scandal going on. That's the reason I'm here this summer, I couldn't even take summer classes."

She reaches over and grabs the bottle of whiskey, refilling our glasses. "Looks like we both need this."

"Thanks." I hold my glass up to hers.

She takes a sip. "So when are they going to tell you something?"

I shrug. "Don't know. They are doing a huge investigation. Hopefully in the next couple of weeks. I'd kinda like to know where my future lies. You know?"

"You'll be fine. What about the draft? They've been scouting you for the NFL since your freshman year."

"Look who was watching stuff about me." I wink at her.

"I had no choice living in the house with dad. You'd have thought his own son was playing." She laughs.

"I would have been damn proud to be Tom's son. I would have entered the draft this coming up season. If I don't play, it'll never happen, so my football career is more than likely over. Whether I want it to be or not."

"Hey, you don't know that. You can go back this season when it all gets straightened out. You can still go pro."

I shake my head. "The thing is, once word gets out on the scandal, and it will, I'm surprised it hasn't already, I'll be damaged goods. Even though I'm not guilty of anything. It won't matter, no one will come near me."

"I'm sorry. I didn't realize." She wipes a tear from her face. "So what about your classes?"

I tilt my head back. "Well, there is a possibility I can finish if they don't suspend the entire program. If they do suspend the program, then I'm screwed. My scholarship is athletic. No athletics, no degree."

"Fuck, I'm sorry. You could finish up at State here. I'm just piddling along myself, you know."

I adjust her so she's curled into me on her side. "So, what is your degree in?"

"Business. With a minor in sketch and design. I like tinkering with blue prints and stuff. What about you?"

I laugh a little. "Business Management."

"Why are you laughing?"

"Most people laugh when I tell them. They expect me to say like Physical Therapy, Sports Medicine or something sports related."

She smiles. "Oh, well other people are stupid. Maybe you'll hear something soon. You can always enroll here and apply for financial aid to help pay for your classes."

I nod. "Yeah, that may be my only options."

"I'm glad you're here."

I kiss her forehead. "Me, too. You know, when I told Tom about my problems, he said 'When God closes a door, sometimes he opens a window.' I guess that applies here."

She nods. "Yep." She turns around until she's straddling me. "Can we go slowly this time? Not that last time wasn't off the charts, but I'd like to enjoy it longer."

I nod. "Oh, so you think that I'm some sort of foregone conclusion now?"

She shakes her head. "Nope, but I need you."

Simone

He tugs off his t-shirt and I pull my tank top off. He takes off my bra as I unbutton his cargo shorts. Grabbing my shorts, he slides them and my panties down my legs. He lays me back on the dock as I use my feet to slide his shorts and boxers down.

He slowly takes time kissing and licking my breasts and neck. “Hmm, you taste so good, baby.” He works his way down and when he gets to my pubic bone, he stops. “What does this say?”

I look up at him. “Savor Me, in Italian.”

He chuckles. “Oh, I plan to. Just not in Italian.”

We both let out a small laugh. Mine quickly turns into moans as his tongue flicks my throbbing clit. “Oh. Mmm. Silas.”

He hums as he’s sucking and licking my labia. I start to feel my insides tighten and my breath shortens. “Silas. I need you inside me.”

He slides up my body, entering me in one smooth stroke. “Happy to oblige, ma’am.”

I giggle for a moment, but it turns into moans and passionate pleas as we make love. I say making love because it’s slow and meaningful.

A little while later, we lay in silence, wrapped in each other’s naked bodies. Looking up at the stars over the lake, it all comes rushing back to me.

My voice breaks when I say his name. “Silas, my daddy is dying. I’m scared.”

I start crying in his chest and he strokes my hair, kissing the top of my head. “Shh, baby, it’s okay. I know. I’m scared, too, but we’re gonna get through this together.”

I look up into his eyes. “What am I gonna do if the chemo doesn’t work? Will I be able to run this resort by myself?”

He smiles at me. “Baby, you’ve been running this place since you were a kid. Plus, I’m gonna be here for you. I’m gonna help you.”

I shake my head. “I can’t ask you to do that.”

“You’re not asking me, I telling you.”

“Silas, what if it all gets worked out with school? You can’t pass that up.”

“Since I haven’t heard anything, I’m not thinking it’s good news. I should probably go ahead and do what you suggested about State.”

I nod. “I’m sorry all of this happened to you. I’m sorry you came home in the middle of this shit storm.”

He kisses me gently on the lips. “Hey, I’m where I’m supposed to be. You and Tom are the only family I have left. Dee Dee is just a person that takes up space in my life, she doesn’t really care about me. I mean, I don’t think she wants me dead or anything, but she doesn’t care. Grandma was the only person who really cared besides y’all.”

“You know that’s the reason I was so broken. You were the only person I could count on besides Daddy. I really don’t know what I’d do if you weren’t here.”

“You’d get through it, with or without me. You’re the toughest person I know. I’m just going to try and lighten your load if you’ll let me.”

With that said, we lie there until we fall asleep. I wake up sometime in the middle of the night. “Silas.”

He stirs and looks at me through dreamy eyes. “Mmm. I like waking up to you saying my name.”

“Hey, we should probably get home. Don’t need any of the customers coming out here finding us naked and passed out.”

He stands up, pulling up his boxers and shorts. “Yeah, Tom wouldn’t be pleased.”

I laugh as I’m putting my own clothes back on. “Nope. I don’t think so.”

I walk him to his truck. “Are you okay to drive home?”

“Yeah, baby, I’ll see you at the office first thing.”

I lean up on my tip toes and kiss his lips. “I like the sound of you calling me baby. I think.”

As he climbs in the truck, he looks at me. “Get used to it.”

I watch his tail lights go down the drive way and think about the last twenty-four hours.

I also think about the time I have ahead of me. Looking around the house I grew up in, I wonder how this will work when he’s gone. Will I be able to stay here? I know we own almost everything, but what if I fail? What if no one wants to come here when he’s gone? What if I suck at it? All of these doubts linger in my head as I try to go to sleep.

~*~*~

To say my sleep last night was fitful would be a massive understatement.

Between this new thing with Silas, my daddy and this business, my head may explode before today is over.

I know Silas and I were able to straighten out a lot of misunderstandings and miscommunications last night, but part of me is scared. I'm scared that he doesn't really feel as strongly for me as he thinks he does. That he feels a sense of duty to my father. That he's just trying to the hero, since his world is falling apart, too.

I hear the chime on the office door and I look up to see the man in question. He swaggers over to my desk and pulls me up under my arms without saying a word and kisses me like a fool. "You look worried. Don't be worried. I got you. Don't get wrapped up in your own head."

I sigh out a breath I didn't know I'd been holding in. "Thanks. Is that all that was for?"

"Nope, I'm doing it anytime I want to now."

I bark out a laugh. "Oh, you are?" I look up at him. "What if I say no?"

He smirks. "Then I may have to resort to begging."

He pulls away about the time we hear the door chime again. I look up to see my daddy walking in. "Hey, kids. Jack dropped off my schedule this mornin'." He hands it to me. "I thought you'd want to look over it so you could put it on your almighty calendar." He laughs.

I get picked on for writing EVERYTHING on my desk calendar, but oh well, it's kept me from messing things up numerous times.

I smile and kiss his cheek. "Thank you. This will help Silas and I make our schedules so I can go with you."

"Now, you don't have to go every time."

I look at him with a death glare. "I'm going. I may have to hire someone for a few hours on those days to grab the phones so Silas isn't overwhelmed, or I may have to redirect the calls to my cell and carry a planner or my tablet with me, but I will be there."

My daddy looks at me amused. "You trying to scare me, young lady?"

Silas laughs and I look back at my daddy. "Nope. Just stating the facts, young man."

Silas looks at me and dad. "If there is a day that she can't go, then I'll go. One of us will be with you. We are all in this together. You guys are really the only family I have, so I'll do what I can."

With that said, he walks out of the office to get to work. Daddy and I look at each other and shrug. I hug him tight. "Daddy, I love you."

Silas

I didn't sleep for crap last night. I was hurting, I knew Simone was hurting, and I knew we were both scared as hell. Tom has been our constant.

Along with all the fear I was feeling last night, I also couldn't help thinking about Simone's naked body and mine wrapped together. Our climaxing together, all of the words we whispered in the throes of passion. I love her, I'm just not convinced that she realizes how much I do. I worry that she feels like this is all because of Tom.

To top it all off, I had an email from the university waiting for me this morning. We have a meeting in one week that all athletes have to attend. I don't know how I feel about going back. I feel like I don't want to leave Simone and Tom.

All of those things are the reason I snatched her up and kissed her like crazy this morning. I needed her to feel me, feel my heart beating only for her. I want her to know that I'm in this all the way.

I shake my head and go over to the dock to start working on the new steps. After a few minutes, Tom comes into my view. "Hey, Silas. Everything going okay?"

I nod. "Yes, sir. How's it going for you this morning?"

"Good, I feel like some weight has been lifted off my chest. I didn't like keeping things from her. I just didn't want her to worry if it wasn't necessary."

"I understand." I say, looking over the lake. "She'll be fine, she's a lot tougher than she gives herself credit for."

He chuckles. "I know. I'm just glad you two have gotten your friendship back. I know how much y'all meant to each other and no matter how many times I told her stubborn ass just to go to you and talk, she wouldn't."

"I'm just as guilty." I shake my head. "I wish I had it to do over."

He shakes his head. "Son, those mistakes are what make you know it's worth fighting for."

I look back over the lake. "I told her about school."

"You did?"

"Yeah, she says she supports me, whatever happens. When I have time, she's going to help me apply to State here and for some grant money and stuff."

"Good. You remember what I said about God closing that door?"

"Yes, sir. I've been thinking about it a lot. I know that even if I go back, once the scandal hits the media I'm done just for being at that university. No Pro team will come near me, so no matter what, I'm done with football."

He nods. "Do you think you could spend the rest of your life here and be happy?"

"For years, I didn't know. I thought I shouldn't come back here. Like I'd be a failure if I did, like the town would laugh. Now, I don't care. My momma is going to be a bitch about it, though."

"Hey, don't call your momma bitch. I know she's not the greatest person in the world, but don't call her a bitch. Your grandmamma would tear your tail up."

I nod. "You're right."

Now he looks over the lake. "I love this place, have since I was a kid. My momma and daddy bought this place back when I was about ten.

I've been to see my lawyer. I don't want Simone to have to deal with her momma when something happens to me."

I nod. "Okay. I think Simone can handle her, though."

"Yeah, but I don't want that damn woman to have a leg to stand on. I want Simone to have as little worries as possible."

"I understand. I'll take care of Simone."

He looks at me with almost tears in his eyes. "I know you will." He looks back out at the lake. "When Jack first got suspicious of my blood work and talked to me about it, I prayed for answers, for guidance, for peace about Simone, I just prayed. Then you came here and asked for your old job back. Like I've always said, God laughs at our plans while he's making his own."

I nod. "Yeah, I know what you mean."

"I always thought I'd grow old here and watch my grandkids play in this lake like you and Simone did."

"Hey, you said yourself we don't know anything for sure yet. God has a sense of humor, he might just leave you here for us to deal with." I chuckle.

He laughs. "Yeah. Well, I better get back to work before she fires me."

I laugh. "Yep, she'll crack the whip on you, that's for sure."

~*~*~

I feel lighter after my conversation with Tom this morning. I know in my head I'll be staying here, no matter what they say at the meeting next week. My life is here and I'm okay with that.

I make my way up to the office to see what Simone is doing tonight. As I make my way through the door, I see her on the phone, working the computer and writing notes on the in-between. She's incredible.

Once she hangs up with the customer on the phone, she smiles at me. "Can I help you, Mr. Manning?"

"I don't know. I've got this problem with this beautiful girl. She won't get out of my head, I'm having trouble concentrating on work."

"Hmm. Well, what can I do to help?"

"Well, how about going out with me tonight? On an official date."

She looks a little thrown off her game. "Where would we go?"

I shrug. "Where ever you want, as long as it's not Ruth's Chris or something."

She laughs. "Oh yeah, because they just put one of those in by the Piggly Wiggly here in Richter's Crossing."

I pop her butt. "Smartass."

"Yeah, what about it? My brain is smart, too, not just my ass."

I laugh. "Okay. How about I pick you up at six? We'll go over to Samson, maybe eat at Outback since there isn't much to choose from here. Maybe we can stop back by the Tavern for a night cap or some dancing."

She smiles. "Okay. I haven't been to the Tavern since the other night. I hope Tuck is working, I can't handle Claire right now."

I smile. "Whatever she throws, we'll catch and just throw it back."

She laughs. "Wow, how elementary school of you. Next thing I know, you're going to jump up to her and say, 'I'm rubber you're glue, whatever you say bounces off me and sticks to you.'" She shoves my arm.

"Hey, if it works. It would definitely challenge her intelligence."

She rolls her eyes. "A can of concentrated orange juice challenges her intelligence."

I laugh and kiss her forehead. "I'm heading home to shower and get ready, see you soon."

"I'm about to head out myself, see you in a bit." She smiles, biting the corner of her lip.

Simone

I make my way up the path to our house. What am I going to wear on this date? I haven't been on an actual *date* in a long time.

I'm still nervous about this whole thing between Silas and me. It is really hard for me to trust people, but the more he explains, the more I understand.

As I enter the back door, I hear Daddy cussing the umpires on TV. The Braves must be playing. I round the corner to find I'm right and my daddy is busy calling the umpire a no good piece of shit with the vision of a blind man.

"Hey, Daddy, what's the score?"

"Bottom of the 7th, 3-3."

"Well maybe they'll pull it out."

He takes a swig of his beer. "Yeah, if they can get this ump to pull his head out of his ass."

I laugh. "Are you supposed to be drinking beer with your treatments coming up?"

"I honestly don't know, I figure I'm going to enjoy this ball game and my beer before I start them, though."

I shake my head. "Well, I'm going to get ready."

"Where are you going? Down to the Tavern?"

I give him a twisted smile. "No, I'm going on a date with Silas." I wait for his reaction.

"Well, it's about damn time the two of you got off your asses." Then he turns back to his ball game.

I shake my head and leave the living room to get ready for my date.

After showering and doing my hair and makeup, I stand in front of my closet trying to figure out what to wear.

Silas has seen me at my worst. Most of the time when I dress to go out, I'm either looking to be left alone or looking for sex, period. I would dress just provocatively enough to entice someone. Other than that, I really didn't care.

Now, I do, so I choose a new pair of *Miss Me* jeans and coral colored tank with a tan crochet cover over it. Now, to decide on shoes. Maybe my wedges, but then I see my brown cowgirl boots. I grab my boots and throw them on.

Stopping in the bathroom, I check my hair and makeup one last time. I head out into the living room, seeing that Silas is already here and watching the game with my daddy.

"Gentlemen, what's the score now?"

Daddy looks up. "Top of the 9th, 4-3 Braves. If they can get this last out, they've got it."

Silas stands up. "You ready to go?"

I nod. "Yeah. Daddy, you want me to bring you back something?"

He shakes his head. "No, y'all have fun. I'm gonna hit the hay after this finishes."

I put my hands on my hips. "Daddy, did you eat anything or did you just drink beer?"

"I had some left overs outta the fridge, Miss Bossy Britches."

I roll my eyes as I head for the door. "Lord forbid I try and take care of you."

Silas and my daddy laugh as we walk out the door.

Once we get in his truck, I giggle. He looks at me. "What?"

"I just feel like a little girl in this truck. It's been a long time since I've ridden in it."

He smiles. "Glad you still like it."

I nod, reaching for the radio to scroll through the iPod he has hooked up. "I do."

"You look very sexy tonight, by the way. I wanted to tell you that as soon as you walked in, but I just couldn't say it in front of Tom."

I laugh. "Well, if it makes you feel better, he's happy we finally got off our asses to go out on a date."

He laughs. "He pretty much said the same thing to me while you were finishing up. He did say that if I hurt you, he'd kill me. Even if he has to come back from the dead to do it."

I shake my head and roll my eyes. "He would say something like that."

I fiddle some more with the iPod when I come across the song *Backroad* by Corey Smith. I start laughing and hit play.

When the first lyrics come out, Silas looks at me. "Really the perfect date song, huh? But I think it's me that's supposed to play that song."

"Hey, this is an equal opportunity date, silly. Hey, I'd love to love you on a back road." We both start laughing.

He looks over at me. "Well, let's eat first. I'm kinda hungry."

I nod and laugh. “Sure, lightweight.”

He grins at me. “Oh, I’ll show you lightweight later. You’ll regret that remark, young lady.”

I know I’m getting to him, so I start singing with the radio.

If we get too hot and heavy, there's a place where we can go. Down this worn out hunting trail a half mile off the road. And we might not make it back there in this little two wheel drive. But judging by the way you're kissing me, it's at least worth a try.

“Hey, Simone?”

“Yeah.”

“Who sings this song?”

“Corey Smith, duh.”

“Well, you should let him sing it. Just saying.” He laughs.

I punch him in the arm. “Asshole.”

“Do you think you can keep your hands to yourself until we get to the restaurant, ma’am? I’m not all about being violated and beaten in my own truck.”

“Oh, but you’d like to be beat otherwise? That makes no sense.”

He laughs. “Well, you never know, I might be into some kinky shit like that.”

“Hey, if you wanna strip me down and fuck the shit out of me against a hard surface like you did the other night, I’m all game. That was the hottest thing ever.”

“Thanks, now I have a very uncomfortable situation to deal with through supper.” He chuckles.

We ride for a few more minutes in silence. I scoot over on the bench seat. Reaching down, I rub his crotch through his jeans. "Weren't lying, were you? This must be very uncomfortable. Let me help you with that before we get to Outback."

I unbutton and unzip his pants, pulling out his erection. He groans. "Simone-."

I sink my mouth down before he gets another word out.

Silas

After a rather interesting ride to dinner, we had a great dinner date, now we are off to see what else the night holds.

Pulling in to the Tavern, she looks over at me. “I really don’t want to deal with Claire. I’ve got too much else going on in my head to deal with her.”

“I know, we’ll just slip in and grab a drink, maybe she won’t even be working.”

She sighs. “Hopefully.”

We make our way into the bar and see that Tuck is working behind the bar, thank God. I grab Simone’s hand and pull her to me. “Hey, lets grab a drink and get a booth.”

Getting a couple of beers from Tuck, we grab a booth. She slides in and I slide in right behind her. I want everyone to know we are together, no question about it.

“Silas, everyone is staring at us.” She tries to hide behind me.

“Hey, who cares if they are looking?” I pull her face to mine and kiss her.

Jake and Zack make their way over to our table. Zack speaks up first. “Hey, y’all. Looking mighty cozy.”

I look up. “Thanks, we are.”

Jake looks down at Simone. “Hey, Simone. Dad told me about Tom. I’m sorry to hear it.” His dad, Jack, is Tom’s doctor and they’ve been friends since they were just kids.

She nods. "Yeah, I appreciate Jack doing all he's done." She stops and looks down. "We're just hoping that the treatment maybe will give us a little more time."

Jake nods. "Yeah, maybe so."

Zack looks down with a hint of pity in his eyes for her. I can tell he decides to leave it all alone.

Jake and Zack sit with us and we talk about random things for a little while. I hear her irritating ass voice before I see her. She makes her way over to me, not seeing Simone in the booth with me.

"So Silas, you wanna get out of here and relive old times?"

"No, not with you, Claire. Go find another table."

She steps further around to see Simone sitting there. "Oh God! Don't tell me you fell for her lines? Well, I guess you are considered an out of towner now, so she'll be with you just once."

Simone finally speaks up. "Claire, shut your fucking botched Botox face."

"Oh, honey, everyone's always saw how you chase after him like a pathetic puppy." Claire snarls.

I've had enough. "Oh, is that why you were so intimidated by her that you told people she was gay? I doubt that, you knew I loved her, so you did whatever you could to fuck it up."

Claire laughs. "Oh, honey, you weren't complaining or telling me you loved her when I got you off all those times."

"No, I didn't complain the one time we had sex, or even touched, for that matter. I should have, though, because me and several other team members had to take a trip to the health department thanks to you."

She looks like I just hit her with a Taser. "OH MY GOD! YOU FUCKING LIAR! It was probably her." She points to Simone.

I shake my head and Jake speaks up. "No, it was you. How embarrassed do you think we were when we had to explain it all to my dad?"

Simone looks up. "Claire, high school and all the bull shit that goes with it is over. Has been for a few years now. Maybe you should get the memo. Sometimes there are things a lot more important than ourselves."

Claire turns her head to the side, making a smart ass sad face. "What, did you get all holy and healed because your daddy's sick?"

Simone tries to climb over me to get to her but I push her back. Zack stands up and glares at Claire. "Get the fuck away from us, Claire, no one wants you here. If you come over here again, I'll personally talk with Tuck and Jerry. Your ass will be looking for a new job."

She glares back at him. "It doesn't matter, Silas is a washed up has been. I saw the news this afternoon. No more football for you, huh? Cheater."

I'm so pissed. I stand up as calmly as I can, taking Simone's hand. "Let's go."

She nods. "Sure."

Claire looks like she is going to say something else, but before she can, Simone slaps her across the face. "Don't, bitch. He's not a cheater, but you are a fucking cunt."

Once we get to my truck, I kick the fender. "FUCK!"

Jake and Zack have followed us out. Jake looks at me full of sorrow. "Sorry, man, I thought you knew about the news this afternoon."

I shake my head. "No, we were told to keep quiet until it was sorted out. What did they say?"

"It came on ESPN right after the Braves game went off. They said there was a cheating scandal with the football team, along with all of the other athletic departments at the school, and it looks like this year there won't be a football team." Jake shakes his head. "I'm real sorry, man. I know you aren't a cheater, you just got caught up in this shit."

Zack nods his head. "Yeah, Tuck made them turn the TV on in the bar."

I nod. "Thanks, guys. We left for our date right before the Braves game went off, so we just missed it. We are going to get out of here."

Jake and Zack both nod. Jake smiles. "You guys finally pulled your heads out of your asses, now take care of each other."

I slap his arm. "We will."

Simone and I climb in my truck and head towards her house.

Once we are on the road, she looks over at me. "I hate tonight ended in such a disaster."

I shake my head. "I knew it would come out before our meeting next week. I just had a feeling. I hate Claire said all those things to you, though."

"Whatever. I mean don't get me wrong, I still want to kick her ass, but she's not worth it. I just won't go back in there while she still works there."

I take her hand. "As pissed as Jake and Zack were, I'm pretty sure if they have anything to do with it, she won't have a job there."

She squeezes my hand. "I'm glad I have you."

"Me, too, babe."

Simone

We both need a break from what just happened. "Let's go hang out at the boat house for a little bit. I'm not ready to go home. You probably need to take some time going home so maybe Dee Dee will be asleep. I'm sure she's gonna throw a fit with the news tonight."

He sinks back a little. "Yeah, she's already made her opinions known about how big of a failure I am. I really don't feel like hearing it tonight."

I have an idea. "Hey, swing by my office real quick, then we'll go out to the boat house. I have a plan."

He nods and smiles. "Okay, thanks."

I giggle. "You don't know what I'm doing yet."

He shakes his head. "I can only imagine."

We pull up to my office and I run in and grab a bag, throwing some necessities in it. I lock the door behind me and jump in the truck. "Okay, let's go."

When we get to the boat house, I go in and flip the switch for the single light bulb that hangs from the rafters. "Okay, so I brought us a couple of blankets, some snacks, some beer and water. We are having a camp out, like we did when we were kids. Well, except we didn't have beer back then."

He smiles. "Thanks. I feel like a real douche right now. My life plans are changing, you're losing someone, and you're taking care of me."

I put my arms around him. "Hey. This is happening to you right now. I can't get down and wallow about something that may happen soon. Daddy is going to do the treatments. They might work. But the life you had planned is officially gone."

"Yeah, but I'm glad if it had to change, that I have you now."

I snuggle into his chest. "Hey, besides, I need to take care of you. I do have a feeling I'm going to need you more when it all boils down." I pull back.

I spread the blankets out and then our snacks. "I grabbed what I had in my office. So it's Ritz crackers, spray cheese, chips and oh, I did have a left over wrap from lunch yesterday."

He smiles. "You're awesome" He sits down by me on the blanket and kisses me. "Well, we didn't do that when we were kids, either." He lays me back and we start a full-fledged teenager make out session. He rubs his hands over my breasts and then to my jeans, unbuttoning them. "Seems like I owe you from earlier today." He strokes over my throbbing clit.

All I can do is moan. "Mmm." I shake my head. "We. Didn't. Do. This. As. Kids, either. Oh."

"I gotta few other things I'd like to do that we damn sure didn't do as kids." He kisses my neck.

I roll over on top of him, grabbing the hem of my cover and tank top and pulling them over my head. We roll back over with him pulling my boots, socks, jeans and panties off in what seems like one swift movement. I grab his shirt, pulling it over his head and we both work quickly to get his pants down.

He sinks into me. "Fuck, baby. You feel so good."

I look into his eyes. I know he said this earlier tonight but I need to say it now. "I love you, Silas."

He pumps into me. "I love you, too, baby. I always have."

I feel everything building inside of me. I roll us over so I'm on top. I start riding his thick cock, harder and faster. All of my emotions boil up as I feel my orgasm coming on.

He looks up at me. "Fuck, baby. That's it, take it." He grabs my breasts, tweaking my nipples.

I lose control at that point screaming his name. "Silas! OH God! Silas." I lose myself. When I come down, I realize I'm crying.

I'm curled into his side when he brushes my cheek with his finger. "Hey, are you okay, baby?"

"Yeah, that was just intense."

He nods. "Yeah, it was."

"I've never felt all of the emotions like I just did."

He kisses me on the lips. "It's because it's different when you're in love."

I reach and grab our beer. Handing him one, I take out the snacks. "I figure we need a little refuel."

He laughs. "Oh, so do you think I'm just so easy that I'll give into your wicked ways again?"

I smile against his lips. "Hmm. I'm counting on it."

He looks over at me sadly. "Do you think if you have time in the morning, you could do those applications for me? I would but I promised Tom I'd do some equipment maintenance tomorrow. I figure with the news out, I should take care of it soon."

I nod. "Sure, just leave the information on my desk in the morning. I'll take care of it."

He kisses me. "I know you think things like paper work and applications for me are no big deal. The thing is, no one has ever done anything like this for me before. I love you."

I smile. "It's nothing for someone that you care about. I love you, too."

~*~*~

Waking up wrapped in his arms is where I want to be for the rest of my life.

He pulls me tight to his chest when I start moving. I giggle. "We have to get up and get ready for work. I need to be at the office in a couple of hours. You better get me home."

He grunts. "I wanna just lay here with you and never leave."

I smile as I'm grabbing my clothes. "I know, and one day we will."

Walking in the door at my house in the morning after a night out isn't something I'm not accustomed to. It's just different with my daddy knowing I was out with Silas.

I run to my bathroom and grab a shower, throwing on my typical shorts and work shirt.

I grab a cup of coffee and some toast. My daddy is reading the paper. "Must've been a good date last night, since you didn't come home."

"Well, he needed to get away after the news and we kinda fell asleep in the boat house." Well, we did, I just didn't include the activities that led up to said sleep.

"I know, I saw the report after the game. Did anyone say anything to him?"

I roll my eyes. “Just that good for nothing slut bag bitch, Claire.”

“She is a nasty little piece of work, isn’t she?”

“Yes, sir, but I gotta get to the office. I’ll see you in a little bit.”

He nods. “Okay, sweetie.”

I make my way down the path to my office. Once I get there, I’m looking over dad’s chemo schedule and my schedule.

Silas has that meeting to go to next week. I don’t want him thinking that he can’t go. I have to find someone to work part time while dad’s taking chemo, that’s all there is to it.

I sit back in my chair and sigh, praying that we can afford to hire someone. Daddy has always been in charge of most of the money. I use the small operating account for the bills and expenses. I’ve never had to mess with the payroll account, he’s always taken care of that.

Silas

I'm changing the oil in the lawn tractor when I hear her.

"Well, looks like you did a real good job of fucking up this time."

I look up at her. "Well hey, Mom, how are you doing? Hope your day isn't as shitty as mine."

She throws her hands on her hips. "Silas, you have been nothing but trouble for me since I found out I was pregnant with you."

I shake my head. "Thanks Mom, love you, too."

"Do you have that hundred dollars you borrowed when you first got here?"

She never ceases to amaze me. I bought groceries for her house with that money. Which, I'm not sure I have it in my wallet after going out last night. "I don't have it on me. I'll have to go by the ATM."

She shakes her head. "Just wanted to let you know I'm moving in with Damien. So you'll need to get your stuff out of the house before the first of the month, the landlord said."

"Really, Mom? That's so motherly of you."

"Really, it's time you grew up and started taking care of yourself. I've given up my entire life for you. All of my plans, everything."

I'm pissed, I've had enough of her mouth. "You know I've been raising myself since Grandma died. You never gave up anything for me other than the six weeks you were out of commission after you had me. So just leave. I'll have your money to you by the end of today and I'll have a place to go by the end of the day."

"Good. I don't know what you plan to do with no future and no skills, but whatever."

I sling my shop rag on the ground. "I have skills, damn it. I fix things around this lake, I'm changing the oil in this tractor right now. I'm also finishing my degree here in the fall. Just because I won't be playing football doesn't mean my future is shot. It just means the free ride you've always dreamed of is."

"Go to Hell, Silas, you ungrateful little shit."

About that time, Tom steps around the barn. I've never in my entire life seen him look so angry. "Dee Dee, here is the money. Silas will go get his stuff out of the house right now. You can get the hell out of here and never speak to him again."

She snatches the hundred dollars from him. "What business is this of yours, Tom Whitman?"

He steps closer to her. "This is my damn property, he's my employee, and you are disturbing him. Besides those facts, you are the most disgusting excuse for a human being and mother I've ever met."

"You can go to Hell, Tom Whitman. Everyone else in this town might feel bad that you're sick, but I don't."

Tom shakes his head. "This has nothing to do with me being sick. Wait, it might. I seem to want to tell the truth a lot more now. How about you tell Silas what the deal really was with his daddy?"

That gets my attention. "What?"

My mom looks like she could set him on fire. "Nothing."

Tom glares at her. "Your daddy wasn't an NFL player that died in a car accident. He was a married politician old enough to be her grandfather at the time. He died just after you were born. His family gave you a chunk of money and Dee Dee here went through it." He looks back at my mom. "Gotta love small towns, huh."

With that, Tom turns and walks off. I turn to look at my mom. "Really?"

She shakes her head. "Just have your shit out by this afternoon."

She storms off and Tom steps back around. "Okay, I'm taking back my statement the other day. You are allowed to call her a bitch. 'Cause she ain't nobody's momma." He shakes his head. "You go get your stuff from her house and move in the spare room at the house."

"Tom, you don't have to do that. I can find a place." I push my hands in my pockets.

"Silas, it's not a big deal. Plus, maybe I won't have to worry about Simone staying out all night." He laughs, then his face turns serious. "Plus, when I start these treatments, she's going to need you there for moral support."

I nod, understanding now. He's afraid that Simone will be alone when and if something happens to him.

I love that girl, she's my life. Always has been since we were kids sharing snacks at recess. I'm so glad we're on the same page now, or well I hope we are.

"Alright, I'm gonna go get what little bit of stuff I have left there. She packed most of it up when I went to college so it shouldn't take long."

He nods. "Okay. You need me or Simone to go with you?"

"No, sir. Oh, and thank you for telling me the truth about my dad. I knew so many things never added up with her story, but it doesn't surprise me that while my Grandma raised me, she robbed me blind."

He puts his hand on my shoulder. “I’m sorry, son. I just couldn’t handle her talking to you that way. You’re a good boy and you don’t deserve it.”

I nod, getting in my truck and making my way to my mom’s house.

I go in our storage room on the back of the house and load up all my boxes from my grandma’s. That has my pictures and everything from the time I was born until she died. I load the few boxes she packed up out of my room when I went off to school. Then, I make my way to my room, packing the few things I have in here.

When I’m finished, I look around this house. It’s sad that it only takes me one load in a pickup truck and a little over three hours to pack up my entire life.

Simone

Dad comes blowing through the door of my office and I can tell he's pissed. He never gets that way often, so I'm curious when it does.

"Daddy, you okay?"

"That damn Dee Dee, she showed up here."

I stand up from my desk. "Is she still here?" I'm about to go throw her ass off the property.

He shakes his head. "No, I told her to get to steppin'. She was ugly to that boy for the last time in my presence. He's gone to go get his stuff, he's moving in the spare bedroom."

I nod. "Okay. What happened?"

"She came to tell him she's moving and for him to get his stuff out. So I gave him a place to live."

I slowly nod. "Okay. Listen I need to talk to you about something."

He sits down. "Alright, shoot. How much more we gonna throw at an old man today?" He chuckles.

"Mine isn't bad. I don't think." I look down at my calendar. "Daddy, I think we are going to have to hire someone to help me in the office while you are doing treatments. I'm hoping we can afford it. I've never asked you about that kind of stuff because I never really thought it was any of my business. Just looking at the calendar with your schedule, mine, and what Silas will need to be doing around here, I just think we'll need someone. If we can't afford it, I can do what I said about transferring the phones and all. I just know people staying here like someone being in the office during the day."

He smiles. "Slow down there, girl." He shakes his head. "Baby, we have plenty to hire someone. I've never hired someone because you always had it under control. You've always taken care of it. You never asked for much. Hell, I had to make you take that Jeep as a birthday present. This place makes a pretty penny, it has for years, and I've invested some. My parents left me a good nest egg. When I'm gone, this place and you will be well taken care of."

Sadness fills my heart. "Daddy, don't talk like that. The treatment might work."

"Honey, there is one thing for sure. Whether this cancer gets me or something else, ain't nobody made it out of this world alive yet. So, one day I will be going and you'll have this place. Now, go hire somebody."

"I think I have someone in mind. I just gotta go talk to her."

He nods. "Okay. How old is this person?"

"She's around my age. She's kinda quiet, I knew her in high school. She's worked at the Pig for years, she's good with money, great with customer service, and I think anything else she could learn. I know she's still taking classes like I do."

He nods like he's thinking. "Sounds okay. Just make sure I meet her before you give final word."

I smile. "Yes, sir."

"Hey, why don't you stay in here and grab the phones for a little bit? I'll go on down and try to catch her. I'm gonna grab some stuff to make stir-fry for supper. You don't need to be doing a bunch of outside stuff while Silas is gone anyway."

He slides down to my computer. "Okay. Sounds like a plan. Silas has damn near done anything I could think to do outside, anyway."

"Alright, well I'll just plan to go straight home after I pick up the groceries and get started on supper. If you can close up here for me?"

He kisses my cheek as I reach down to grab my purse. "Sounds like a plan, baby."

As I climb in my jeep, I see Silas pulling up. He smiles getting out of his truck. "Hey there, sexy."

I smile. "Hey."

"Where are you off to?"

"I'm gonna run to the Pig and grab a few groceries. I think I'm gonna make stir-fry for supper. I heard you are my new roommate. I'm a little excited." I grin.

He puts his hands to his chest like he's embarrassed. "Don't think you're going to be sneaking in my room and having your way with me."

I laugh. "You wish. Anyway, while I'm there, I'm gonna talk to Mary about working here some. We're gonna need a little help when Dad starts treatments."

He kisses my lips and smiles. "I was thinking that you're gonna need more than me."

"I talked to dad and okayed it. I think Mary would be a good fit. What do you think?"

He thinks for a minute. "Yeah. She seemed polite and nice the night I was in the Pig. I know she said she's in school, I think."

I nod. "Yeah, she's in school, but she's been at the store a long time." I shrug. "So I think it might work."

"Yeah. So where is Tom?"

"He's in the office. I asked him to watch it while I was gone. Especially since you weren't here, either. I don't want him out by himself."

"Good. I'll see you at home later."

I smile, kissing him on the lips and talking against them. "I like the sound of that." I wink. "See you at home."

~*~*~

Once I'm inside the store, I look to see if Mary is working. She is, thank goodness. I gather up the necessities to make beef stir-fry and a few other items we needed at the house. Well, quite a few more. I've always bought just enough for dad and me, but now we have another member of our family.

Making my way to the front, I see Claire standing there giving Mary a hard time while she's checking out. I get in Mary's line and Claire turns around.

"Well, if it isn't the bitch that got me fired."

I roll my eyes, shaking my head. "Shut up, Claire, no one cares. You should have kept your damn mouth shut. Besides, I didn't do shit."

She grabs up her bags. "Whatever, Simone. Enjoy Silas while it lasts."

I look to see the relief in Mary's eyes as Claire storms out of the store almost knocking over a young bag boy.

I mumble. "What a bitch."

Mary giggles. "I'm just glad someone else thinks that."

I laugh. "Honey, we aren't in the minority of people that think that."

“Thanks.”

I smile. “Listen, I wanted to talk to you about something. I’m going to need someone to work in my office at the resort. My dad is starting treatment for cancer and I’ll have to take him in. Silas will have to be working outside. I was wondering if you might be interested. When school starts, we can work around your schedule.”

She lights up. “Would it just be while your dad is in treatment or would it be something kinda permanent?”

“It would be permanent and probably turn into closer to full time later.” I shake my head. “Look, I’m honestly not sure how well dad’s treatments are going to go. I’ve been reading online and it’s scary, I have to be realistic. I may need someone while I’m taking care of him at home, too. I like how you treat people in here and I’m sure you know how to count money, the rest you can learn.”

She smiles. “Sounds great. What do I need to do?”

“Well, I need you to come by and talk with dad, but I’m sure he’ll be okay with you. Then, just finish out whatever you need to do here. When you make your schedule for fall semester, just get it to me.”

She grins. “You’ve just made my day! Thank you so much. I love most of the people in this town and I don’t mind waiting on them, but when people like Claire come through, well, it just gives me no hope for the entire human race.”

I laugh. “Yeah, she has a way of doing that. Can you stop by tomorrow during the morning?”

She nods. “Yes. Tomorrow is actually my day off here. So if your dad is okay with it, you could show me some stuff tomorrow.”

“Sounds good.” I get my receipt and my bags.

“See you in the morning.”

Silas

I like that she's excited about me living with her. Once Tom and I have finished everything for the day, we talk on the way to the house.

"So, Mone told me she's going to talk to Mary about working here some."

He nods. "Yeah. I'm afraid y'all are gonna need help. Jack will help get me to and from treatments, but Simone says no."

"You might as well not argue with her. You know you won't win." I laugh.

He shakes his head and laughs. "I know. I know. I raised one stubborn girl." He looks over at me. "You know this treatment is like a 5% chance, right?"

I nod. "Yes, sir. I did some reading on it. I'm pretty sure she has, too."

He nods. "I figured she had or else she wouldn't be preparing. Have you met this Mary?"

"Yeah, she went to school with us. I didn't know her very well but she was nice to me at the store. If Simone thinks highly of her, that must say something."

"You're right. Simone is harder to break through than you or I." He looks back forward. "You're gonna take care of Simone, aren't you, Silas? I can depend on you to do that?"

I nod. "Yes, sir. I promise I'll take care of her for the rest of my life, if she'll let me."

He nods. "Good. It makes facing all of this easier. She loves you and I know you love her." We make our way on to the porch and in to the house.

I smile when the smell hits me. Home cooked meals are something I could get used to.

Simone is standing in the kitchen at the stove. Tom heads to the fridge to grab him and me a beer. I kiss her on the cheek. "Smells good, baby. I could get used to this."

She shoves me. "Yeah, well don't get too used to it. I don't cook every night or anything. Especially when I'm in school."

I hear Tom chuckling. "Now, you two, I don't want to have to do random bed checks around here since Silas is staying here."

Simone puts her hands on her hips. "What makes you think I'd wanna share my bed with his stinky ass, anyway?"

I laugh. "Oh, well if I remember correctly, you snore like a freight train, so no thanks."

He chuckles, going to the living room to turn on the Braves game probably.

A few minutes later, we sit down to the table and start eating. Tom looks at me. "So what do you think they are going to say at your meeting now? Since the news last night?"

I sigh. "Probably the same thing, that our football program is suspended for the year and the same with some of the other sports. For people like me on scholarship, it'll be to find out if we are staying and footing the bill ourselves, or if we are transferring."

Simone looks at me. "Well, I submitted your application this morning for State and for the financial aid. Hopefully you'll hear back from that soon." She puts her hand on mine. "Don't get down about it. Okay?"

I nod. "Okay. It's just everybody will have their own opinion of me and I don't like it."

Tom smiles. "Son, people are gonna talk. Look at it this way, if they are talking about you, then they are leaving some other poor soul alone."

We all laugh and discuss Mary coming in tomorrow for a working interview of sorts. We talk about my trip to the university. I tell Simone about what Tom told me about my dad.

I could get used to this. Having a family and someone care about me is all new. I haven't had that since my grandma.

~*~*~

Tom has been doing treatments for four weeks now. He's getting blood work done today. The chemo has been horrible on him. He's been so sick, and sometimes he doesn't even get out of bed. This isn't like him at all.

I'm glad I moved in with them. I would have hated for Simone to face all of this alone. Helping Tom up when he falls in the floor, when he can't get out of bed, or when he needs help getting to the bathroom. Simone shouldn't have to shoulder that herself.

I got accepted to State with full financial aid, we both start in a few weeks. Mary is working out great at the office. It has really helped us out, especially letting Simone spend time with Tom.

Mone has been seriously talking to her dad about some of the ideas she has for adding a total of six cabins eventually. She wants to do two a year, that way they can help pay for themselves as they're being built. She's also talked about adding in that small snack bar, or it'll be more like a small café. People staying here can get a limited breakfast, lunch or supper. She is so damn smart.

I can tell this is starting to take its toll on her. She's been really down the past few days. Her appetite has been up and down, and the doctor warned her about her own immune system the other day. He said that people let themselves get run down when they are taking care of a loved one, almost like depression. He wants her to get some blood work done today while her dad is.

With all the cancer stuff going on, he'd like to get a clear picture of her wellbeing, and so would I. I have a surprise for her. Her dad gave me her grandmother's wedding set the other day. I'm asking her to marry me tonight at the boat house.

My phone rings and I see it's Simone. "Hey, baby, what's going on?"

I hear her crying. She doesn't say anything. "Simone, baby, what's going on? Where are you?"

She sobs. "Jack's office."

"I'm on my way."

"Okay."

I radio the office and let Mary know I have to leave.

My head is running crazy with thoughts. Shit, Tom's blood work is bad. Oh my God, her blood work is bad. I don't know if I can handle it if she is sick.

I pull into the parking lot of Jack's office pretty much on two tires.

I can't lose her. I just got her back. I'm asking her to marry me tonight. God, please don't do this to me.

Once I get inside, a nurse takes me back to the room Simone is in. I rush through the door, pulling her into my arms. “What’s wrong, baby? Where is Tom? Are you okay?”

She wipes her face. “I don’t know about dad, I haven’t talked to him. He’s down the hall, I wouldn’t let Jack get him. I don’t want him worried about me.”

It’s bad. I know it’s bad. “Baby, you are scaring the life out of me. Please tell me what’s wrong and we’ll face it together.”

She looks up at me. “I’m pregnant.”

For a minute I’m shocked, but then relief and excitement take over. I grab her under the arms and kiss her. “Really?”

She nods. “I didn’t think you’d be happy about this, and I don’t know how my daddy is going take it.” She shakes her head. “What if this is too much for all of us? What if it’s not the right time?”

I stroke her hair, pulling her to my chest. “Hey, we’ll figure it out, we always do. Now, I have something for you.”

She looks up. “What?”

I pull the box out of my pocket. “I was going to do this tonight at the boat house, but now seems right.” I drop to my knee. “Simone Whitman, I have loved you since you shared your gummy bears with me at snack in kindergarten. This was your grandmother’s, Tom gave it to me when he gave me his blessing. Will you marry me?”

She looks up at me through tear soaked eyes and nods. “Yes.”

Simone

Six Months Later…

I look around my old room that is now set up for a nursery. I shake my head. Boy, I'm glad I hired Mary. I was not planning on this when I did.

Silas and I got married in front of a judge a few days after he proposed. When Daddy's blood work came back, it wasn't good. If I wanted him to be there, then I needed to go ahead and do it. No big deal to me, I never wanted a big wedding. I just wanted my daddy there.

He was so excited about Silas and me having a baby. It seemed to make him happier in his last days. He made me find out as soon as we could what we were having so he'd know, and then got the nursery decorated so he could watch.

He passed away the week after the nursery was finished. I swear the reason he hung on was to find out what I was having and give me one final gift.

I was 21 weeks along. That last week he mostly slept, but right before he went, he asked me to name this little girl after his momma. Then he promised to watch over her and never let anything happen to her.

I lay her coming home outfit on the dresser. He bought it the day we found out she was a girl. He knew he wouldn't make it to see her born.

I turn the light off and close the door.

Silas comes down the hall. "Baby, you okay?"

I nod. “Yeah, just sorting some of the baby stuff that keeps coming in from Amazon. Letting my daddy loose with a computer while he was bed bound has proved a wealth to us in diapers.” I laugh.

“How are your online classes going?”

I sigh. “Fine, I hate finishing my last semester like this. I’m fat, tired and swollen. The bad part is I’m not done yet, I’ve still got eight weeks.”

He laughs. “Baby, you’re beautiful, and you can get as big as you need to. I want my baby girl to be healthy.”

“How were your classes today?”

He shrugs. “Fine, I’m glad this is the end of them. I went by the office and checked on Mary, she has an appointment in the morning. She said she’d take the office cell with her.”

I shake my head. “No, I can go down to my office for a little bit tomorrow. This house is starting to get to me anyway.”

He nods. “Okay, I’ll let her know. Also, I wrote a check to the construction crew. They finished the second cabin. So we should be able to start reserving it now.”

I smile. “That’s great. What about the café?”

“I talked to the appliance people and they’ll be done within two weeks. After that, we’re just waiting on the inspections, then we’ll be up and going.”

I clap my hands like a little kid. “Yay! I’m so excited!”

He kisses me. “I’m happy this is all working out for you.”

I nod. “Me, too.” I kiss him back a little more aggressively. These pregnancy hormones are no joke. I find myself horny as hell part of the time. Silas calls it *Horny Day!*

He groans. "Mmm. I guess today is a horny day, huh?"

I laugh and nod. "Yep."

He picks me up, carrying me to our bedroom. "How do you want it today, babe?"

I snatch my dress over my head. I grab my bra, undoing it quickly as he snatches my panties down. I look back at him once I bend over. "I want it hard and fast."

He shoves his pants down. "Yes, ma'am. I aim to please."

I snicker until he slams into me. "Oh. Fuck." I cry.

He reaches around me, grabbing my breasts. "Mmm. I love horny day." He keeps pounding into me from behind.

It doesn't take long before we are both screaming each other's names in passion.

Lying here wrapped up in each other's arms, I look over at him. "Silas, I'm so glad you came back home last summer. I couldn't have done the past ten months without you."

He smiles at me and kisses my forehead. "Same goes here. I'm just so glad you forgave me."

Falling for Autumn

A Richter's Crossing Seasons of Change Novella

By: S.M. Donaldson

For anyone who needed a do-over in life.

Falling for Autumn

A Richter's Crossing Seasons of Change Novella

Cover by SM Donaldson

Image from shutterstock.com

Editing by Chelly Peeler

Introduction

• Due to mature subject matter this book is for readers 17+.

•This book is written in a true southern dialect, from a true southern person. Therefore, it is NOT going to have proper grammar.

Let me start by saying I hope you enjoy this novella. Each Novella in this series will center around a season of the year. Also, it will release during the coordinating season. They will all be based in the town of Richter's Crossing, but they will be able to be read in any order.

This is a new adventure for me and I'm excited.

Autumn

Just my damn luck. I'm still seven hours from my parents' house and this fucking heap of shit I'm driving overheats. I just pulled into some small god forsaken town called Richter's Crossing. I can't even find it on the map. My cell provider has no coverage here and even if they did, I'm not sure who I'd call. Plus, the radio is talking about some late season hurricane that is headed up the coast.

When I left Charlotte I wanted nothing more than to leave my past in my rearview mirror. I'm going to Florida to start a new life, find new shop to work in and stay the hell away from men.

Checking my face in the mirror, I see that my bruises are healing, my make-up covers the ones on my face pretty well.

Less than a week ago I was happy working in a small tattoo parlor on Monroe. I started working as an apprentice in a tattoo shop for some friends of my parents when I was still in high school. As soon as I could get my work permit, they let me start. They retired a year or so ago, around the same time my parents did. The owners and my parents all retired to Florida. I'm only twenty-one, I wasn't ready to run my own shop. I wanted to stay in Charlotte, so I went to work for another established shop in town called Body Designs.

How was I to know going to work in that shop would change everything? That I'd end up dating some asshole who'd ruin everything for me?

Eric Vander was a clean cut college guy that came in not long after I started working there. He wanted his fraternity letters done on his chest. *How original?* He was a nice guy, though. He flirted with me while I was giving him his tattoo and a week later he came in and asked me to dinner. After that it was like we were inseparable, mainly because he said he never wanted to be without me.

Slowly I realized he was becoming my entire life. It started out sweet, like showing up at my work to make sure I was *safe.* Little by little things changed. He started picking out my clothes. He liked me in long sleeves when we went out to dinner because they covered most of the tattoos on my arms. I couldn't hang out with the other tattoo artists when I got off. He hated me talking on the phone with my parents for long periods of time and he talked me into changing my hair to all one color. He was isolating me from the rest of the world, controlling me like a puppet. When he actually approached the subject of me quitting Body Designs to find something *reputable* to do, I said that was enough. I told him that we'd moved too fast and that I needed some time to myself. He wasn't very happy with me. He said a lot of mean and hurtful things to me.

That was three months ago. I thought I was done with him, that he'd moved on. I even saw him walking arm and arm with some blonde one night. Seeing him with her and it not hurting me at all made me realize I was never really in love with him.

A couple of weeks ago I had the eerie feeling someone was watching me but I just shrugged it off. Then on Monday, I was closing up the shop...

"Excuse me. Are you okay?"

I'm snapped from my angry memory rant and I see a tall muscular guy with dark brown hair. *He's like a stranger porn fantasy come true. A hot guy comes to the rescue of a stranded motorist.*

I suddenly remember I'm standing beside the highway with a car that's broken down. Hmm. A southern gentleman.

"Oh, I'm fine. This stupid car just died, it overheated. I'm not sure why. I don't have great cell service here to call a tow truck."

He smiles. Holy crap, what a smile. "Well, I have a buddy that owns a shop." He sticks his hand out. "I'm Jake Callahan. If you'll give me a minute I'll call my buddy and we can get you towed in."

Damn it! No men! No men! I smile. "Thanks, that would help a lot. I'm Autumn Byron."

He takes out his phone, explaining to his friend about my car.

"He'll be here in about ten minutes." He grimaces. "But he did say that it would be tomorrow before he could do anything to it."

I smile. “That’s okay, I understand. Do you know of a motel or somewhere I could crash for the night? Oh, and a number for a cab?”

He shakes his head with a sexy grin. “Yeah, I know a place you can stay for the night. Only thing is, there are no cab companies in this small town.”

“Oh, well maybe the tow truck driver can give me a ride to the hotel.” I sigh.

He chuckles. “I can give you a ride.”

“Oh. Um. Okay, thanks.”

He laughs again. “I promise I’m not a killer or anything.”

We both laugh and I wink. “Well that’s good to know, being hacked to pieces in the middle of nowhere would put a damper on my plans.”

His friend pulls up on the tow truck and gets out. “Hey, Jake.”

They do the back slap thing. “Hey, Zack man. This is Autumn Byron. She is the young lady I called about. I told her you couldn’t get to her car until tomorrow so I’m gonna take her in to town to stay the night at Twin Oaks.”

Zack nods. “Alright, well write your number down and I’ll give you a call about it tomorrow.”

I smile. “Let me get your number, too. My cell provider has crappy service in this area so I may have to use the hotel’s phone.”

Zack smiles. “Oh, I’ll just give you a call there then. How does that sound?”

I nod. Everyone here is so nice. “Thank you.”

Jake

I was beat. I've been working all day with my dad at his office. I'm in school to be an ARNP and my father is a doctor. He's had an influx of flu cases and needed help.

I was on my way out to our farm when I saw a car with its hood up and smoke boiling out of it. Hmm. A hot red head in a white tank top and cut offs. She was so angry and staring off into space, she wasn't even paying attention.

I can't stop looking at the intricate tattoos down her arms. I really would love to pull this truck over and trace those tattoos with my tongue. It makes me hard just thinking about her naked tattooed body.

Now I'm in pain and giving her a lift over to Twin Oaks Inn, an old style inn that my mother owns. My friend Zack is going to check out her car tomorrow.

There is an uncomfortable silence and I look over at her. I can see what looks like bruising on her face and I definitely see one on her arm. "So, where are you from?"

She looks out the window. "I'm from Charlotte, but I'm moving to Florida."

I nod. "Wow, so what do you do?"

She chuckles. "I'm a tattoo artist."

"Well, you have awesome work on your arms. Did you do most of it?"

She nods. "What I could reach. The spots I couldn't, my Uncle Paulie did."

"Oh, so you have an uncle that's an artist, too?"

She shrugs. "He's not really my uncle, but he gave me my start. He's friends with my parents."

"Oh cool."

We pull up to the inn. I reach and grab her bags from the back seat. “Follow me and we’ll get you set up.”

“Oh thanks, but you don’t have to do that. I can manage to get my own room.”

I try to laugh. I sense from the bruising that she’s having some trust issues. “Just follow me.”

“Really, I can get my own room. I don’t need your help.”

We step inside and I call out. “Hello!”

My mom comes from the back. “Hey, sweetheart.” She kissed my cheek. “What’s going on?”

“I brought you a guest.” I motion to Autumn. “Mom, this is Autumn Byron. Autumn, this is my mom and owner of Twin Oaks, Drucilla Callahan.” They shake hands and exchange pleasantries. Autumn looks at me like she is in shock.

“Autumn’s car broke down on her out by the main highway. I was on my way out to the farm. Her cell didn’t have service so I called Zack for her. He is looking at her car so she needs a place to stay for the night.”

My mom claps her hands together and brings them to her chest. She’s always been a little bit of a dramatic southern belle. “Well, I declare. Jake, I’m so glad you found her.” She takes Autumn over to the counter and I follow them with her bags. “Here sweetie, just fill this out.”

Mom reaches behind her. “Here Jake, she’ll be in room 7, be a gentleman and take her bags in.”

Autumn’s head pops up. “Oh, I can get it. He’s already done so much to help me.”

My mom shushes her with her hand. “Oh stop. I’m glad he saw you. Lord only knows what could’ve happened out there by that highway. They have prisoners working on the road gangs out there all the time.”

Autumn hands her the registration slip. “Thank you for your concern. Is there a pay phone I can use? I’m traveling to my parents in Florida. I still don't have great reception on my phone and I really don't want them to worry."

So she's moving to Florida to be with her parents.

My mom tilts her head and smiles. "That is so sweet. Honey, you can use this phone right here, everyone has unlimited long distance now anyway. You just go ahead and call them. I'd be worried half to death if you were my daughter. Oh, we have breakfast in the morning from 6 to 9."

Autumn smiles. "Thank you."

She makes a quick call to her parents and meets me in the hall. I hand her the key. "You're in room 7, I put your bags on your bed." I follow her back down the hall to room 7 and we stop at the door.

She giggles. "I feel like I should give you a big tip. In the past hour you've been triple A, my chauffer and now, my bell hop."

I grin and lean closer to her in the doorway. "What can I say, I'm a jack of all trades. How about instead of a tip, you let me take you out to dinner tonight?"

She smiles as if she's thinking about it, but then steps back suddenly. "That's really nice, but I've had a long day and I'm really tired."

"Come on. You have to eat. This is just two people eating. I don't expect anything more."

She puts her hands out. "Look, I appreciate all you've done for me today. I'm not sure what I would've done."

"Hey. Hey. It's okay. I was just offering. I just know you don't have a way of going, so I thought I'd offer."

She looks defeated. "I'm sorry, I'm just a little on the defensive side. I'm really sorry, I have my reasons."

I nod. "Okay, I'm gonna go help my mom get ready to finish up her day."

She nods. "Thanks again."

I make my way back down the hall to the front desk. "Hey Momma, why don't you go on home. Dad was beat when we left the office."

"Hmm. Why do I think it's not your parents you are worrying about right now?"

"Momma, I'm serious. We saw a ton of patients today and Dad was beat. Go make sure he is a doctor to himself so he doesn't get sick, too."

"Alright, fine. I'm just glad to see that you might have an interest, that's all." I give her a glare and she just smiles back. "You're right, he'll be a big ole' baby if he gets sick. You know how to shut down the office for the night?"

"Yes, ma'am."

She gathers her things and takes off. I sit around watching ESPN and reading a sportsman magazine until dark.

I guess she is never going to come out of that room.

I just find myself wanting to talk to her more. I roam around and end up at her door. I knock softly in case she's really asleep.

She answers in some lounge pants and a t-shirt, sans bra and shoes. So fucking sexy. She's washed her face and I can noticeably see the bruising on her face now.

"Well, I was going to ask you again about going to dinner but I see you're already dressed for bed."

"I told you. It's really sweet of you to ask, but I don't really want to go anywhere." She tries to turn away.

Now I know I have a master plan she can't say no to. "I tell you what. Why don't we go to the kitchen and find some food here? I'm sure if nothing else we can have brinner."

She looks confused. "Brinner? What's brinner?"

I laugh. "Breakfast for dinner, of course."

She laughs at my comment and doesn't seem to fight when I take her hand, pulling her to the kitchen.

Autumn

After Jake has cooked up a pile of bacon, scrambled eggs and some pancakes, we sit across a small table from each other.

He is so damn sexy, I can't seem to think straight around him. That is the reason I didn't agree to have dinner with him earlier. I made myself a promise of no guys, not even to blow off steam. I need to be *me* for a little while anyway. Why couldn't I've met him a few months from now?

I try to smile. "Thanks for everything that you've done today. This *brinner* is great, by the way."

He gives me a full smile. "You are very welcome. I hate you've had such a shit day. I guess everyone has one every now and then."

Maybe he is genuinely nice. I should try to make small talk with him. I mean, I'm getting out of here tomorrow. Just get through tonight, keep my pants on and make conversation. "So I told you what I do. What do you do?"

"Well, I'm in school to be an ARNP and I work at my father's practice. That's where I was coming from today when I saw you."

"Wow, so your father is a doctor and your mom owns this inn?"

"Yeah. This inn has been in my mom's family forever. I think she would love for my sister Camellia to take it over one day."

"Wow, real small town royalty, huh?"

He hangs his head a little. "I guess so."

Crap, I've made him mad or something. "I'm sorry. Did I say something wrong?"

He shakes his head. "No. It's just most people don't see the expectations we have to live up to. I'm set to a completely different set of standards than the rest of the community. It's just a lot to carry around. Everyone is always watching what I do and how I do it."

Wow, he has a lot on his plate. "So you said you were headed out to the farm when you saw me. You guys have a farm, too?"

"Yeah, just on the edge of town. It was in my father's family. Sometimes my parents stay here at the inn if it's full. When there are only a few people, like tonight, either myself, Camellia or one of the workers stay."

"That's kinda neat. It'd be cool I think to be so surrounded by family."

He speaks as he's biting into a strip of bacon. "So is that the reason you're moving to Florida? To be with your family?"

I don't know why I want to tell this guy everything. We don't know each other and we won't. I haven't told a soul what happened at the shop on Monday, I just called up my parents and told them I was coming for a visit. I left my furniture in the apartment I was renting and packed up all of the rest of my belongings that would fit in my car and left town. I did text my boss at Body Designs to tell him I was taking some personal time, that I had a family emergency and would be in touch.

I decide I need to be honest with someone. Who better than a total stranger? "Yes and no. I do want to see my family, but that isn't the main reason. I'm sure you see the bruising on my face."

"Yeah. I noticed it in the truck but you seem private, I didn't want to pry."

I give a small smile. "That's really nice of you. I honestly haven't told anyone why I'm on my way to Florida."

He leans back in his chair. "Well, I'm all ears."

"I had been dating a guy for a little while. I didn't notice how controlling and abusive he was until a few months ago. He wanted to change too much about me so I broke up with him. He wasn't happy about it, but he seemed as if he'd moved on. Until Monday night when I was closing up the shop. He came in and attacked me."

He looks at me serious. "Attacked you how?"

I shrug, I'm not ready to give the details to anyone yet. "He just did. Then I got the hell out of town. That's pretty much it."

He starts cleaning up our dishes. "Well, I'm kinda glad you're here. It's nice to have a new face in this town every once in a while." I can tell he's trying to lighten the mood a little.

I help him pick everything up. "Thanks *again*. I'm going to go to bed, though. I've had a long couple of days and I've got some driving ahead of me tomorrow."

He turns, putting us in close proximity of each other. "Well, have a nice night. If you need anything, I'll be just down the hall. The only other guests are the newlyweds in the cottage behind us."

Crap, so I'm alone in this place with a strange man. This is the shit horror movies are made from.

I try to calm myself down. He's nice, he hasn't made me feel the least bit uncomfortable all day. *Well, except for the uncomfortable throbbing in-between my legs.*

Yep, he's been nice all day but that doesn't mean he won't kill you in your damn sleep.

I shake all the thoughts from my head about the sexy southern gentleman. I step back and put a little distance between us. "Thanks." I say as I turn to go to my room. I close and lock the door behind me.

I lie down, trying to shake all the thoughts I'm having away. Jake seems super nice, but so did Eric. I've known this guy less than twelve hours and he has me wanting to spill my secrets to him, have sex with him and possibly his babies. It's like something out of a cheesy romance novel.

ARGH!

Finally, my tired eyes start to win and I close my eyes.

I shut down the computer for the night so I can finally head home. This always seems like the victory point of the day. Then, I hear the bell from the front door. I've already shut down some of the lights in here so it's dim. I finally make out that it's Eric who has came in. FUCK.

"Eric, what are you doing here?"

He gives me his signature spoiled kid smirk. "Came to try and talk to you."

I stand my ground. "Well, I don't want to talk to you. I told you before, we are finished."

He glares at me. "Look, I have given you some time to come to your senses." He switches to his endearing voice. "I've missed you. My fiery little red head."

I shake my head. "Eric, I can't do this with you. I saw you dating a blonde, what happened with her?"

"She wasn't who I wanted. I only want you."

I grab on to the counter. "But see Eric, that's the thing you don't want…ME. You want who you can make me turn into."

I see his eyes change. I need to get him out of the room. "Come on, let's go. We can grab some coffee tomorrow or something."

He grabs my arm as I walk by. "No. I want to talk here. Now." He presses me against the desk. "You know you've missed me."

I shake my head. "No. Now Eric, you need to go."

I taste the metallic flavor after he hits me. I shove him as he tries to push the skirt I'm wearing up my legs. "I came to remind you of what's mine."

I shake my head and try to get away as I feel his hand on my panties. "No. Eric." He pulls his hand out from under my skirt and backhands me. His other hand is still tight on my arm. Finally, I wiggle enough to knee him in the balls. Grabbing the glass paperweight off the desk, I slam it into his head.

He stumbles back. "You bitch!"

I grab the phone and start to call 911. "I'm calling the cops. I wonder how your parents are going to like this?"

He glares at me. "Fuck you, this isn't over. I'll be back." He runs out the door. I run and lock it, sliding down the wall behind it.

BAM! BAM BAM! Oh God, he's back.

BAM BAM BAM, "AUTUMN! AUTUMN! ARE YOU OKAY?!"

I'm startled awake by someone beating on my door. Shit! Where am I? I breathe. Okay, I'm here in a little town with my car broken down.

I jump from the bed and swing the door open to find an out of breath, sexy, disheveled Jake.

Jake

I was startled awake by moaning and screaming. At first I thought someone had broken in, but then I got my bearings.

I take off running down the hall to room 7 where Autumn is staying and I hear her screaming. I bang on the door. *"AUTUMN! AUTUMN! ARE YOU OKAY?!"*

The door to her room flies open. She's standing there panting, shaken and scared. For some reason I want to take her in my arms and hold her.

But that's not me, I never want that again. I should just comfort her like a patient.

I reach out to touch her arm but she jerks away. "Hey, are you okay?"

She nods. "I'm sorry I woke you."

I want to reassure her, but she doesn't want that right now. "Hey, it's no problem that you woke me. It just scared me. That's all."

She puts her hands out. "I'm fine. I just had a little nightmare."

I lean against her doorframe. "You sure?"

She nods. "Yeah, I just wanna go back to sleep."

I step back. "Okay. I'll be just down the hall."

"I know, thanks." She says as she quietly closes her door back. I hear the lock turn as I walk back to my room.

I lie back down on my bed, but I'm too fitful to sleep. I grab some of my notes from class and start studying. I can't help thinking about the girl down the hall.

My thoughts are consumed by her for some reason. She seems so hard on the outside with the tattoos and bright red hair, yet her eyes and body language seem so sad and vulnerable. I know her ex attacked her. I don't know all the details but she doesn't seem like the type of girl who is going to talk about them willingly, either. I just feel like she needs me.

Get it together, Callahan, she's only here for one night. Why would you even try to start this up now? All it would be is sex. You had your chance for something more years ago. You blew it. You have no right to move on.

I don't know what is going on in my damn head. For the past five years I've done nothing but concentrate on school. Every once in a while I go have a beer with my buddy Zack, but for the most part school has been everything. I've had the occasional one nighter with a couple of girls from town, but nothing permanent. *Nothing will ever be permanent.*

I haven't wanted anything permanent since the summer after I graduated high school. I wasn't exaggerating when I say being small town royalty sets you to a different set of standards. Sometimes they're impossible to live up to.

~*~*~

I hear her laughing from the passenger side. "Jake, if you don't have me home soon my daddy will whip us both."

"I know Jess, I'm working on it. We'd have more time if you wouldn't have raped me for the second time tonight."

She winks. "Can't rape the willing. You know, if you'd just agree to go pre-med, your daddy said he would buy you a new truck. Then you wouldn't have to keep working on this old farm truck."

"Yeah, well I don't want to be a doctor like him." I say looking out from under the hood through the windshield.

She steps out of the truck. "Yeah, well what's so wrong with being a doctor?"

I shrug. "Nothing, that's just not what I want to do. I want to teach."

She smiles and kisses my cheek. "I love you, Jake Callahan."

I snap up in my bed. Text books fall on the floor. I rub my face with both hands. "Fuck."

I'm sweating. Actually fucking sweating.

It was so real. I could feel her touching my face. I gotta get out of here. I jump in the shower and then snatch some clothes on.

Walking out of our private quarters, I see that my mom is already here. She looks up and smiles. "Hey, sweetie. Did you guys have a good night?"

I grabbed a piece of bacon off of the breakfast bar my mom is setting up. "Mom, it was nothing. She just crashed here. I did cook us something to eat but that's ALL."

She rubs her thumb down my cheek to wipe off a crumb. "Baby, I know, it's just time to move on. You know?"

I shake my head. "No, Mom. Jess will never be able to move on, so I'm not going to either."

She shakes her head. "Baby, that's not healthy."

I can't listen to this for the hundredth time. "I'm going to work. I'm sure Dad's office will be packed again today. Then I've got class tonight."

She smiles, handing me an insulated lunch bag. "Here, your father forgot to take some lunch this morning. I put you something in there, too."

I kiss her cheek. "Thanks, Mom."

"What about the young lady? Autumn. What do you want me to tell her?"

I stop at the doorway. "Nothing. Just make sure she can get to Zack when her car is ready." She gives me her look. That look that says I'm full of shit. "Mom, seriously, I was just helping her out. There is nothing between us. She's leaving to go live with her parents in Florida."

My mom shakes her head, turning back to set out food. "Okay. Go on or you'll be late and your Daddy will be on his butt."

As I'm walking out to my truck, my sister Camellia pulls up. She grins getting out. "Hey, Momma already here? I need to see her real quick."

"Yep. I'm heading to work."

She shrugs. "Okay, nice chatting with you, Jake-off douche monkey."

I sit down in my truck. "Screw you, Camellia Deville."

She blows me a kiss and I smile.

Yes, my sister and I have a strange relationship but it works for us.

We talk shit to each other all the time, but nobody has our backs like we do each other's. She's the only one who has even tried to understand what I've been through. Where everyone else thinks that I'm just supposed to magically get over Jess and everything that happened, she just tells me that I'll know when I'm ready to move on and that I may never be, but that no matter what happens, she has my back and she loves me.

Driving back through town, I see my old high school. I flashback to the hallway after class one day at the end of my sophomore year.

"Just go talk to her, man." My friend Silas says.

"Man, you are the star football player around here. You are the one destined to leave here on a full ride, not me. Girls don't fall at my feet."

"If you don't take your ass over there and talk to her, I'm gonna get Zack to go talk to her and you know how that will end up." Everyone knows Zack is a man-whore.

"Fuck you, man. Zack is a whore. You know he wants to hook up with Simone, right?"

His face turns hard. "He better stay the fuck away from Simone." He turns to walk off. "Go talk to her, man."

As she walks by to go to her next class she smiles at me.

Fuck, it's now or never. I catch up with her. "Hey, Jess."

She stops and turns to me. "Yeah."

"Hey, um, I was just wondering. Would you, I mean, do you wanna go out maybe one night this weekend?"

She gives me a mega-watt smile. "Sure. I have to ask my parents, but if they say it's okay, then sure. I have to help my momma with the church yard sale on Saturday, but Saturday night would be great. Is that okay?"

I give her a timid grin. "Yeah, that sounds great. Can I pick you up at six?"

She nods. "Yeah, give me your number and I'll let you know what they say."

Fuck, back to reality where I work and go to school. I'll never see that mega-watt smile again.

Autumn

Waking up to the smell of food cooking is certainly a change. I take a shower and grab my things to put them in my bag when there is a soft knock at my door. I look at my watch and see that it's eleven o'clock. Fuck, I'm probably going to get charged extra for late checkout.

I snatch the door open and see Drucilla, Jake's mom. I start apologizing. "I'm so sorry. I guess I was really tired. I'm gathering up my things to check out."

She smiles. "Sweetheart, calm down. It's no problem. I just came to tell you that Zack is on the phone about your car." She hands me a portable phone.

I let out a breath I didn't really realize I was holding in. "Oh. Thank you. Hopefully I'll be out of your hair soon then."

"Honey, you are no trouble. When you're finished just bring it back to the desk."

Putting the phone up to my ear, I speak. "Hello, this is Autumn."

"Hey Autumn, it's Zack. Listen, I looked at the car first thing this morning and you are going to need a radiator. Fixing it is no big deal but the problem is I can't get one here until Tuesday. With today being Friday, they'd already sent out their delivery trucks before I could get a call in. They deliver late on Monday's so it will be Tuesday before I actually get it in the shop. I should be able to have you up and going by Wednesday morning. I'm sorry. I thought it would just be a hose and I could replace that and you'd be on your way this afternoon."

"It's okay I understand. Is there not another place to get the part?"

"Normally, yes. The problem is the year model of your car. That year they changed the hook-up for the radiator and they only did it for two years, so it's kind of an odd part."

I nod to myself. "I should've expected that. I've had other mechanics tell me that car is a pain because of stuff like that. I guess that year was like test monkey year or something."

He gives off a deep chuckle. “Yeah, something like that.”

“Okay, well thank you for calling me, Zack. I’ll check with you at the first of the week. I need to go see if I can get my room for a few more nights.”

He laughs. “Okay. Yeah, I’m sure you won’t have a problem doing that. Mrs. Dru will make some room for you, I’m sure.”

“Thanks again.”

I hang up and go to the front desk. “Mrs. Callahan?”

“Sweetie, call me Dru.”

“Um Dru. I’m going to need to check in for a few more nights if that’s possible? Zack can’t get the part for my car until late Monday. So the earliest he’ll have my car ready is Wednesday.”

She smiles. “That is certainly possible. Why don’t you go ahead and call your parents to let them know so they aren’t worried? Then come on in the dining room and eat you some lunch.”

I nod and smile. “Thank you.”

I dial my parent’s number and hear my mother pick up. “Hello.”

“Momma.”

“Oh Autumn. I was hoping you’d call me once you got on the road today.”

“That’s why I’m calling, I can’t get on the road today. The mechanic won’t have my car ready until Wednesday morning. The part won’t get here until Monday late.”

“Oh sweetie, I’m sorry. I told your daddy when he bought that car it was going to be nothing but problems.” I hear her moving stuff around as she talks. “Actually, with this hurricane heading in, it’s probably best that you stay in one place. Well, are you okay on money? Do I need to wire you some or anything?”

“No, ma’am. I’m good. You’re right though about the hurricane, traffic was already picking up yesterday.”

I hear her let out a deep sigh. "Okay. Well, I wanna ask you about something. I know you said you're coming here for a visit but Mark from Body Designs called here to double check our mailing address last night. He said you didn't pick up your check the other day and figured you might need it. He said you were taking some personal time, but that when he went to your apartment, you'd packed up. Honey, please tell me. Is something wrong?"

"I, ugh." I try to stall.

"Honey, please. I'm worried about you. This isn't like you."

I exhale loudly. "Eric and I broke up a few month ago. He came into the shop Monday night pretty angry. I just need some time away."

I hear her sigh. "Baby, I'm so sorry. You know we're so excited that you are coming here for a little bit, though. You're daddy and Paulie have turned into beach bums, I swear. Always in shorts and flip flops, gone fishing."

"Well, they both deserve to be a bum for a little while." I say laughing.

"Alright, well you keep me up to date about your leaving and all."

"Yes, ma'am. I'm staying at the same place until my car is ready. It's a place called Twin Oaks in Richter's Crossing."

We finish our goodbyes and I go into the dining room for lunch.

Dru smiles as I walk in. "Everything okay with your folks?"

I nod and smile. "Yes, ma'am. She's just happy I have a nice place to stay until I'm able to leave."

"Okay, well the food is over there on the buffet table. Help yourself."

I nod and walk over, making myself a plate of beef tips and rice with gravy. Grabbing a glass of sweet tea, I sit down at a small table.

A few minutes later Dru stands across the table from me. "Do you mind if I sit here?"

I wipe my mouth with a napkin. "No, of course not." I pick up my fork. "This is wonderful by the way. I haven't gotten many home cooked meals since my parents retired in Florida."

"Well thank you. I'm glad you like it. So, are you just going for a little visit to your parents?"

I shake my head. "No, ma'am. I'm moving there for a little while." I nervously glance off.

She reaches across the table and takes my hand, like only a mother can. "Sweetie, are you gonna be okay? I mean, I know it's probably none of my business, but I saw the little bit of bruising."

I nod, feeling the tears threatening to tumble out of my eyes. "It's okay. Yes, ma'am, I'll be okay. I just needed to get away." I swallow that feeling. I haven't really cried and I'm not going to. Eric isn't worth my tears.

"Okay, well if you need anything you just let me know." She sits her tea glass down. "So now, what do you do for a living?"

I'm nervous to answer this. This lady probably doesn't have a single tattoo and she looks like a fragile southern debutante. Sometimes older people say stuff about my profession. I clear my throat. "I'm a tattoo artist." Now I wait for the reaction.

Her eyes light up. "Oh that's exciting. I noticed your beautiful artwork on your arms. My husband has a few tattoos." She scrunches her nose." It's kinda sexy." She giggles. "My son also has a few. I've never been brave enough, but my daughter Camellia had a camellia done on her ankle a year ago. While I think some people get a little out there with them, I think if they are tastefully done and by someone that is talented, they can be quite beautiful."

Okay, that's a shocker. I chuckle at how vibrant her words are about my profession. "Well, if you ever decide to get brave enough, give me a call. I actually have my kit in my car if you decide while I'm here."

She gives me a huge grin. "I just might think about that. You know, shock my husband and kids."

I laugh and shake my head. “You gotta keep them on their toes, you know.”

She sighs. “You know what, if you’re serious, I’ll run you down to Zack’s so you can get your kit after we finish lunch. That way if I get the nerve we can do it.”

I smile. “Sure, do you have any ideas as to what you might want?”

She nods a little. “I know some things I want to incorporate. Does that help?”

“Sure does. I can sketch some stuff up for you.”

She claps her hands excitedly. “Okay! I’m excited.”

I laugh. “Alright, we will go in a little bit.”

We both go back to finishing our lunch so we can go get my kit.

Jake

I don't know what my problem is today. I can't stop thinking about that fiery red head, Autumn. I know that she'll be gone by the time I get off from here, and then I have class, so I need to pull my head out of my ass.

It's crazy in here again today. This damn flu going around is nuts. I trudge along through the endless amount of patients for the day. I check the clock and realize it's almost three o'clock. We worked all the way through lunch.

Running into my dad in the hall, he looks pale. "Dad, you okay? You need a break?"

He nods. "I'm fine right now. I'm gonna have to talk to the girls though, I think I'm catching this. Your sister just called, she and your mom are sick. I'm gonna need you to take care of the inn again tonight." He starts to walk off. "No, you can't, you have class."

I probably need to be with all of them. I shake my head. "No, I just got a text cancelling it because of the incoming weather. But Dad, if no one is staying at the inn, why don't we just shut it down for the night and I'll go home and take care of you guys. Plus, we are supposed to start getting some weather in from that hurricane."

He shakes his head. "There is a girl staying at the inn. The one you brought in yesterday. She offered to go stay somewhere else but your mother wouldn't hear of it. She actually drove your mother home in her car and one of the guys out at the stable brought her back to the inn. Your mother must trust her if she gave her the keys to come back to the inn alone."

"She was supposed to be leaving today."

My dad nods and is about to say something when he holds up his hand and runs to the bathroom. I slump my shoulders. "Shit."

I walk to the front office. "Tam, dad is throwing up now. I also just found out that Mom and Camellia are sick, too. We need to get the last of these people out of here and call the rest. Send them over to Urgent Care or something. Apologize, whatever we have to do."

She nods, looking a little pale herself. "Sure thing, Jake. We only have the three in the lobby right now. I'll call the rest."

I walk down the hall to check the treatment rooms and Dad comes out in the hallway. "Dad, go lie down in your office. I'm going to see these last three patients and I'll bring you the details. Then we'll get them out of here so we can go home. Tam is looking a little pale, too, so you will probably want to take care of her before we leave."

He nods and heads into his office. "Thanks, son."

I call the last three back to the treatment rooms. Luckily two of them are just here for follow ups and prescription refills on normal meds.

I'm so glad the college required me to get a flu shot for my classes right now. My family and the office staff normally get one, too, but they had a shortage this year so dad had to make sure that some of his elderly and auto immune cases got them first.

After I've finally gotten everyone out of the office and sent dad home, I walk through and soak all the surfaces with cavicide to kill germs. As I'm locking up, my stomach growls. Damn, I still haven't eaten. I should probably swing by and grab something to eat from somewhere for Autumn and I.

I secretly wonder why she didn't leave today. As I drive through town, I notice it looks like we are going to get a thunderstorm.

I make my way into the Tavern Inn, a local bar and grill. "Hey, Tuck. I need to grab some food to go."

"Sure thing, Jake. You look dead on your feet. What ya need?"

I think about the football game that is going to be on tonight. Maybe she would like to watch that, drink a couple of beers and eat with me. I'll swing by the store and grab some beer after I leave here. "I am, the office has been swamped and my whole family has the flu. I have to go work at the inn tonight for Mom. Just give me a large meat pizza, a large order of wings and some bread sticks. Oh, and a bunch of ranch dressing."

He nods. "I'll get right on that."

A few moments later, I hear probably the one voice I hate more than anything. *Fucking Claire.* She is like a damn leech. She rubs up beside me. "Hey, Jakey."

I try to politely put a little distance between us. "Hey, Claire."

"So what are you up to tonight?"

"Just waiting on some food so I can head to work at the inn."

She smiles. "Oh, well maybe I could come keep you company later."

I shake my head. I had sex with this girl one time in high school and she still tries to cling on to any of my friends that are willing. "That won't be necessary, Claire. I'll be working. We have a guest out there."

She winks, turning back to her mixed drink. "Okay, sexy."

A few minutes later Tuck comes out with my food. *Thank God!*

"Here you go, man. Better get out of here before that storms comes in. Hope your momma and them get better soon."

I nod. "Yeah, me too. Dad has to get better, his office will be full again on Monday."

He nods. "Alright, man. Take care."

I nod, grabbing up the food and making my way out to my truck. I swing into the corner store and grab some beer and sodas.

I make my way down the lane into Twin Oaks. I see the light on in the sitting room. Parking my truck in front, I make my way on to the porch of the inn. *I need to come back out and get all the shutters closed up before it gets worse.*

I walk in the door and see Autumn sitting on the couch and drawing in a sketch book. "Hey, I brought some take-out in case you're hungry."

She smiles, looking up and chuckling. "Thanks, looks like you're ready to feed an army."

I laugh. "Oh, I'm starving. I didn't get to eat lunch today and I figured you could share with me. We could watch the Dawgs play tonight and have a couple of beers."

She looks at me weird. "The Dawgs?"

"Yeah. Georgia Bulldogs are playing tonight for some reason. I guess maybe they decided to go ahead and play tonight because of the incoming weather or something."

"Who are they playing?"

"Some no name college I think. Probably the reason they could move the game so quick."

She nods. "Okay, I'll watch but just so you know, I'm a Clemson girl through and through." She winks.

I put my hand to my chest like she's giving me a heart attack. "You've got to be kidding me."

She gives me a pouty face. "What, you worried about the game this year?"

I snort. "No, I'm just thinking had I known you were a Clemson fan, I might have left you beside the road."

She laughs as she opens a beer, taking a sip. "Oh well, you're stuck with me now. It seems the universe is against me getting to Florida."

"Yeah, I thought you were leaving today."

She sighs. "Zack won't have my car ready until Wednesday." I guess she can see confusion on my face. As we set out the food in front of the TV, she explains what Zack told her about her car.

"Damn, that sucks. I know you were looking forward to getting to your parents. It's probably best though with the weather. On the way here it started to look like the bottom was going to fall out and we are going to be on the east side of the storm. It's the worst, you know."

She relaxes a little and sits back. "It's okay. Everything happens for a reason. Like I'm glad I was here today when your Momma got so sick, she worried me a little. I'm glad I could drive her home."

I hand her a napkin as I sit down on the couch by her. "Thanks for that. I'm glad you were here. My dad is sick now, too."

She nods. "Yeah, your mom said that she thought he was and your sister is as well. I guess you're the lucky one."

I look at her seeming so much more relaxed than yesterday. So sexy. I want her even if it's only for tonight. "Yeah, I guess I am."

Autumn

As we sit on the couch watching college football, I also work on the sketch I'm doing for his Mom. It has started raining and I hear the wind picking up outside. I keep glancing over at his profile, he's so chiseled, so beautiful, so fucking ruggedly sexy.

He sits his beer on the table. "So what are you working on over there?'

I chuckle. "Something for your mom."

He looks at me questionably. "My mom?"

"Yeah. When she found out that I'm a tattoo artist, she got all excited. We went and got my kit out of my car today. She wants a tattoo so I'm drawing some stuff up for her. She got sick before we could get started on it today."

He eyes me, obviously shocked. "My mom. My mom, Drucilla Adams Callahan, member of the DAR and Women's League, wants a tattoo?"

I laugh and nod. "Yes. She wanted something very family oriented. She said she's always wanted one, she was just nervous."

He shrugs. "Okay. I mean I knew she never freaked out about any of ours, but my mom just didn't seem like the type to want one. You know?"

"She's always thought your dad's were kinda hot." I roll my shoulder. "She said she really has always wanted one that would represent both families. So I've been working on this." I pull the pad out and show him.

His eyes get large. "Wow. That is just wow."

"Do you think she'll like it?"

He smiles. "I don't know actually, considering I never knew my mom would want a tattoo to start with. But I think it's awesome."

I look at the sketch and back up to his face.

He smiles. "So explain it to me."

"Well, I thought the twin oak trees would be a nice tribute to her family, especially since she loves this place so much. We wanted to figure out a way to incorporate the Callahan name, too. She found a picture of the family crest for me. Since your dad's heritage is Irish and family crests are big to them, we decided to incorporate it somehow. So I thought about putting it on one of the trees as if it's carved, then putting all of your names on the other tree trunk because she wanted her children in it, too."

He looks shocked. "Wow. That is just fucking awesome. I mean, you put so much thought into this."

I nod. "Well, that's part of my job. I mean this is artwork someone is going to be stuck with for the rest of their life." I shrug and sit back into the couch, taking another sip of my beer. "Don't get me wrong, working in a shop you always get the people who want stupid shit like fraternity letters, logos, emblems from stupid stuff and crap off the wall. I love doing stuff like this so much more."

He shakes his head. "Hell, I may let you put this on me too before you leave. Well, if my late bloomer mom doesn't want to hog it all for herself. Do you do that? Give people the same tattoo?"

I laugh. "Yeah, I had a motorcycle club that I did some work for, they have a specific tat that all of their members get. I also had a group of brothers come in and get a crest done a few years ago. Your mom said you had some work. What do you have and where do you have it?"

He laughs and starts to pull his shirt over his head. Holy fuck, he has a cut chest. He must work out some. I mean I can tell he doesn't live in a gym and eat nothing but cardboard, but he's definitely fit. *My panties just got uncomfortable.*

I smile. "Okay, so explain."

"Well this." He points to a military guidon. "Is for Zack's brother, Wade. We all grew up together with our friend Silas. Wade was killed in Kabul last year, it's my most recent piece. He was practically my big brother, too. Silas, Zack and I all have this. It's the guidon for his unit with his name. The guidon is-."

I stop him. “The flag that represents his unit.” I point to myself. “I’ve done several military tattoos, I know most of the jargon. Several veterans come in and get ink. Especially living in the Carolina’s. We have all of the branches.”

“Yeah speaking of that, I thought for sure you’d be a Tar Heels fan or even a Blue Devil fan.”

I shake my head. “Nope. Just because you live in a state doesn’t mean you have to like that team. Look how many *Crimson Tide* fans live in Florida or how many *Gator* fans live in Georgia. Now back to your tats.”

He chuckles. “Fine, Miss Impatience. After Camellia got a camellia on her ankle, I got one here,” he points to his chest, “for her.” He points to a tribal band around his arm. “Just turned eighteen and picked some crap off the wall as you put it. Like I said, I’d kinda like the one you’re doing for my mom to represent my entire family.”

I lean over closer to him. “What’s the script say?”

He shakes his head, quickly putting his shirt on. “It’s a friend’s name, a friend I lost.”

“Is that Spanish or Italian?”

“Italian.” He looks away taking another drink from his beer.

I can tell he doesn’t want to talk about it so I drop it. “Jeez, the way your mom talked you and your dad were covered.”

He laughs. “No, my dad has some old school stuff from when he was in the army. This is all I have and my sister just has the one on her ankle. Well, as far as I know anyway. So what about you?”

I shrug. “Sadly I’m just as guilty of random stuff. Well, it’s more like stuff I create and I like, so I end up putting it on myself. Some are from my early days when I was learning. I do have my Uncle Paulie’s old shop logo on my shoulder blade. I had him do it before we closed his shop. Just a little something from where I started.”

“Can I see the logo?”

I'm not modest by any means. When you pierce and tattoo people, plus have tattoos and piercings, modesty kinda goes out the window but I'm nervous to pull my shirt up around him. I hesitate for a minute. "Um, yeah." I reach and pull up the back side of my shirt.

I feel his finger start to trace the logo. "Wow. That's pretty awesome."

I feel an almost electric current surge through me from his touch. He starts to trace out some of my other tats and I let out a deep sigh. The shock surges through my body, making in between my legs throb. I squeeze my thighs together.

A loud clap of thunder sounds, seconds later I see a streak of lightening through the window and the power goes out. The entire house just vibrated.

I scream from being startled and he grabs my hand. "You okay?"

"Yeah, it just gave me a little scare."

He's moved his hands from my back, so my shirt slides down. "Alright, I'm gonna go grab us some candles and flash lights. It'll probably be a little while before it comes back on. We are on our own little drop line so normally we are the last ones they worry about."

"Do you need any help?"

"No, I know my way around here in the dark better than you. I'll be right back."

Now I'm left alone in the dark with my thoughts and right now my thoughts are consumed with Jake.

FUCK! This throbbing won't go away.

Jake

I dig around in the kitchen until I find a couple of flash lights. Then I grab the candles and light them around the sitting room. “Sorry. This kinda sucks, I know. At least we’ve got plenty of food.” I laugh.

She giggles. “Yeah and with the help of those three beer I drank, I’ll probably just go ahead and crash.”

I flop down on the couch next to her. “No, let’s keep talking. I mean we might as well.”

“O- okay.” She twists her fingers together.

“Do I make you nervous?”

“No. It’s just been a little while since I’ve opened up to someone. Eric, my ex, was probably one of the last ones and that didn’t turn out so great. So I’m a little gun shy.”

I sigh. I know the feeling. “Yeah, it’s been awhile for me, too.”

“So you work at your dad’s office. Are you going to keep doing that when you get out of school?” She asks.

“I think so. I mean, there was a time when that would have been the furthest thing from my mind, but now it’s the only way I see it.”

She tilts her head. “Why would it have been the furthest thing? Did you want to do something else with your life?”

“I didn’t plan on being in medicine at all actually. I originally planned on going into teaching. My dad always wanted me to be a doctor like him, but I never really wanted that. Right after I graduated high school some things happened, and I chose to be an ARNP instead.”

She nods. “Wow. So what did you want to teach?”

“Any kind of Science. I’m good at it.”

She laughs. “Good for you. I hated Science, I was always more of an English or History person myself.”

I shake my head. "So did you always want to be a tattoo artist?"

She shrugs. "I've always been into art. I thought about being an artist, but tattooing just kind of fell into my lap." She laughs. "I'd been drawing on my own skin with pens and Sharpies forever being around my dad and Uncle Paulie. Finally when I was 16, Uncle Paulie took me under his wing."

"That's pretty cool." Suddenly I remember the porch shutters. "Shit, I'm gonna step out on the porch and check the storm shutters."

She nods. "Okay. I'll come help."

I shrug and we step out on the porch. "Let's close these. The wind is coming from the east so these are getting the worst of it. I'm also going to step around on the south end and shut those, too."

"Okay, I guess this is the nice thing about having a wraparound porch."

I nod. "Yeah. I should have closed these sooner." *I was too busy imagining her naked and under me.*

Stepping around the house, I already see a couple of big limbs down in the yard. I feel the hair stand up on my neck and I hear it in the distance. SHIT! I should've had the weather alert radio on.

I take off running around the porch. "Autumn! Get in here now!"

She comes running around the corner and we collide. "Fuck, I hear what sounds like a tornado in the distance, come on we need to get inside and get the weather radio on."

She runs in the house. "Where do we go?"

"Go to the kitchen, we have an old root cellar below the back porch." She runs that way, grabbing her sketch pad off the couch.

I grab the weather radio and a few other supplies while following her. "Okay, wait here for a minute so I can get out there and open the door."

I put the items I brought on the counter by the door. Once out on the back porch, I run to the corner where the trap door is. I finally get it lifted and run back, grabbing the supplies and Autumn. “Here, let me use the light and go down first. It’s been a while since we’ve had to use it.”

I shine the flash light as we make our way down the steps. Once we get down, I light a couple of the lanterns. Turning on the weather radio it starts going crazy. Tornados are touching down in our area, but not right on top of us yet. Then it gives out our area and I hear it. That sound like a freight train. It’s not right here, but it’s a lot closer than it was. I grab her arm and pull her to me. “Stay close by me so we can huddle if we need to.”

She looks at me. “How did you know?”

“I’ve always had a sense. When we were out on the porch I felt the hair stand up on the back of my neck. I also heard it in the distance. I just can’t believe I hadn’t already turned on the radio. I know better than to ignore it.”

It thunders hard, shaking the ground. She jumps in my arms. “Shit!”

I stroke her hair. “It’s okay. That was just thunder.”

She looks up at me through heavy eyes and I see a little fear in them. I sit back against the wall and pull her into my lap while the weather bangs around outside. The weather radio quietens as does the storm. The tornados must be moving along. I guess the adrenaline rush wore us both down. I lean my head back and let my heavy eyes take over.

I wake up from the thunder a little while later. Autumn is still snuggled against my chest.

She’s beautiful, that’s the first time since Jess I’ve thought about someone like that. As beautiful. Not just hot, sexy or good enough to fuck.

I can’t help it, I feel my body leaning further toward hers and I pull her mouth to mine. She wakes up, placing her hand on the side of my face.

We both moan and she moves to straddle my thighs. My hands slide up her ribs, rubbing over her breasts. *Fuck.*

My cock is rock hard as she grinds against my jeans. Her hands run down my chest fumbling with the buttons on my shirt. I put my hand up. "Wait, Autumn." She looks at me through hooded eyes. "Are you sure?"

She nods. "I need to feel something other than fear and hurt."

I take her lips back to mine. "Me, too."

I pull her shirt over her head and unclasp her bra. *Holy Balls! Her nipples are pierced.*

"Damn, that is hot." I put my mouth over one of the rings, sucking in as she cries out.

I lay her back on the ground, pulling her jeans and panties down her legs. I run my tongue down her inner thigh to her core. *Sweet Jesus she has a little ring down here, too.*

"Baby, if you have any more surprises you should tell me now before I come in my pants."

She giggles, but it turns into moans as I bury my face in her soft wet folds.

Flicking the little ring with my tongue, I slide my hand up and slide one finger inside of her. She starts calling out my name and shudders. I come up and lean over her. "Fuck, that was sexy."

Autumn

Of all things, I'm lying on the floor of the cellar, and I'm actually in pure bliss. I've never came like that. People always think that just because I have the piercing I can come in an instant. Not the case at all. You still have to have some digital and oral skills. Believe me, this boy has them.

He slides up over me and takes my mouth with his. I can taste myself on his lips. Our kiss gets more intense and I can feel his erection still covered by jeans against my leg.

I reach down for the button on his jeans. He leans back and takes his wallet out and grabs a condom, then slides off his jeans and underwear. He rolls the condom on and slides back up over me. "Are you sure?"

"Yes. I need you inside me. Now."

I feel him enter me. *Jesus!* He rocks into me over and over. I feel myself climbing toward ecstasy again.

"Fuck baby, you feel so good." He pants in my ear. "It's been a little while, I may not last very long."

What the hell is he talking about? Shit, he's already gotten me off once. Most guys only care about themselves. I feel like I'm about to go again. "Fuck, I'm coming."

I feel his back tense up as he comes, while I'm screaming out to God or whoever is listening.

Lying here wrapped up in a blanket with each other, I keep thinking to myself that this is crazy. I'm here with basically a stranger in the middle of a storm. It sounds like that old *Heart* song. I jump when his thumb touches my face.

"Hey, what are you thinking about over there? You have this intense look on your face."

I sigh. "How fucked up this whole situation is? I'm leaving for Florida. We don't even really know each other. I just got out of a really shitty relationship and we just had mind blowing awesome sex."

He cradles the side of my face with his palm. "Hey, hey. Shh. Calm down. It's okay, we are adults. I think we both just needed this. As far as a relationship, I can't be in one. So it doesn't matter."

That startles me. "What do you mean? Are you already in one? Do you have a girlfriend?" I sit up and bury my face in my hands. "Holy shit, that's it, you have a girlfriend!" I stand up and start putting my clothes on quickly. I have to get out of here.

"Autumn, what are you doing?" He stands up, pulling his jeans on sans underwear.

I look over at him. "I have to go." I start up the steps to the door.

He grabs my arm. "You can't go out in this storm. Come on, let's talk."

I snatch away from him. "No!" I burst through the trap door. The wind and rain are blowing all over the place. I guess in the middle of our tryst the weather picked back up.

"Autumn! You can't be out here." He comes toward me, grabbing my arm.

My heart starts hammering through my chest. He looks angry. I start to shake. I snatch my arm and start running. I don't care about the weather, I'm trying to run across the yard.

"Autumn! Come back, let me explain." He starts running after me.

Fight or flight. Fight or flight.

He tackles me to the ground. "Get off of me! Let me go!" I start shaking and screaming.

He pulls me into his chest. My screams are muffled by his body. "Autumn, I'm not going to hurt you. I'm sorry I grabbed you but you scared me."

"I SCARED YOU?! You just manhandled someone who has just left an abusive relationship."

He cradles my face in his hands. "Oh my God. I'm so sorry. I was just trying to get you to stop so I could explain." He stands up, pulling me to my feet. "Come on, I think we can go back in the house now. We need to get some dry clothes on and I'll start a fire so we don't catch a chill."

Now that my breathing has somewhat returned to normal and I can think straight, I know he's telling me the truth. He may be a bastard girlfriend cheater, but he's not going to harm me. I nod. "Okay."

When we are back up on the porch, he steps down in the cellar to grab the stuff we took down there and turn out the lantern.

Once we are back in the house, we both take a flash light and go to our rooms to grab dry clothes. I have to admit I'm starting to get a little chilly.

Southern weather is crazy. It's humid as hell outside because of this storm, but it's also early November so it does start to get a small chill with the rain.

I think back to him looking down at me while we were in the cellar. His eyes are so hypnotic.

That was the best sex I've ever had. Eric was always so selfish. I've never had someone be so attentive, to make sure I got off just like they did. Hell, I got off twice.

Making my way back into the sitting room, I see he's started a fire in the fireplace. "That feels good." I sit down on the floor next to the fire. "I'm sorry I freaked out like that. I hate that you had to chase me out into that storm."

"Hey, it's okay." He sits on the other side of the fireplace. "I need to explain the relationship thing."

I shake my head. "No, you don't. I mean we just found comfort in a bad situation. I won't say anything to your girlfriend or whatever."

"Autumn. Shut up. I don't have a girlfriend. I haven't in a long time and I never will again."

I shake my head confused. "What? That doesn't make any sense."

"Look, it is a long story."

I look around at the darkness and motion around me. "Seems we've got nothing but time."

He slumps and then stands up. "Okay, but I'm getting something to drink. I'm going to need it."

"Okay. Grab me something, too."

Oh man. What in the hell is he going to tell me? What did that girl do to him or what did he do to her?

My heart starts racing again and I'm imagining a thousand different scenarios.

A few moments later he returns with our drinks and he hands me a glass. "It's Jack and Coke. We drank the beer I brought."

I nod. "That's fine. Thanks."

I take a sip of my drink as he sits on the floor and leans back against a chair letting out a huge sigh.

Jake

Am I really ready to tell someone this? Everyone thinks they all know the story, they all think I'm crazy. They are just waiting on me to snap.

Staring up at the ceiling and watching the orange glow flicker from the fireplace, I decide to start. "Jess and I were high school sweethearts from the time we were juniors. Her family moved to town the summer before. Her family was always a little strange, but she was so beautiful that I couldn't see past that. I didn't know if I would ever work up the nerve to talk to her. When my friend Silas finally coaxed me into it, I thought I'd pass out. I asked her out and she said yes. That was the start of our relationship. Our senior year, my father started pushing me about becoming a doctor. I never wanted to be a doctor and he felt like I didn't understand about money. So instead of them giving me a new truck like they'd said, I had to drive one of the farm work trucks. Which never bothered me except that it was always breaking down."

I look over and see that she's gazing at me intently. "Anyway. One night I was running behind bringing Jess home from a date when the truck broke down. I was on the side of the road working on it. I had noticed that night that she was particularly horny but seemed preoccupied all at the same time. Looking back on it now, it was almost like she knew it was our last night together. She was complaining to me about getting her home on time and that if I would just go to school and be a doctor, my dad would buy me a truck that I wouldn't have to work on all the time. I was telling her I didn't think I would be happy being a doctor. She stepped out of the truck and kissed me, telling me she loved me. That's when a big truck came out of nowhere and slammed into my truck. We were both hit with my truck but I managed to pull myself up and call 911. I got over to Jess, she'd been stabbed with a piece of metal and was losing a lot of blood. I tried to help her, tried to treat her wounds."

I take another big swallow from my drink. "The next few hours were a blur. Paramedics, cops and my parents. Come to find out, her family was on the run from some Detroit gangsters. They'd managed to stay here for almost two years without being found. Her sister told me that they'd planned to leave town the next day after our date, they'd overheard their parents talking. They were pretty sure they'd been found. That's the reason she was acting that way. She knew she'd never get to say goodbye. The Detroit guys were scoping out our town for them. They saw us on our date that night and sent her parents a message…by hurting her."

She sits forward and covers her mouth with her hands. "Did she live? What happened?"

"She did, but she'll never be the same. They told me she'd suffered a lot of blood loss and it had done some brain damage. Also, she'd more than likely be paralyzed. My dad offered to get her into some specialty places, but her family was too afraid of being found again. They said they would handle it. They left and I had to deal with all of the rumors and speculation."

"Did they go into witness protection or something?"

I shrug. "I'm not sure. Every once in a while I get an envelope in my mailbox with a picture and update. It's only about once a year and it's always a plain envelope, no way to trace it. Believe me, I tried."

"So, is that why you said no relationships?"

"Yes. Everyone thinks I should move on, but she can't so why should I?"

She shakes her head. "I don't think that's fair to you. I mean it was an accident. If it's anyone's fault, it's her parents or those gangsters. You should be able to move on."

I shake my head. "No, if I would have just quit being so damn stubborn and took my dad's offer we would have never been beside that road. She might have left, but she'd have been safe."

"Jake, you're not being fair to yourself. She loved you, she'd want you to be happy. What did you mean by rumors and speculation?"

I take another big drink. "Well, you know how I told you about being small town royalty and expectations? Let's just say when they find out the girl you were dating for two years was on the run, you are a topic of conversation. I have people who think it was all a set up and that I know where they are. I have people who said we were arguing on the side of the road and there were no mobsters. There are the ones that think I set the entire thing up. There were actually even some brave souls who acted like my father had set the whole thing into motion to get me to become a doctor."

She wipes the corner of her eye. "So what happened after they left town? I'm assuming the way you talked that they did leave town."

I shake my head, trying to clear some of the memories, I guess. "I had a couple of days in the hospital. I'd broken my arm, cracked a couple of ribs and had a concussion. My parents took me home and tried to play buffer between me and everyone else. I got questioned by all kinds of law enforcement. The entire alphabet soup. Once they determined that I really didn't know anything, they left me alone. The doctor that saw over Jess until she left told me I'd done all the right things at the scene. I'd done everything I could for her, which isn't true. If we hadn't been in that broken down truck in the first place, it wouldn't have happened. So that's when I decided to give up the idea of teaching."

She crawls across to me and puts her hands on my face. "Jake, you can't-."

I cut her off. "I wanted to go to med school, but my parents felt like with my 'experience' I should go into nursing first and see how I like it. If I'm happy as an ARNP, then they'll pay for me to finish up med school."

She clears her throat. "Are you happy?"

I nod. "I like helping people. I actually like working with my dad. I just wish I'd come to this conclusion earlier."

"You were what, 18?" I nod and she shakes her head. "You were a kid, you didn't know what you wanted. Why do you think like 75% of college freshman change their major like five times that first year?" She lets out a big exhale. "Okay, enough depressing stuff. Do you think your mom has anything sweet in there?"

I laugh. "I'm positive there are some cookies in the jar and if the fridge is still cold, there's a pie in there."

She smiles. "Mmm pie."

I pull her up as I stand and we make our way into the kitchen. Knowing that since I've only opened the fridge once since the power went out a few hours ago, I know the pie should be fine. I grab the chocolate cream pie, two forks and a couple bottles of water. Walking back in the sitting room, she's sitting Indian style in front of the fireplace. I hand her the pie as I sit down. "There's only half of a pie left, I figure we can finish it."

She laughs. "Who said I was sharing?"

I shake my head. "You better."

We both grab forks and dive in. When the first bite his her mouth, she moans. "Fuck that's good."

That sound reminds me of us in the cellar earlier. "Don't make that sound babe, or I may take you right here."

Autumn

I giggle when he says that about my moan. “This is really good, though.”

He laughs. “So what’s your story? I told you all my deep dark secrets.”

I look down. “I told you some of it the other day. But okay.” I tell him about meeting Eric, how things progressed into the fight Monday night.

He looks at me with fire in his eyes. “Did he rape you?”

I shake my head and say in almost a whisper. “No. I stopped him before that happened.”

He looks at me now with confusion. “Why would he want to keep you but change you? I don’t understand. You’re wonderful the way you are.”

“I don’t know. He wanted me, I guess just covered up with normal hair. I was like his dream girl, but the real me, the one with ink and piercings, he didn’t want anyone else to know that me.”

“He just sounds like a spoiled ass brat to me. He just wanted things his way.”

I lean back against the chair. “I guess I was his way of rebelling from his parents without them knowing. I really don’t understand him either. I just knew he was serious the other night when he said he’d be back. I can’t have him causing trouble for my boss that way so I decided it was time for a warmer climate. I talked to my boss, gave myself a day or so to heal and pack, and hit the road.”

“He was a dickhead and an idiot.”

I chuckle at little. “Yeah, if my dad and Uncle Paulie had still been up there when this happened, Paulie’s guys would have made him pay.”

“Hell, I think he still needs to pay.”

“That’s all well and good, but once he sees that I’m gone, he’ll drop it.”

He looks at me and lifts his eyebrows. “You really think so?”

I shake my head. "Yeah, he has the attention span of a toddler. So literally it's out of sight, out of mind."

He exhales. "For your sake, I hope so." He looks at his watch. "Shit, it's almost one in the morning. How about I gather us some blankets and we can crash in here? That way if the weather radio goes off, we're closer to the cellar."

I nod. "Sounds good to me."

He goes and gathers some blankets and pillows. When he comes back in the room, I smile and laugh a little. "I almost feel like you're going to build a blanket fort in a minute."

He laughs. "We can if you want to. I'm not above camping inside."

I shove his arm a little. "Nah, let's just get some rest." I think for a minute about what I would've done in this storm had he not rescued me from the side of the road. The reality is I don't know what I would have done. I lean up on my tip toes and kiss his cheek. "Thanks for all of this. If you hadn't picked me up yesterday, I have no clue what I'd have done today during the storm. Hell, I'm not even sure where I'd be."

He gives me a half smile. "No problem."

We lie down on the blankets. It's like there is this strange weirdness between us. We just had great sex, spilled our guts to each other, and now we are afraid to touch each other. Finally, I roll over to him. "Okay, I have a proposal."

He talks with his eyes still closed. "I'm listening."

"I say we just have a good time this weekend. Well as much as we can have during a hurricane. It doesn't seem like either one of us are in a good place to have a relationship but we obviously have some chemistry. So let's just hang out, talk, have sex, cuddle, laugh, whatever we want and then when I leave, I leave. No strings."

He peeks one eye open. "That's all well and good, but most girls get attached."

"Really, were you not listening about my last boyfriend? I don't want an attachment right now. I just need to blow off some steam."

Finally, he nods. "Okay. Well in that case, I think I'd rather enjoy blowing off some steam myself."

Suddenly he flips me on my back and kisses my neck. "I think I'd like to blow off a little more right now."

I laugh. "Sounds like a plan to me."

He reaches for his pants, grabbing his wallet out. "I have one condom left in here. so this is it for tonight."

"Don't tell me that's the end of our weekend. Especially if the stores are closed for the storm."

He kisses my neck. "No, I'm pretty sure I have some in my truck."

I nod as he moves down, taking my nipple in his mouth through my t-shirt, tugging the ring a little. I run my hands up his arms. As he works his fingers into my sleep shorts, I push him up a little so I can sit up. Pulling my shirt off as he slides my shorts down my legs, he smiles. "Fuck, you are beautiful, and all of those piercings just make me fucking crazy."

He works his way down my body to my clit and my hood piercing. As he licks and tugs on it, I come apart. "Oh God. Jake. Jake. Oh God."

He lets go, sliding up over me and into me. I'm not sure when he slid his boxers off, or put the condom on for that matter, but he did. "Shit babe, your pussy is like a glove."

"Oh." That's all I can manage to get out.

After a few minutes, I roll so he's on his back and I'm riding him. He groans. "Shit babe, that's it, ride me."

I start moving faster and rougher. "Oh. Oh. Fuck, Jake." He reaches up and grabs my nipples roughly with his mouth and I come, screaming incoherent jibber jabber. Suddenly, I'm flipped back on my back and he pounds into me.

He leans down into my ear. “You like the way I fuck your pussy, don’t you?” All I can manage to do is nod. He thrusts into me hard a couple of more time before screaming. “Fuck, Autumn! So fucking good!” As he slams into me for the last time.

He rolls to his back, pulling me on top of him. I chuckle. “I think I’ll be able to go to sleep now.”

He laughs. “Did our activities wear you out?”

I close my eyes and nod my head against his chest. “Mmm hmm.”

I feel him pull the condom off. “Let me grab a napkin off the coffee table to put this in.” Grabbing one of the napkins from our dinner and disposing of the condom, he settles back into me and stokes my back. “You have to be one of the sexiest women I’ve ever met.”

Still talking with my eyes closed, I chuckle. “You know I’ve already had sex with you. Flattery really won’t get you anything now.”

“I’m just being honest. Oh and you agreed, I’ll still get more out of my flattery until you’re gone.”

I laugh against his bare chest. “Sure. Mmm hmm.” I say, feeling my eyes get heavier and heavier.

Jake

Waking up this morning with Autumn wrapped in my arms is strange. Not a bad strange either. I don't think I've ever woken up with someone in my arms before. The very few girls I've hooked up with since high school were all kind of *wham bam thank you, ma'am*. No cuddling or morning after. With Jess, we never had the opportunity to wake up together, we were kids. So yeah, I guess this is my first time. Looking down at her face resting on my chest, I brush the hair back off her face.

She stirs. "Hmm." Rolling to her back, she stretches like a cat, thrusting her tits into the air.

I put my hand on her stomach. "You should stop right now if you don't want to get taken advantage of as soon as your eyes open."

She giggles, pulling the blanket up over her chest. "As much as I would love that, I'd really like to find some way to bathe off or something."

"I'm pretty sure we can find a way to do that. I need to get dressed and go outside to see what kind of damage we have."

"Let me put some clothes on and I'll come with you."

We both get dressed and walk outside. It looks like we've pretty much been spared. There are some limbs down and one of the storage sheds has some metal missing, but that's it.

An idea pops in my head. "Wait right here just a minute."

She nods and I run in the inn, grabbing some towels, soap and shampoo.

I come out the door with a bag and she looks at me amused. "What are you doing?"

"We are going to go bathe. We have to go down to the pond and it'll be kinda cool, but at least we can get clean."

She laughs. "Well that sounds chilly but refreshing. I have to say I haven't went skinny dipping in years and surely never in November."

"Well, there is a first time for everything. Follow me, ma'am." A few minutes later we've walked down to the pond.

We strip off and run into the water. She shrieks. "Fuck, that's cold!"

I laugh and try to forget the fact that I think my balls and dick just crawled back up inside me to warm up. "If you'll come over here, I'll warm you up."

She shakes her head. "Nope, I have a feeling if I come over there, you have an entirely different idea for warming me up."

"Oh, I'm coming to get you now."

~*~*~

An hour later we are back at the inn, clean and dressed for a new day.

I look over at her sitting on the couch sketching and I sit across from her. "So I was thinking we could ride out and check on my parents. Plus, they might have power."

"Okay, that would be good. I could take my sketch to show your mom and my kit in case she wants to get started."

A little while later we pull up to my parents' house. I unlock the front door and go in. "Hey guys, Autumn and I are here."

My mom comes around the corner, still looking a little pale. "Hey honey. Is everything okay at the inn?"

"Yes, ma'am. Just some limbs down and some missing metal on one of the storage sheds. We don't have any power out there right now. Did you guys lose power here last night?"

"Yeah for a little bit through the worst of it. I was worried when the weather radio kept going off giving the area close to the inn."

I nod. "Yeah, it got a little rough. I heard a tornado close by. We had to get in the root cellar for an hour or two. How's Dad and Mellia?"

My mother's eyes grow huge. "Oh My Goodness! I hate it got so rough. Your daddy and sister are doing better, so am I." She turns to Autumn. "Sweetie, are you okay?"

Autumn smiles and nods. “Yes, ma’am. Jake did a great job. I brought my sketch I’ve been working on for you.”

My mother’s eyes light up and she claps her hands together. “Yay! I was telling Jack about it last night.”

“Mom, it looks really awesome. I was hoping you wouldn’t mind sharing. I’d like to have her put it on me, too.”

Mom smiles. “Ooh let me see.”

Autumn grabs her pad out of her bag. “I hope you like it.”

As soon as my mom looks at the pad she tears up. “Oh Autumn, sweetie. This is just beautiful. Where do you think I should put it?”

“I was thinking maybe on your shoulder, or I can put it on your leg somewhere if you want to be able to keep it covered.”

I look at my mom. “I think you should do the shoulder, Mom. If you’re sure, that is. I mean what about your friends, what will they say?”

My mom shakes her head. “I don’t give a hoot what they think. I want it on my shoulder. So where were you thinking about getting it, son?”

“I was thinking about over my heart.”

My mom smiles. “Well then, I guess I’ll share my tattoo with you.”

I laugh. “Autumn brought her kit if you are up to it.”

My shrugs. “Maybe not today. Let’s see how I feel tomorrow. Why don’t you guys stay here tonight?” She looks at Autumn. “They never get the power back on at the inn until it seems like very last.”

Autumn looks around. “I don’t want to be a bother.”

“Autumn, we have plenty of room out here and Camellia left this morning to go check on her apartment.” My mom says while smiling her best debutante smile.

Why in the world my sister has an apartment, I don’t know. I mean I have my own apartment in the barn out here on the farm, but she could still live with Mom and Mad. I guess since she’s in college now, she wants to assert some independence or something. All I know is she better not have some damn piece of shit guy shacking up with her there.

I look over at Autumn and mouth. *"You can stay with me in my apartment."* Wagging my eyebrows.

She chuckles out loud before she realizes it and covers her mouth quickly. "Thank you, Dru. It would be great to stay out here."

My mother looks over at me to see what I've said. I shrug. "Actually, you should probably stay with me in the barn. We don't need to run the risk of you getting sick before you have to make your trip."

My mom walks away with an *hmph.* I laugh and Autumn shakes her head.

"You just had to say that didn't you."

I grab her around the waist. "Hey, we agreed I get you for the few days you're here, and I intend to take advantage of everyone minute of it."

Autumn

Hanging out with Jake's parents has been a trip. He and his sister obviously have a close, but funny relationship. His parents tell me about the things they've done to each other over the years, but it's obvious that he'd do anything for his sister.

After he and I make a lunch of soup and sandwiches for his parents, he offers to show me around the farm. It's really a beautiful place, they have cows and horses out here.

"I can't imagine growing up in a place like this. I've never gotten to be around animals like this."

He gives me that southern boy, panty dropping grin. "Have you ever been horseback riding?"

I shake my head. "No. I rode one at a carnival one time."

He bursts out laughing. "That's not the same. Come on, we'll go for a ride."

I'm suddenly excited and nervous at the same time. "Are you sure?"

He motions for me to come on. "It'll be great, come on. Don't get all scaredy cat on me now."

I finally nod and we walk into the horse stable. "This is Matilda, she's very gentle. She's good for a first timer."

After he saddles the horse, I watch him climb up on her. "I thought I was going to ride her."

He laughs. "You are, you are just going to do it with me this time. I wouldn't put you up on here by yourself to start with. Give me your hand and put your foot in the stirrup, then just swing it over."

He reaches his arm down. I grab ahold of it, pulling myself up while I put my foot in the stirrup and slide in behind him on the saddle. I giggle once I'm up on the horse.

"Okay, I think I'm ready."

"I hope you are." And just like that we take off.

~*~*~

The past couple of day have proven to be mentally challenging. I've never felt the chemistry I have with Jake. I mean we are still pretty much strangers, but we are fucking like damn rabbits. He bent me over a hay bale yesterday. How he manages to keep so many condoms on hand, I don't know.

But I've also went horseback riding, and I feel comfortable on my own horse now. I've gotten to feed cows and pet them. It's like a whole other world out here and I love it.

We went out yesterday and checked the inn, along with Zack's shop to make sure my car was still there and intact after the storm.

I know the campus where Jake goes to school got damaged so they are out for a week. The roof on his dad's office had a chunk taken out of it, so they have a crew there patching it up with Jake helping them.

While he's gone, I decide to call my phone and check my messages since it's been a few days with no service.

Message one. Look Autumn, I'm sorry about the other night. I lost my temper. Call me back and we'll talk this out.

Message two. Don't avoid me, Autumn. I'll find you, I don't care what that tattooed up dickhead said.

Message three. Hey Autumn, it's Mark. I hope everything is going okay. That little preppy prick you used to date came in here demanding to know where you are. I told him I didn't know. He got pissed and started showing his ass. I threatened to beat the shit out of him if he didn't leave, hope that doesn't make you mad. And you better not get back with him, he's always had abusive high dollar drunk written all over him.

Message four. Fuck you, Autumn. I'll beat your ass good the next time I see you. I know you aren't living in your apartment, I went by there today. How do you think I liked finding out my girlfriend just up and left fucking town? I'm going down to that shop and that fucker is going to tell me where you are.

Message five. Hey, Autumn. So I called your parents to get your mailing address down there, I saw you moved from your apartment. That is probably a good thing. I think you need to stay with your parents for a little bit. Preppy prick went off his rocker again last night. I had to call the cops on him for tearing up my shop. His daddy is not thrilled with him or me.

Message six. Hello Autumn, this is Mr. Vander. I would like to speak with you on a matter concerning Eric. Please give me a call at your earliest convenience.

Message seven. Hey girl, it's Mark again. I know that Mr. Vander is trying to get in touch with you. Call him back. I guess he finally realized how off his fucking kid is. He wants to get him in some treatment facility for his anger. So you need to call him. I hope you're being safe. Your mom said that you broke down and with the weather, you haven't made it to Florida yet. Keep in touch.

Fuck, I guess I should call his dad. "Dru, I need to make a couple of more calls. Is that okay? I need to return some messages."

She fans her hand. "Sure honey, no problem. Can we do my tattoo later this afternoon? I know you are supposed to be leaving day after tomorrow."

I smile. "Sure."

I take the phone and step into the den. I dial Mr. Vander's number.

"John Vander."

"Mr. Vander, this is Autumn Byron. I was returning your call."

"Yes, Miss Byron. I know that you've left town and I gather from your employer that it may have had something to do with my son. Can you enlighten me?"

"Well, I'm not sure if you're aware, but Eric and I broke up a few months ago."

"No, I didn't know that."

"Well, we had some problems. He became controlling, belittling and verbally abusive. The other night he showed up at the shop out of nowhere and demanded that I go back out with him. When I said no, he got physically abusive. He tried to force me to have sex with him. He didn't stop until I hit him over the head with a paperweight and threatened to call the cops, knowing that you wouldn't like the publicity he left. A couple of days later, I left town."

I hear him let out a deep sigh. "I'm sorry this happened, Autumn. I'm also very sorry that he went into your workplace. I take it since the owner didn't mention the attack on you, he doesn't know about it."

"No, sir. I was trying to keep my private life private. I figured you felt the same way."

"Yes, I do, and I appreciate your privacy on this matter. We are sending Eric to an anger treatment facility. He had some problems when he was younger but we honestly thought they were under control. I'm sorry all of this has happened. I hate that you felt like you had to leave your home in fear."

"I appreciate your apology and for what it's worth, I hope Eric can get some help. I know I was never the kind of girl you had pictured for Eric, but I don't wish him or your family any ill will."

"Thank you, Autumn. You have a nice day."

"You too, Mr. Vander."

I call Mark back and apologize for all that's happened and I fill him in on what happened to cause me to leave. He understood and told me that I'll always have a booth in his shop, if I want it. I told him I felt like it was time to move on for a little while.

I'm going to start a new chapter in Florida. I wipe a couple of tears from my eyes and make my way back to the kitchen. "Alright lady, when do you want to get started?" I pick at her.

Her eyes light up. "Now!"

Jake

After helping the crew patch the roof on Dad's office, we go inside and check to see if we have any damage. One of the treatment rooms is a mess. I tell Dad I'll take care of it so he can go on home. He's doing better, but I don't want him to push it.

Autumn is leaving the day after tomorrow. I've never had this connection with someone. We are addicted to each other's bodies, I swear. It's like a drug. The intensity of the passion we have is euphoric. It's not just that, though. We may still be basically strangers, but I feel like I can tell her anything.

If I were anyone else, I'd ask her to stay here forever. Stay with me, move in with me and make babies. But that will never be my life. Jess doesn't get that so neither will I.

My dad comes in the office. "Son, I'm going to go on home. I just wanted you to know that I'm happy you seem to be moving on with this girl."

That shocks me. "I'm not moving on. We are spending some time together while she's here, but she'll be leaving soon and that will be that."

"Son, what happened to Jess wasn't your fault. You don't need to keep living your life as some kind of penance for what happened."

I shake my head. "If I hadn't been so stubborn and just agreed to medical school, I wouldn't have been broken down by the road."

"Well, then this is my fault, too. I should've never put that much pressure on you. I should've gotten you the truck we promised."

Is he crazy? How could even think that.

"Dad, this couldn't be your fault. You weren't there, you didn't hit us with a truck. You just wanted what was best for me."

He looks at me in the eyes. "Exactly. You didn't hit you guys with a truck either. Her parents were the ones involved in this. You were just part of the collateral damage."

"But-."

"Son, don't let the good things in life slip by. Our time on this Earth isn't guaranteed from one day to the next. Now, I'm going to head out and check on your mom. I'm pretty sure she was going to get that girl of yours to do her tattoo today."

I chuckle. "So, how do you feel about mom getting a tat?"

"If she wants one, she should get it. She said you want the same one."

"Yeah, have you looked at it? It's awesome."

"No I haven't, she wants it to be a surprise."

I shake my head and laugh. "Alright, well I'm going to get this treatment room cleaned up and then I'll be home."

"Okay."

I mop up the floor in the room and start working on sanitizing everything in the room, all the time thinking about my life. Thinking about Jess, her beautiful smile, the things she would say to me. I think about her and I laugh. She was the blonde haired, blue eyed all-American girl. She would put hot sauce on everything. She would only drink clear drinks, I could never convince her to even try sweet tea.

My thoughts drift over to Autumn. She's a totally different girl. The red hair that's different shades, the tattoos that drive me wild, and those piercings do something for my libido that I never thought possible. It's like just thinking about them makes me hard. She always listens to what I have to say, never seems to be picking it apart like most girls, trying to figure out *what I'm really saying*. I don't know why girls do that. I'm saying what I really mean. You may like it or not like it, but that is just the way it is.

I try to concentrate on what my dad said, I could move on and start over with her. It's just Jess is holding me back. If only I knew where she was, how I could say I'm sorry.

I spend the rest of the afternoon cleaning up the rest of the office. I swing by the inn and see that they've finally gotten the power back on. I clean up our mess from the other night and turn on the fans to get the stuffiness out of the rooms.

Finally around six, I make my way home. I don't see the lights on in my apartment so that means she's at my parents. Making my way inside, I see her watching a movie with them and it really warms my heart. My mom sees me walk in. "Hey, sweetie. You hungry?"

I nod and she follows me to the kitchen. "I fixed some pork chops, mashed potatoes and field peas. Fix you a plate."

"It looks great, I'm starving. So did you get your tat today?"

Her eyes light up. "Yes!" She shrugs her shirt around so she can pull down the shoulder.

Just like I knew, it's the most beautiful piece of artwork I've ever seen.

"Looks awesome, Mom. Are you gonna share with me?"

She winks. "Yeah, I think so."

She walks back in the living room and I scarf down my food. We watch another movie with my parents and then head over to my apartment.

Autumn brings her kit with her so she can do my tattoo at my place. Once we are settled in, she sets up and I lie back on the couch for her to work.

I watch her facial expressions and the looks in her eyes as she works. She's so sure of herself. So confident. I want to be that way about something.

I'm jarred from my fantasies of her when she sits up. "All finished."

I go look in the bathroom mirror. "Holy shit, Autumn, this looks even better than Mom's."

She shakes her head. "They are the same. It's just the placement. I do like it, though. Looks very sexy on your chest."

I grin, pushing her toward my bed. "Wait. We have to cover this first." She says, putting cream and a cover over my tattoo.

Once we are in bed, we play around and I know I want this forever. I can't stop myself from saying it, either.

"Autumn, would you consider staying here? I think I'm ready to move on. I want to do it with you."

She looks at me with doe eyes. "I don't know. How do you know you're ready? I mean, just a day ago you said you'd never let yourself have happiness."

"I don't know, I just am." Before she can answer, I take her mouth with mine. Soon I'm dragging her pants and panties down her legs. I lick that little hoop through the hood of her apex and she cries out. Before long, I'm pounding into her with both of us screaming out in ecstasy. I slam into her one last time. "Forever. I want this forever."

I pull her into my side, she doesn't say much before we fall asleep.

~*~*~

The sunlight coming through my window wakes me. I roll over to put my arm over Autumn, but I'm met with a cold bed. Instead of her, I find a note.

Jake,

I know you're going to be upset with me for leaving like this. I hope you understand though. The last relationship I was in, my partner wanted me to be someone else. I can't do that again. If I stay, I'm worried that I'll always be a substitute for Jess. I know you would never do it on purpose, and believe me, it would be so easy to stay here. I love it here. Your parents are awesome, this town is great and you aren't too bad, either.

When you know for sure that you're ready, not just a spur of the moment, sex-filled decision, you come find me. I had to leave after last night. I laid awake most of the night wondering and going over scenarios of what could happen. I know that I need to get some distance to make the right decision and for you to make a decision.

Zack had called me yesterday to say that my car was ready a little early. I was going to stay, but I knew if I did that I would be here forever. Do me a favor, find your inner peace, then come find me. I feel like you know me, the real me, even in just a few days, it's crazy.

Who knows, after I leave here you may not miss me at all. If that is the case, that is fine, too. Just know you're special and a wonderful man and you deserve to be happy.

Yours,

Autumn

I storm out of the apartment and into my parents' house. My dad meets me in the kitchen. "Come in here, son. Let's talk."

"Did you know she left?"

"I took her to get her car. Now come sit, we need to talk."

I want to scream and throw shit, but this is my parents' house. Instead, I nod and sit down. "Okay, talk."

"I know you love Autumn."

"I'm not sure it's love, I mean we just met."

"Sometimes it happens that way. You've talked to her more in three or four days than you've talked to anyone in four years. She pulled you out of that deep dark place you'd sequestered yourself to." He adjusts himself on the couch. "I'm going to tell you something and I know you aren't going to like it."

"Okay."

"I know where Jess is. I've known the whole time." I feel my skin growing hot with anger. "Now before you blow up, I didn't want to tell you to start with because you would have been all in the middle of things and her parents didn't want that. You would have stayed out of guilt. I've talked to them, kept in touch. She's in one of the facilities I suggested for them. Now, I'm going to give you the information, and I'm hoping you use it to give yourself some closure." He gets up and hands me a card and walks out.

Fuck

I grab my phone and make plans to get to Arkansas as soon as possible.

Autumn

Three Weeks Later…

Watching the waves crash over and over again from the Gulf of Mexico is very therapeutic. I sit here most days wondering if walking away from him was the biggest mistake of my life. I laid there in that bed all night trying to figure out how I felt. If only I knew if he was really moving on past the whole Jess thing.

I cried for almost the entire trip here. I came so close to turning around several times but I just couldn't do it. His dad was so sweet and helpful about leaving. His mom was so upset. I just knew that it was what I had to do. I gave his parents my address so he could find me if he really wanted to and I left.

My parents have been great about me being here. My Uncle Paulie was so excited, he wanted me to give him and my dad some matching pirate tattoos since I guess they want to live like retired pirates now. So now they have a bad ass old school Jolly Roger tat on their calves. I've looked around trying to find a tattoo shop that I would fit in, I just haven't found one yet.

Looking at my phone I see it's about supper time, so I should make my way back to the house. My daily afternoon pity party is over.

As I start walking back down the beach, I see someone walking my way. They are still pretty far away, but there is something familiar about the way they walk.

Once I get closer, I see him. I can't help myself, I take off running and jump in his arms. We fall over with me landing on top of him. "Holy shit. I can't believe you're here."

He laughs. "Well, I'll take that as you are happy to see me."

I nod through tears. "Yes."

He wipes the tears from my face. "Hey, hey, hey no crying."

"I'm so happy you're here. I just hope it means what I think it means."

"Let's talk." He scoots and we sit beside each other. Now I'm nervous.

He looks at me. "When you left I was ready to tear everyone and everything apart. But Dad reined me in and gave me the shock of my life. He had known where Jess was the entire time. He told me he knew if he'd told me earlier, that I would have given up everything and stayed with her in Arkansas out of guilt. He felt like after you, I was ready to move on. So he gave me the contact information for closure.

"I left out the next day. I knew what you did was right, as much as I hated it. I knew I had to get my shit straight before I could give you the life you deserve. I got to the facility she's in. It's a great place and she's not completely paralyzed. She has some fine motor skill issues and some brain damage, but she lives a relatively happy life. Will she ever live on her own or have a husband and kids? No, but she was happy. I got to see her smile.

"Her parents came in while I was there and they talked to me for a little while. They told me they never blamed me for any of what happened, and that they knew Jess had always been happy with me. That if she had to live the rest of her life like this, they were glad I made her happy so early in life, that she actually got to live some before everything was taken away. Her father started crying, telling me that he was to blame for all of this. That it was his connections that brought the entire family danger."

He swallows hard. "I spent a couple of days there watching her and I realized I was ready. She may have been my first love, but I want you to be my last."

"Are you sure? I mean, how do you know for sure?"

"I want you to come back with me. I found a location and put a deposit down. A location that would be great for you to open a shop in town. If you don't like it though, we'll find another place. We've always had to go out of town to get ink so I think you'd do okay. I would move here to be with you, but I'm starting medical school next fall. I've already been accepted to the program at State. I finish my ARNP stuff this coming summer. It gets a lot of stuff out of the way and I'll move a little faster in the medical program."

I smile. “Wow. You’ve figured out so much in three weeks. All I’ve done is give my dad and uncle a tattoo and figure out that I wouldn’t fit in any of the local shops and miss you.”

He nods. “I had a lot more shit to clear up than you did.”

“So you want me, huh?”

He shakes his head. “Autumn, you’d have to be nuts to not see that I’m falling for you so fast I can’t catch myself.”

Jake

Autumn's Ink Grand Opening…

I think I'm more nervous than Autumn. This is her dream, and I want it to be perfect. She's spent the past four months getting this place exactly like she wants. She's already been seeing people. My mom let her use one of the rooms at the inn since it's hardly ever full. We all thought it would be a good idea for her to go ahead and start building a clientele.

Since she's been here, my sister and dad have gotten the family tattoo. Right now we are staying in my apartment, but we just broke ground on the farm to build a house.

My dad was right, we never know if we are going to be here tomorrow and I don't want to waste a single minute not being with Autumn.

I walk into the bathroom and see her double checking her hair and make up for the grand opening. "You look sexy, babe."

"Yeah it's the red hair. I have to give the guys that old school pin up girl kinda thrill, you know?" She laughs.

"Well, the old guys will definitely like it." I kiss her neck from behind. "You know, we have a few minutes..."

She laughs. "Baby with you it's always more than a few minutes."

"Thanks, babe. I take that I'm not a minute man as a compliment."

"Well good because I meant it that way."

I hear the front door jingle as someone comes in. My parents are the first to arrive. I'm not shocked, they are so proud of Autumn. Her parents, her Uncle Paulie and her aunt came in yesterday to surprise her for the big day. They'll be here in a little while. She's so happy. If I ever had any doubts about us, I surely don't now.

When I'm around her my heart feels like it may explode with happiness, just sheer happiness.

After being open a few hours, my sister has helped her schedule appointments. Her next couple of weeks are going to be full. She did a small tattoo on me today for everyone to watch. I got the Caduceus Symbol. I've wanted it for a little while, but today just felt right. It's the medical emblem most hospitals or medics have.

After we lock up, she smiles as we look in the mirror. "That looks so good, but I think you always look good. I'm kinda partial."

I grin, kissing her on the lips. "You know, I kinda think you always look good, too."

We kiss for a minute and I grin at her. "Well, it looks like you are going to be very busy for a few weeks."

"Yes, I even had one of the ladies from your mom's DAR group schedule an appointment."

I laugh. "Holy crap. My little sexy red head is going to turn my small town on its head."

She smiles. "Yep. I guess so. Oh and I got several compliments from the retired men about my outfit. They said they always liked it better when women looked sexy and left a little to the imagination."

"Dang, I'm going to have to watch out for old guys on rascals now, too. But just for the record, I think this look is sexy as fuck and I'm going to show you just how sexy."

I boost her up on the counter and work her panties down her legs. After slipping the condom on, I slide into her. She kisses me hard on the lips. "I'm so happy you came for me."

"Autumn, I had no choice but to fall for you. I don't think it was ever up to me."

She grins. "Thank God."

I keep thrusting into her until we both come. I smile. "Well, we've christened the shop."

She giggles and wraps her arms around me. "Let's go home."

I look down at her and smile, knowing I could do this for the rest of my life. “Okay.”

Holiday with Holli

A Richter's Crossing Seasons of Change Novella

By: S.M. Donaldson

For anyone who needed a do-over in life.

Holiday with Holli

A Richter's Crossing Seasons of Change Novella

Editing by Chelly Peeler

Introduction

• Due to mature subject matter this book is for readers 17+.
•This book is written in a true southern dialect, from a true southern person. Therefore, it is NOT going to have proper grammar.

Let me start by saying I hope you enjoy this novella. This is the first in a series. Each Novella in this series will center around a season of the year. Also, it will release during the coordinating season. They will all be based in the town of Richter's Crossing, but they will be able to be read in any order.
This is a new adventure for me and I'm excited.

Holli

"Sweetheart, had you told us that you were planning to come home this Christmas we would have remembered."

I shake my head knowing I told my mother that I was planning to come home for Christmas, just like I always plan. I just wouldn't take no for an answer this year, so she decided to do what she does about anything that doesn't go her way. She ignored it. My parents have never had, nor made time for me. I spent most of my holidays growing up with my Gran, and I miss her all the time. She passed away right after the end of my freshman year at college.

I could just stay at school like I have most years, but no one will be here. I have one friend here, and that's Jules. She and I became friends my first year here. She was the only person who was willing to look past my pretentious wardrobe. She even asked me to come home with her this Christmas, but I'm not anyone's charity case.

My parents aren't horrible people, they're just people with a certain set of expectations. They just expect me to go to the proper school, date the proper boys and dress a proper way. Their lives are broken up into assets and liabilities. If you aren't an asset, you are a liability.

"It's fine, Mother."

I hear her exhale loudly through the receiver. "Well, I gave the staff Christmas off, so you'll be here all alone."

"It. Is. Fine, Mother."

"Well, if the Mitchell's weren't expecting us in Aspen tomorrow we would try--."

I have to stop myself from laughing, my parents haven't cared about even attempting to do Christmas with me since I was eight and found out there was no Santa. Well, mom told me there was no Santa is more like it. After that it was just me and Gran.

"Mother, it's fine. It'll give me some time to rest before I go back to school."

"Yes, dear, that is a wonderful idea. I'll make you an appointment at the spa for a day while you're here. A little rest and rejuvenation for my sweet girl, help you get rid of those stress lines. You know this is your last semester in college. All of that worry and stress will cost you in the long run."

I know that and I'm thrilled. "Yes, I'm so ready to stop writing papers and start doing the work I've set out to do. I actually get to work in a pharmacy this upcoming semester."

"I know, that's lovely, dear, but what I'm saying is you're running out of time to find a nice boy. You're twenty-one, dear. Have you thought anymore about seeing Christopher or Scott again?"

She acts as if I'm a dried up old maid. "I know how old I am, Mother. No, Christopher and I had nothing in common or to even talk about, it was a dreadful date for both or us. Scott is a complete jerk."

She doesn't need to know that Christopher reeked of scotch when he picked me up and had more hands than a darn octopus has tentacles. That he openly smacked our waitress on the butt during our dinner and tried to swallow my face when he dropped me off. He then proceeded to call me a tease, because I wasn't willing to just fall into bed with him. Then, there was a huge incident in his car. As soon as I climbed out of his Jag, he barely gave me time to get the door shut before he sped off.

However, Scott I thought I liked and that he felt the same. As it turns out he was more interested in taking my virginity and hoping that would be enough to get him an interview with my father's company. Well, he was right on both accounts. He got my virginity. Then, he did get an interview and a job with my father's company. No one knows that he and I slept together, if that is even what you'd call it. He got me completely drunk and I was almost passed out until he broke through my hymen. That is one of the biggest regrets I have in my life. That is the one time in my life I've allowed myself to be really vulnerable, and it won't happen again.

Rather than argue with her and let her know more into those jerk's lives, I just pacify her. "Yes, I intend to get plenty of rest this break. I'm going to try and find a nice guy next semester. Okay?"

I can almost see the smile on her face through the phone. "Yes, dear. I'll set you up for an entire day over at Merlot's. Sandra will give you the full day treatment." She squeals like a giddy school girl, "I just wish I was here to go with you. I'll leave the information about your appointment on the message board by the office phone."

I nod my head as if she can see me. "Yes, ma'am. Thank you so much." I give the best cheerful sound I can through the phone.

After hanging up with my mom, I lie back and relax on the chaise lounge in my living room. I think about my life. I'm finishing college way earlier than I should. They wanted me to be a good student, so that is just what I did. I worked really hard, took all AP classes in high school. I graduated a year early and since I took college level courses in high school, I was almost two years into my degree when I started college.

I've always done what they expected of me and more. I just kept my head down, smiled and nodded, playing the part. Being an only child to a wealthy family can be a bit of a burden to carry sometimes. I get jealous when I look around the campus and see parents helping their kids move in and out their dorm rooms. My parents would have never helped me move and I was forbidden to live in a dorm. They bought me a nice apartment in a secured complex just off campus, hired an interior decorator and hired a moving company to move my personal items. I have managed to make one friend since coming here but Jules didn't really give me an option. She sat beside me in Orientation and that was that.

Standing up, I put my feet in my slippers and tighten the belt on my robe. I think about the girls around school dressed in gym clothes, lounge clothes or even just jeans and t-shirts. They look so happy, so relaxed. My parents would die of heart failure. I own one pair of jeans, I bought them for a western night at my sorority. My mother always believed you dressed for success even when you went to bed. Jeans were only for cowboys and cashmere should be like a second skin. I look at myself in the full length mirror on my bathroom door, I dress like I'm forty. My blonde hair has soft curls and is just past my shoulders. I stand here in a peach and cream nightgown and matching robe, with slippers. Really, I look like a politician's cookie cutter wife. I could be Christopher's wife, the wife who sits at home while her husband is out screwing his secretary and drinking scotch with his friends, the private joke in his office, but I'm not going to be.

I have a long drive ahead of me tomorrow to get home to Northern Georgia, and with holiday traffic it'll take me even longer, so I should get some rest. Placing my slippers by my closet and sliding my robe off, I watch myself in the mirror and begin to wonder. *Will someone ever find me sexy? Will I ever get those wild nights of romance like I read about?*

I shake the thoughts from my head and place my robe on the wingback chair in the corner of my room. I climb into bed and stare at the ceiling until sleep takes over.

It feels like I've just closed my eyes when sunlight comes through my blinds. I shuffle to my shower and turn on the warm water. Stepping under the spray, I think how it would be to shower with someone else. To feel that passion. Once again shaking those kinds of thoughts from my head, I finish my shower and wrap a towel around my body, until I'm dry enough to put my robe on.

Once I've finished my hair and my makeup, I slip off my robe. I pick a pair of cream linen dress pants with an aqua sweater and a pair of nude pumps. Most people would travel in comfortable clothes, but not according to my mother.

I grab my phone and shoot a quick text to Jules that I'm about to leave and to have a Merry Christmas. She left a couple of days ago, her family is going to the mountains for Christmas. Finally, I make my way down to the parking garage, pop the trunk on my BMW and place my suitcase inside. Sliding into the driver's seat, I place my wool coat in the passenger seat and set off for my hometown Richter's Crossing.

Zack

I'm running the diagnostics on Mr. Jacob's Audi when my dad comes into the garage. "Okay, son, I'm gonna go home, grab my bag and hit the road. Are you sure you're alright with this?"

"Dad, he's one of your oldest friends. This is probably his last Christmas, go see him."

He nods. "Okay, we'll have a steak dinner when I get back."

I shake my head. "Sure thing, Dad."

It's just been Dad and me for a while. My mom died when I was a toddler and my dad never remarried. My older brother, Wade, died overseas a while back. Dad and I own this shop together. He's hung in there with me through everything. I have to give him props, I wasn't the easiest teenager to have. I partied, drank and slept with anything that had a slit between her legs.

I still go out for a drink most nights at the Tavern Inn. Sometimes I meet a few of my buddies from high school, sometimes I don't, and my sex life is still pretty much a revolving door. I've just never found a girl that would hold my interest longer than the time it took to have sex.

I'm finishing up the diagnostics on the Audi when my cell phone rings. I grab it up and swipe across the screen.

"Caraway's."

"Zack, this is Marcus Brown."

"Hey, Mr. Brown. How can I help you?"

"We left for Aspen today for the holidays, I need you to run out to our place and pick up my wife's Volvo. It needs servicing and I would prefer it be done while we are gone. The keys are on the hook in the garage. You have the code, right? No one will be there to let you in."

"Yes, sir. I still have the code. I'll run out there this afternoon and pick it up. When will you guys be back?"

"On the second of January."

"Okay then, well y'all have a Merry Christmas."

"You too, son."

I shake my head after I hang up the phone. Never in my life did I want to be Marcus Brown's do-boy but he pays damn good money. I don't like how he calls me up like I'm his servant who can just drop everything to suit his needs. We are the only shop in this little town who is certified to work on foreign cars. That works to our advantage most of the time. It also means that we stay pretty busy.

Taking out my cell, I send my friend Jake a text.

Me: Hey can you give me a lift out to the Brown's? He wants her car serviced while they are out of town and dad left already.

Jake: Sure. I'll be leaving the office in thirty minutes. Will you be ready then?

Me: Yep. Thanks man.

Jake: No problem.

I close up the doors to the shop and lock everything up. I scrub up and grab some disposable covers to lay in the Volvo. I shut down the computers and meet Jake outside.

I climb up in his truck. "Thanks again, man."

"So, Marcus called ordering again?"

"Yeah, if he didn't pay such damn good money I'd tell him where he could stick his orders."

"Has he ever said how Holli is doing? I haven't seen her since we graduated."

"No. Which he wouldn't say anything to me, anyway. It's not like she and I ran in the same social circles. She probably moved to some Convent."

"She wasn't that bad, Zack." Jake rolls his eyes at me.

"She dressed like she was older than most of our teachers. Her clothes probably cost a hell of a lot more, too. She never gave me the time of day, she acted like it was a chore to even speak to people."

He chuckles. "That's because you were such a prick to her. You terrorized her."

I shake my head. "No I didn't."

"Dude, you called her Frosty."

"Because she acted so cold towards everyone."

He shakes his head as we are turning up the drive to the Brown Estate. "Look, she probably didn't have the easiest time fitting into her parents' standards. They don't seem like the type to be very supportive. It's not fun living your life under a microscope. I should know."

I shake my head and jump out of the truck. "Thanks, man."

"Sure, no problem. You going to the Tavern tonight?"

"Not tonight, probably tomorrow night, though."

He nods his head. "Alright, I'll try to swing by."

I shut the door and he pulls off. I walk around to the back side of the house and punch the code in the keypad. The garage door rolls up and I see the blue Volvo sitting in its normal place. I notice an extra car, a BMW, and I guess Mr. Brown got something else.

I reach up to the hook and grab the keys for the Volvo. As I'm about to open the door on the vehicle, I sense someone behind me. Before I can turn around, something hits me and everything goes dizzy for a minute.

I lean up against the car trying to regain some sense of direction. About that time, a screaming blob of blonde hair comes at me again. This time I catch it.

"What the fuck?" I yell while I'm still trying to focus.

"If- if you don't let me go, I'm calling the police."

I shake my head trying to see one of everything. “And tell them what exactly? That I was supposed to come out here and pick up a car to service for Mr. Brown and you assaulted me?”

“No one told me anyone was coming out here.” I recognize that voice now.

I sigh, “Your father called me today and asked me to come pick up your mom’s Volvo to service it while they are in Aspen for the holidays. He said no one would be here.”

She half chuckles, shaking her head. I can see a sadness in her eyes. “Fine. Sorry I hit you. I wasn’t expecting someone to be here.”

I notice for the first time how much more attractive she’s become as she’s gotten older. She was always pretty, but now. Wow. “Yeah well, the next time you think someone is stealing a car you should probably come at them with more than an umbrella. You should at least use a croquet mallet.”

She rolls her eyes. “Thanks for the heads up. Should I expect you to be breaking in again over the holidays?”

“Yes, I’ll be returning the car before your parents get back.”

She crosses her arms, which pushes her breasts up in her little sweater. “Well, thank you for the heads up. I’ll try not to hit you next time.” She looks hollow in her eyes.

I shake my head as I put the disposable covers on the seat and floor of the Volvo. “Anytime, Frosty.”

She snarls as I shut the door and back out of the garage.

Holli

Zack Caraway is still the same butthole he's always been. He's always called me Frosty and I really have no idea why. I never did anything to him in school, but I wasn't exactly popular. When you had to dress like you were going on a job interview instead of going to high school, you didn't make many friends. I was friends with a few people from the AP classes I took and from the academic bowl team, but Zack was a football player and he and his friends ruled the school.

Hearing a commotion at the other end of the hallway, I look to see what's going on. I see Silas, Zack and Jake horsing around. Claire runs up and jumps on Silas's back. A locker to my left slams. I turn to see Simone glaring at Silas. She loves him. Too bad he doesn't seem to have a clue. I hear her mutter something about a 'stupid skank' and 'a fucking dick'. She storms off just as someone smacks my rear end. I spin around and Zack is there. "Hey, Frosty."

My voice trembles a little and I look down. "H- Hi, Zack."

"Are you coming to the game tonight?" Jake and Silas are laughing.

My shoes are really interesting. "Um, no."

"Yeah, I didn't figure so. We don't have box seats at our little stadium." He touches my arm. "Damn, just as cold as an ice block. Have a good day, Frosty."

Shaking my head, I bring myself back to my current place. Walking around my parents' house is more like walking around a museum than a house. My mind begins to wonder. Why was Zack the one picking up my mom's car? Who does he work for that my dad trusts? My dad used to always take the cars over an hour away to get them serviced because he didn't trust "Podunk Mechanics" with his quality machine. Well, Podunk was the word my mom always used to describe the town.

Also, what the heck did my dad mean there wouldn't be anyone at home? Did he forget I would be here? I know Mom told him I was staying here without them. I'm sure she made a huge production of telling him.

I guess I need to go see how much food is here. I'd literally just walked in the door when I heard the garage opening again.

I walk in the pantry and look around. I know Sylvia does the shopping each week, I'm sure there won't be anything sweet in here. Yep, no Little Debbie fat cakes or anything like that. I check the fridge, there's nothing to even make a simple sandwich and no Coke. God forbid this house have a darn bag of Doritos in it. I'll have to make a trip to the store later to get some *junk* as my mother would call it.

I can hear my mother now. *"Holli, I know you're small now but one day all of this junk will catch up with you and no man is going to want you. Water is essential, along with some healthy dehydrated veggies."*

Yuck. Why would anyone think that was a substitute for a nice fudge covered brownie?

Looking at the oil painted canvas of our family, I have to laugh. It really is a joke. We are supposed to look like some all American family but in reality we are strangers. I think about Jules's family. I've met them before, I actually went home with her last Thanksgiving. To me they look like a Norman Rockwell painting, just the Latino version. They bake cookies together and tell funny embarrassing stories about each other.

It makes me miss my Gran even more. She and I used to bake cookies for Santa, it always made my mother furious.

I smile thinking about that. I grab my keys and decide I'm going to get the stuff to make cookies.

My cell rings as I'm backing out of the garage. I hit my Bluetooth.

"Hello?"

"Hey Deb, how's it going?"

I shake my head and chuckle. "It's going fine, Jules. Are you ever going to quit calling me Deb?"

"No, because you, my dear Holli, are the poster child for a Southern Debutante. Glistening vapors and all. So what are you doing?"

"On my way to the store to pick up some groceries, or junk, as my mother would call it."

She laughs. "Ooh. Marsha is going to be pissed." She always compares my mom to Marsha from *The Brady Bunch*. '*Marsha Marsha Marsha.*' My mom Lenora Brown would have a heart attack at the comparison.

"Well, she would be even madder had I really hurt the guy they didn't tell me was coming to pick up her car for service. That I hit over the head with ann umbrella."

A roar of laughter comes through the speaker. "You didn't?"

I laugh. "Yes I did, and to make matter worse it was this guy I knew from high school."

She's laughing even harder if that's possible. "You, my feisty little Deb, are too much."

"I'm glad you think this is so funny. I think I almost had a heart attack."

She clears her throat. "So was it a hot guy from high school?"

"Really, Jules?"

"Yes, really. Maybe a little bow-chicka-bow-bow would brighten up your holidays."

I laugh. "I don't think that will be happening. Yes, he was one of the hot guys from my high school, but it's not like they ever gave me the time of day. Also, he's still the same a- butthead I remember him being back then."

She giggles. "You know you are an adult. You can cuss if you want to."

I shake my head. "It's not appropriate."

"No, what's not appropriate is how your parents have made you this person who is scared of your own shadow. Now, I have to go, one of the demon twins is trying to smoke on the back deck before our parents get back. I've got to go stop him."

I laugh. "Okay. Tell him tobacco use leads to impotence."

"If it was only tobacco."

My mouth drops open and I laugh as she hangs up. I wish I had a set of crazy twin brothers like hers, they are always doing something. Jules comes from a pretty big family. She has two older brothers and then the set of twins, who are seventeen.

I grab my list as I park at the local Piggly Wiggly. It's funny I never really went in here when I lived here. Our housekeeper had always done our shopping. The only reason I even know how to grocery shop, or cook anything for that matter, is because of Gran. I grab my buggy and smile at the older lady doing the same. As I turn around I see Claire coming in. She sees me and sneers.

"Well, if it isn't Ms. Holli Brown. What are you doing shopping with us lowly working class?"

I'm about to say something when a voice speaks up from the side. "If by working class you mean spreading your legs like you…oh wait, you don't charge, do you?"

I cover my mouth, trying not to laugh at Simone. Claire rolls her eyes. "Fuck off." She grabs her buggy and walks away.

Simone laughs. "Welcome home. Some bitches don't change. They think they're still living in their glory days of high school."

I laugh, "I guess you're right on that one."

We both start walking in the direction of produce. "So, are you just home for the holidays?"

I nod. "Yeah. A little down time before my last semester."

"Wow. Is your family doing something big this Christmas?"

I shake my head. "No. It's just me this Christmas."

She smiles, knowing that my family always leaves town for the holidays. "Well you should come down to the Tavern tomorrow night. It's karaoke night, it'll be entertaining to say the least."

I smile, because it's nice to be invited somewhere. This is what Jules is always on my ass about doing. Getting out of my comfort zone. "Um, sure. I'll try to make it out there."

She pushes her cart on. "Good, see you then."

I stop and turn around. "Wait, is Claire gonna be there?"

She laughs and stops. "God, I hope not. If she is we can just ignore her. I'd really like someone *normal* to hang out with."

I nod. "Okay, I'll really try then."

I know that this is what I need to do, I need to work on my people skills. I'm going to the Tavern tomorrow night. I guess I'll be buying a pair of jeans on my way home since the only pair I own are at my apartment.

Zack

After getting wacked in the back of the head today, I decided the best place to go was home. So I did just that, after I dropped the Volvo off at the shop. I caught up on *NCIS*, ate a couple of *Hungry Man* dinners, and drank some cold beer. A nice relaxing night, or it was supposed to be, but my mind keeps wondering back to Holli.

Why did her dad tell me no one would be there? Did they seriously forget she would be coming in for the holidays? Yes, my dad is gone for Christmas, but he sees me every day and his friend is dying. It's not a trip to Aspen. Maybe she didn't want to go, she probably wanted to go to an island or something. This is her little fight of defiance. Yeah, probably. Princess Frosty can do whatever she wants. But when she talked she looked so- lost.

She got freakin' hot after she went to college though. I can't stop thinking about her breathing heavy when she was scared. DAMN!

"Fuck, I'm going to bed." I say to myself. I lie down and thanks to the beer, sleep comes easy.

She's crawling up my body in a white teddy with garter belts and stockings. She's going to make me blow before anything. "Holli, you are so fucking sexy."

"Really?" She says as she grinds against my erection.

I groan. "Fuck yes."

She starts to peel off the teddy. "I'm not too frosty?"

Shaking my head, she laughs and suddenly she's getting further and further away. Laughing harder and harder.

~*~*~

After a long night of tossing and turning, and waking up from one hot dream of Holli to the next, I gave up about five and went for a run.

Now I'm at work and nothing seems to be going like it should be. The computers are acting crazy, I slammed my hand in a door and busted my knuckles turning a wrench. Today is not my fucking day.

I finally just say fuck it and decide to break for lunch. I walk down to the little café on the square, where I eat almost every day. Jake is eating lunch with his dad and he motions for me to come over and join them. I slide into the booth on the side with Jake. "Hey, Dr. Jack. How's it going?"

He smiles. "Good, son. How are you doing? Work keeping you busy?"

I nod. "Yes, sir. As much as I can handle anyway. Dad went to visit his friend in the VA hospital for Christmas."

He sips his coffee. "Well that's good, I know he was hoping he would make it before his friend passed. You should come out and join us at the farm for Christmas dinner."

"Thank you but I'm thinking a nice relaxing Christmas alone will be good for me."

His dad stands up, putting money on the table to cover all of our lunch, even though I haven't ordered. "Well, the offer is there if you change your mind."

"Thank you, sir." I shake my head, Dr. Jack never lets us pay for our lunch.

Jake's family has always treated us all like that. I didn't have a mom growing up and our friend Silas really didn't have anyone but his grandma, so the Callahan's called us their chosen kids.

Jake motions to me as I slide into the other side of the booth. "So are you coming to the Tavern tonight?"

"Yeah, might as well, not much else to do around here."

"Did you get the Brown's car to the shop and all?"

I laugh as I motion to the waitress that *I'm here*. "Ha. Well as it turns out Holli is home, she thought I was stealing the car and wacked me over the damn head with an umbrella. Once she finally believed what I was saying I got in the damn car and left."

He sits back, laughing hysterically at me. "So you guys hit it off right to start with again, huh?"

The waitress brings over my usual order as Jake is still trying to catch his breath. I toss a french fry at him. "Fuck you, man, really." I start putting my burger together. "And to top all of the shit off, she got fucking HOT at college."

"Oh this is just getting better and better."

I shoot him the death glare. "Really man, go to hell."

"I just think it's a good punishment for you, you were always an ass to her. Now she's hot and you are having perverted dreams about her."

I glare up at him. "How did--."

He snorts. "I was just fucking with you, but you had dirty dreams about Holli!"

I put my head in my hands. "Shut up or I'm removing you from my life."

"You couldn't remove me from your life. No one else will put up with your ass." He laughs as he's getting up. "I've gotta get back to the office and then out to the farm. They say we are supposed to have some sleet and ice tonight, so dad has me wrapping pipes this afternoon."

"That's what I heard too, have fun with your pipes. See you tonight, man."

"Yeah."

I finish my lunch and head back to the shop hoping my afternoon goes better than my morning has. As I'm walking back, I see Holli's blonde hair duck into one of the local shops. I peer through the display window, knowing in my head I'm just hoping to catch a glimpse of her. I feel my pants tighten.

She catches me looking. I hurry on past the window, shaking my head.

What in the hell am I thinking? She is fucking off limits.

Once I walk back in the shop, I kick an empty five gallon bucket. “Damn it!”

Getting pissed off with myself for my dick getting hard at the sight of her blonde hair does nothing to make it go down.

Grabbing up my latest issue of *FHM* magazine, I make my way to the bathroom to take care of my problem.

What a fucking day.

Holli

Looking in the mirror, I don't even look like myself. I did my hair and make-up a little more than I normally would wear. Chasity, the sales girl at Southern Chic, helped me pick out some really cute *Miss Me* jeans. Along with an awesome sweater that makes my boobs look magnificent, or so Jules says from the pictures I text her. I put on my knee boots to complete my outfit. I smile at the girl in the mirror and leave the room.

Tonight I'm turning over a new leaf. My parents don't seem to care or even remember that I'm here. I'm an adult for crying out loud, why am I so worried about what they think? I shouldn't be. Well, they do hold all the keys to my future. No wait, my college was paid for with my scholarships. Yes, without them I would have had to apply for grants and housing, but I could have done that just as easily. Jules is always telling me that I need to get out of my comfort zone, I just wish she was here to help me.

Twenty minutes later, I'm pulling into the parking lot of the Tavern. The Tavern Inn is a local bar and grill that everyone goes to. It's a rite of passage in this small town. Needless to say I'm being initiated tonight.

Getting out of my car, the butterflies in my stomach are suddenly starting to feel more like bats. I stand here for a moment trying to gain my courage.

"Hey girl, I'm glad to see you came out."

I look across the roof of my car to see Simone. "Hey, yeah I decided to come."

She smiles. "Alright, well I'll see you inside. Your first drink is on me." She calls over her shoulder as she walks toward the entrance.

I take a few deep breaths and start walking to the front doors. I feel my heart about to pound out of my chest as the gravel parking lot crunches under my feet.

As I enter the bar, I hear karaoke is already in full effect. There is an older lady on the stage singing that old Loretta Lynn song *One on the Way*. Simone was right, this should be some nice entertainment.

I make my way to the bar and order a Midori Sour. Simone reaches over me. “Hey Tuck, put that girly drink on my tab and six shots for my table.” She smiles at me. “I told you your first one was on me tonight.”

I smile. “You don’t have to.”

She shakes her head. “I know but I want to, and you are going to join us at our table.”

Shoot. “Oh- um, okay.”

She laughs. “Come on, everyone will be glad to see you.”

I follow her to the table and see some people from high school along with some new faces. I take the shot that Simone is determined that I take and sip on my drink.

I feel him before I see him. I caught him staring at me today while I was looking at jeans. I’m just waiting for the jackass remark he’s going to make. Why does he hate me so bad? I’ve never done anything to him.

“Well, little Miss Holli came down from her ivory tower to hang out with us common folk at a bar.” He puts his hand over his mouth. “Oh, what will Mr. and Mrs. Brown think?”

Simone shoves him in the chest. “Shut up, fucktard. She’s here tonight on my invite. So sit down and shut up before I shove your tongue down your damn throat.”

He smirks and mumbles. “I hear you get a lot shoved down your throat.”

Thank God Simone didn’t hear him. I look at him with an evil glare. Simone grabs my hand. “Come on, let’s go sing.”

I shake my head. “Um no thanks.”

She laughs. “Come on.”

“No, I haven’t had near enough liquid courage to do that.”

She smiles and heads to the bar. Jake laughs. "I think you screwed up there, Holli."

"Crap."

My skin crawls when I hear the next voice. "ZACK!"

I turn to see Claire climbing on Zack's lap. I don't know why but it makes me mad, but it does. At the same time Simone returns with a couple of shots and me a new drink. I gladly take her up on that and barely notice Zack pushing Claire out of his lap.

Simone looks at her. "Go spread your STD's elsewhere."

Claire rolls her eyes. "Bitch."

"Didn't the health department serve you with a cease and desist order?" I giggle at Simone, she's fiery.

Claire looks back at her. "Fuck you, Simone. You think if you make friends with the rich bitch it will do you any good? You'll always be shit."

Simone jumps up and everyone snatches her back into her chair. I grab her hand "Let's go sing now." What the crap? I really just said that. Wow, those shots are going to my head.

She smiles. "Come on."

A few minutes later, we finally decide on *You're So Vain.* I'm not too worried about how I sound, I know I have a decent singing voice. Also, from what I remember Simone has a pretty good voice, too. It's just being in front of these people for the first time in almost four years that racks my nerves.

I feel like those shots are going to come back up. Taking a couple of deep breaths, I look out across the bar and I see Zack staring at me. He's pissing me off. Simone looks at me and gives me a grin when the song begins.

You walked into the party like you were walking onto a yacht
Your hat strategically dipped below one eye
Your scarf it was apricot

You had one eye on the mirror as you watched yourself gavotte
And all the girls dreamed that they'd be your partner
They'd be your partner.

By this point almost every female in the bar is singing along with us. After we finish, Simone hugs me. "That was fun."

I smile. "Yeah, it really was."

As we walk back over to the table, everyone claps. Zack winks at me. "Nice set of pipes you got there, Frosty."

I smirk back at him. "Just exactly what in the heck is your problem with me?"

"Just teasing you girl. Don't get your sensible cotton panties in a twist."

Simone pulls me down in a chair and I try to ignore him as she flips him off.

She looks at me. "You really have to learn to cuss if you are going to get your point across."

"I just was always taught-."

She grins. "I know, you were taught not to use such degrading language. With an asshat like Zack, you have to use words that he will understand."

I laugh. "That actually makes sense."

About that time my phone weather alert goes off. "Shoot, they are about to start closing roads because of the ice. I guess I should get out of here."

She looks at the alert on my phone. "Yeah. I guess we should let everyone know that we should all get going. Are you okay to drive? I know you aren't used to drinking this much."

"Yeah, I think my nerves from singing sobered me up."

She nods. "Okay, if you're sure. Be safe going home."

I smile. "You, too. Thanks for tonight."

She laughs. “Yeah, it was fun.” She grabs a napkin and jots something down on it. “Here is my number, text me and let me know you got home okay. Also, call me while you’re in town and we can grab lunch one day.”

I smile. “Thanks, I will.”

Zack

I watch her great ass walking toward the door. I look up at Simone. "So I guess she's had enough?"

"No, smartass. We should actually all get going, they are closing roads from the ice."

Something hits me hard inside my chest. I grab Simone's arm. "Is she okay to drive?"

She smiles at me knowingly. "She said she was. She has my number to text me and let me know she's made it home or that she needs me."

I grab my coat and try to play off what she thinks. "Good, I wouldn't want to be blamed by her parents if she wrecks her little beamer."

She shakes her head and rolls her eyes. "Yeah, I'm sure that's all it is." She laughs. "You are such a douche nozzle, you know that, Zack?"

I smirk. "Yep, but you love me."

She shakes her head. "Yeah, almost as much as I love poison ivy."

I grin. "Awe. Don't be like that, Mony."

She turns and glares at me as I make my way to the door.

I reach my truck after almost busting my ass a couple of times from the ice. Hell, there is no way she'll make it home. She's not used to driving after a few drinks and surely not in these driving conditions.

"SHIT! SHIT! SHIT!" I hit the steering wheel.

I pull out of the parking lot headed toward the Brown's. At least this way I'll know she's safe at home.

Why do I even freaking care? Why can't I get her out of my head? Fuck, she has a sexy singing voice. A gorgeous smile, a brilliant set of fucking tits and an ass that just won't stop fucking haunting my dreams.

As I turn down Standland Road, my heart starts to feel like it's going to jump out of my chest. Then, I know why. As I make the turn on to

Brownsville, I see her little white car off the side of the road. I hit the accelerator and slide off the road behind her car. I jump out before I'm even sure the truck has stopped moving. I make it to her door and snatch it open. Her forehead is bleeding.

"Holli! Holli, are you okay?" I say touching her arms.

She looks around confused. I'm pretty sure she checked out for a minute. She nods her head. "Yeah. I think so."

I reach for her hand. "Come on, get out of the car."

"A deer-."

I look at her confused, worried she hit her head harder than I thought. "A deer?"

She stands up. "A deer ran out in front of me. I couldn't stop, because of the ice."

I lean her up against the car. "Stand right here."

I walk around and see the deer off the side of the road. Suddenly it jumps up and runs off into the woods. I check out the damage to the front of her car. She must've gotten her bearings enough to walk because she's looking at the front of her car now, too.

"That deer did a pretty good job banging up your car."

She's still a little shaken. "Y- yeah." She shivers.

"Let me move it over to the side of the road and tomorrow I'll bring my tow truck out here and pick it up. Then we'll go get your head cleaned up."

She nods a little, unsure. "Okay." It's barely a whisper.

I get the car off the road and call the local Sheriff to report the deer hitting her car. I told them that I would be out in the morning when the roads opened back up to tow the car. I guess they've had a busy night with the roads icing over, so they understood.

I guess I'll have a busy day tomorrow after they open the roads. I see her shiver again.

I grasp her arm. "Let's go get you cleaned up. Your car will be fine here until in the morning. It's warm in my truck."

She gets in the passenger side of my truck and I drive her to her house. Once we get to her place, I open the garage and walk her inside. After we are in the kitchen I ask, "Where can I get a first aid kit?"

"In the cabinet by the sink." She steps over by the sink with me. "Really, you don't have to do this. I can do it. You've done enough."

"No, I need to make sure you don't have a concussion."

"Why are you doing this? You don't even like me. You've always hated me."

"I'm just trying to be a good person."

She rolls her eyes and something hits her. "Wait. What were you even doing headed out this way?"

Shit. "I wanted to make sure you made it home. I saw you had had quite a few shots and I just wanted to make sure you were okay. You don't strike me as the type to have a big tolerance for alcohol."

She looks at me as I start to clean the cut on her forehead. "But why?"

"Look, I don't want something to happen to you. And I didn't hate you." I say as I place the bandage on her forehead.

"Then why? Why did you always treat me like some kind of leper?"

I sigh, "You just always seemed closed off and wouldn't speak to us. I was just trying to get a rise out of you. You acted like you were so much better than us."

"I did not." She looks at me in shock.

I widen my eyes. "Really? Then how would you describe it?"

She turns her face from me. "Self-preservation. I was introverted and shy. I'm still that way. Tonight is one of the first times I've ever really stepped outside of my comfort zone." She spins back around with tears in her eyes. "Do you think it's easy living your life like some kind of prized show pony? I'm told where I can live, how I can dress, who I should date and what I should eat."

I honestly don't know what to say. I knew her parents probably played a hand in how she acts, but I never would have imagined this much. "I'm sorry, for what I said and how I treated you in high school. I guess I only saw what I wanted to see about you."

"Yeah, most people only look at the display laid out for them to see. They never take the time to discover what it's made of." She turns walking into the living room.

Holli

I'm blaming the alcohol. That is the only reason I would've said something like that to him. With the exception of Jules, I've never talked about my family life with anyone.

I can feel him in the room looking at me. I turn to see him handing me a bottle of water. "Here, you should drink this and take these Ibuprofen. Not only will it help ward off the after effects of the shots, but also it'll help with that bump to the head."

I take the pills and the water. "Thanks. I'm sorry about being such a witch in the kitchen. You've only been trying to help me."

He shakes his head. "Don't worry about it. You had your reasons. I haven't been the easiest person to get along with in your life. I can be a real jackass sometimes."

I see him moving to the couch. "What are you doing? You can go now."

"No, I'm staying here tonight. I'll have to wake you up every couple of hours to make sure you don't have a concussion."

He's trying to be nice, I know this, but I'll be just fine alone. "Really, Zack. I appreciate your help, but I'll be okay."

"Holli, you are here all alone. Someone needs to check on you." He touches my shoulder. "Look, I would do the same thing for Simone, Jake or Silas. We can crash here in the living room. After I'm sure you're okay in the morning, I'll go to my shop and tow your car in. We'll get it fixed in time for you to go back to school. How does that sound?"

He's really trying. This is the point where Jules is always telling me I should trust someone. I bite my lower lip in a nervous habit. "Um. Okay. I'm going to change and I'll grab some blankets, but we'll have to go to the entertainment den. My mother would die if she found out someone slept on her Italian sofa."

He chuckles. "Okay. Just go get in some lounge clothes and we'll watch a movie or something to relax."

I nod and make my way upstairs to my room. I realize after I make it in the room that I don't have *lounge* clothes. I dig through my clothes and find a set of satin pajama pants and camisole. At least the house is warm. I cannot stand to have a bra on with something like this, much less relax. I grab my robe to put on over it just to be on the safe side.

I take another minute to glance in the mirror and gasp. "Oh God." I see that my face is starting to bruise a little and the Band-Aid on my forehead looks hideous. Good thing he's not interested in me, because I wouldn't be winning any beauty contests tonight. He's just trying to be nice and be a friend.

After my pep talk, I go back down to the entertainment den after stopping by our linen closet. *Well, it's more like a small room.* Zack has already found his way in here.

He turns when he hears me come in. "Hope you don't mind I found my way in here?"

"No, it's fine."

"Here, let me help you with those." As he takes the bundle from me, his hand accidentally brushes across my nipple, causing it to harden.

Thank God he doesn't say anything. I would be even more embarrassed.

I want him to be comfortable, too. "Um, would you like for me to go see if my dad has some pajamas you could use?"

"No, I've actually got a fresh gym bag in my truck I'll grab, it has some sweats in it. Thanks, though."

My stomach is fluttering all over the place. I'm so dang nervous right now. A guy, a hot guy whom I've always thought hated me is here. Not only does he not hate me, but he's here staying the night with me to make sure I'm okay.

He comes back in with a bag, he unzips it and grabs some items out. "Where can I-?"

I point down the hall. "First door on the right."

He nods and leaves the room for just a few minutes. When he walks back in, my breath catches. He's not wearing a shirt. *Holy crap! His chest is so cut, so firm. What is that tattoo of?*

"Holli?"

I jerk my head up. "Sorry. What?"

He looks at me strange. "Are you sure you're okay? You kind of dazed out for a minute there."

I nod. "Yeah, just thinking about things."

"Okay, I was just saying that I was sorry. I thought I had a t-shirt in the bag but I don't."

"It's okay. No big deal. You're a guy, you can run around without a shirt on all the time. It would be different if I didn't have a shirt." I laugh nervously. *Oh my God, did I really just blurt all of that out?*

He chuckles. "Yeah, that would surely be different." I feel his eyes roam over my body. "But I can't say it would be a bad thing."

I feel my face redden. "Um- you can look through the on demand or if you'd like, there is a cabinet full of DVDs over there."

He nods. "Sure. You don't want to pick?"

I shake my head. "I don't really watch many current movies. I'll go grab us some snacks."

He nods and I go in the kitchen, grabbing some of the junk food I bought the other day along with the container of cookies I made.

I go back in the den with my arm load and he laughs as I come in.

"Do you think you have enough for us?"

I nervously chuckle. "Well, I didn't know what all you would like. I've never really hung out with a guy to watch movies before."

He shakes his head. "Good plan. Plus, if I'm going to stay awake to check on you, I guess I should have some snacks."

We both laugh casually as we sit down. “So what movie did you choose?”

He shakes his head and winks. “You’ll just have to see.”

I’m kinda nervous and scared. I don’t think I have any movies in there that could be that risqué but I’m not sure.

As soon as the movie starts, I burst out laughing. I look at him and raise my eyebrows. “*Footloose*? Really? Mr. Jock, you like *Footloose*?”

He shoves me playfully. “Don’t talk shit about Kevin Bacon.”

“I’m not talking *shit* about Kevin Bacon. I’m just shocked you like this movie.”

He points at me. “Oh, you said shit. I’m shocked about that.”

I shove his arm. “Let’s just watch the movie, butt face.”

“Mature, real mature.” He says as he turns back to the movie.

Zack

I can't help but realize the parallels between Holli and Ariel in the movie. What she was saying earlier about her life and how she's *expected* to live it. I guess I always did exactly what she said, I looked in from the outside.

I grab one of the cookies she brought in. "Damn, this is good. Where did you get these?"

She smiles. "I made them."

"Wow. These really are great. I didn't know you could bake." Shit, I'm only looking from the outside again. "Sorry. I'm doing it again."

She shakes her head. "No, it's okay. It's not like I didn't know this is how people thought."

I touch her hand. "But still, I shouldn't have jumped to conclusions."

"I'm serious, it's fine. I'm not even sure my parents know I can bake. My Gran taught me, she was my dad's mom. If it was up to my mother, I wouldn't know what a cookie was, much less how to bake one." She looks sad.

"So you were close to your Gran, then?"

"Yes, I spent most of my holidays with her or any free time I had. My parents were always busy flying all over the place."

"When did you lose her?"

She frowns a little, still trying to be strong. "Just after my freshman year in college."

I want to know more about her. "So what do you do normally for the holidays then? Well, since she passed away that is."

"I've been home a couple of times with my friend Jules. Her family is great, but I really wanted to be here this Christmas. I can't explain why, I don't know why, but I just felt like I needed to be here. Does that make any sense?"

"Yeah, I get it. What are you majoring in?"

"Pharmacy. I'm going to be a pharmacist."

I relax into the couch a little. "So no big jet setting plans for you, then." Shit, that sounded bad. "I mean you don't plan to travel a lot."

"No, if the day ever comes that I have kids, I want to be around. I want to be involved in their lives. Not just stop in once a month to tell the housekeeper to quit buying junk food. That my daughter might be skinny now, but if she keeps eating like that it won't be the case long."

I shake my head. "Seriously? Did your mom do that?"

"Yeah, if it were up to her I would live on boneless, skinless chicken breast and grilled fish. I have my Gran's bone structure, which means I will never be rail thin like my mother, or like she thinks I should be. She would have a fit if she looked in her fridge right now. Between the Cokes, deli meats and cheeses, plus the bread, cookies and chips I put in the pantry, she'd probably kick me out. She'd be afraid she'd get fat just from having it in her house."

Wow, she doesn't know how beautiful she is. Her mother must be crazy. "You are perfect just the way you are."

She looks at me like I've grown another head. "You're crazy. Look, I know I'm not ugly, alright, but I also know I'm not beautiful by any means."

I shake my head. "We'll have to agree to disagree on that one." I say as I steal another cookie.

She nibbles on a cookie. "I have to ask. What is the flag on your chest for? It's not one I've ever seen before."

"It's a guidon. A guidon is the flag for a military unit. This was Wade's. After he died, Silas, Jake and I got a tattoo of it."

She looks down. "I'm sorry, I didn't know your brother was killed. I vaguely remember you having a brother."

I nod. "Wade was older and he wasn't as outgoing as me. He didn't get into as much trouble as me. We were kind of like night and day." *And I think it's seriously screwed up that I lived and he was being a hero and died.*

"I always wondered what it would be like to have a sibling."

"It was fun, we always kept my dad on his toes."

Her eyes shoot up. "Should you call your dad? Will he be worried about you tonight?"

I shake my head laughing. "No, Dad and I are pretty good roommates, but he's out of town anyway. He has a friend up in the VA hospital that is terminal, so he's visiting him."

She nods. "Oh wow. That is sweet. So do you enjoy working with your dad?"

I nod. "Yeah, after I got all of my certifications, I got him to update all the equipment in the shop and step into the world of foreign automobiles. Works out great for the people around here. They don't have to drive so far to get their cars serviced or worked on." I shrug. "So it's kind of a win-win."

She chuckles. "Yeah, that will surely come in handy for me now. Since Bambi decided to attack my car."

I laugh. "Yeah, I suppose so. So what about you? Where do you think you'll end up?"

"I'm not sure, I haven't really thought about that. I've been so busy studying, but this semester I get to work in a real pharmacy. I'm excited about that."

Liking how relaxed we've gotten over the past little bit, I wonder. "Have you ever thought about coming back here?"

She's staring at the drink in her hand and then looks up at me through her eyelashes. "No, not really. There has never been much back here for me."

Fuck, this is getting deep. "Well, Mr. Jenkins has been talking about retiring, but he's worried about a big retailer coming in. I was just thinking it might be a good business opportunity for you."

She turns to me, pulling one leg up and curling it in. Her robe falls open and I see the little cami she's got up under it. Her voice breaks me from staring. "Oh, well I may check into that." She chuckles a little. "Is this crazy? I mean, us here having a conversation without trying to rip into each other."

"Nah. I think it just means we are moving on, to greater things."

She nods. "Thanks. Well, my eyes are trying to close on me. I'm just going to get a little sleep."

I grin. "Okay, I'll check on you in a couple of hours. Then you can go right back to sleep."

She nods with her eyes closed and sighs. "Thanks."

A few minutes later, her breathing has become steady and she looks even more beautiful just sleeping so peacefully. Her cami has slid down even more and I see a small peak of her rose colored nipple.

I feel my dick trying to rise, good thing these sweat pants are loose. I need to push those feelings away. She's not the kind of girl you have a night of fun with. After covering her with a blanket, I make sure the timer is set on my phone and try to catch a few winks myself.

Holli

I feel someone brushing the hair off my face. It feels nice. Wait… who is brushing the hair from my face? I sit up in a bolt.

"Shit. Holli, I'm sorry to scare you, I was saying your name. I guess you were in dreamland." I'm looking into the beautiful eyes of Zack Caraway. Yummy.

Head injury, stupid. He's checking on your head injury.

He smirks. "Yes, I am checking on your head injury, but you're not stupid."

Oh my God, I said that out loud.

He puts his hand on mine. "Hey, it's okay. You're a little loopy. Go back to sleep. It's a little after four, I was just checking on you."

I nod, still confused. "O- okay." Closing my eyes, I snuggle back into the blanket I'm guessing he put over me. I'm a little nervous, trusting someone like him, or anyone for that matter, is a little out of my character. My eyes get heavier and I know sleep is winning again.

"Holli, do you want to go through the rest of your life being a prude?" Scott says close to my face.

"Yeah, you're so damn cold, I almost get frostbite." Christopher grunts out.

I feel like my throat is clogged and I can't say anything. Like something is choking me. I try to scream but there is no sound. "Leave me alone!" I finally manage.

I feel Scott's hand run up my thigh. "Don't fight this, Holli."

Christopher has his hand on my face. "Don't fight this."

"Holli, are you okay? Ouch. Don't fight me."

My eyes pop open and Zack fills my vision. I realize I just kicked him and slapped him.

He gently puts his hand on mine. I jerk it away shivering. “Holli, talk to me. What’s wrong?’

I shake my head. “I’m sorry, I must’ve been having a bad dream.”

“Holli, this was more than a bad dream. You screamed like someone was killing you and then you started shaking and yelling for someone to leave you alone.”

Shaking my head, I look at him. “No, it was just a bad dream. Nothing to worry about. What time is it?”

He looks at his phone. “A little after seven.”

I try to sit up and every part of my body feels sore. “Wow. I feel like I’ve been hit by a truck.”

“Hang on, I’ll go get you some more medicine and water.” He walks away going to the kitchen.

I shake my head. This is all crazy. If you would have told me twenty-four hours ago that Zack Caraway would be here taking care of me after an accident, I would have thought you were crazy.

He breezes back into the room, looking sexy as ever. Those sweatpants hanging on his hips showing that V. His chest is hard and sculpted, not like he lives in a gym, just works hard. *Yummy.*

He looks at me. “What’s yummy? I know you aren’t talking about the pills.”

Holy crap, I said that out loud. I’ve got to get a grip. “I was being sarcastic about the pills.”

He hands them to me. “Here, you tensed up during the wreck so even if you didn’t hit anything inside the car, you’ll still be sore. You need to take these every four or five hours. Drink lots of water, too.”

“Wow, you know a lot about this. Pills are supposed to be my job, remember?” I chuckle.

He laughs, "Just talking from experience. Football injuries and a lot of stupid mistakes as a high school idiot, make a great poster child for Ibuprofen."

I giggle. "Thank you so much for your help last night. I don't know what I would've done if you hadn't been stalking me," I say with a grin.

He laughs. "I was not stalking, I was trying to make sure your pretty little ass got home."

I stand up and my robe slides off my shoulder. I feel this urge stirring between my thighs. *I hear Jules in my head. "Get out of the comfort zone."*

I shake my head walking past him and grin. "When did Zack Caraway become such a good Samaritan?"

He pulls his shirt from last night on as I turn around and he's standing there in a pair of red boxers. He starts putting on his jeans from last night and he winks. "Babe, I'm always *good* at anything I do."

I laugh as I walk into the kitchen, purposely putting a little swish when I walk. I reach over and put water in the Keurig. I pop one of the coffee cartridges in. "Would you like some coffee?"

"Sure, that would be great. I gotta head out soon. From what the dispatcher at the Sheriff's office said last night, I'm going to have a busy day today. I'm gonna go pick your car up first. I'll try to have your mom's Volvo finished later today and get it out here to you so that you'll have something to drive while I fix your car."

"Thanks, that's sweet but if you don't get to it, don't worry. It's not like I have somewhere super important to go. If I really need to go somewhere, I'm sure I can call Simone." Then it hits me. "Shit!" My hand flies over my mouth and Zack almost falls off the stool he's sat on.

"Oh lord, I'm a terrible influence. We've barely been together for twelve hours and already you're cussing."

I laugh. "Shut up. I just realized I never texted Simone last night. She's going to be mad, or worried, and I don't want her to be either with me."

He shakes his head. “I texted her last night once we got settled in here and explained what happened.”

“Oh. Thanks.”

He laughs again. “Jeez, you got so worked up you cussed.”

I shake my head. “Quit laughing or no coffee for you.”

He puts up his hands to surrender. “Sorry.”

I pass him a mug of coffee and reach up in the cabinet for a large travel mug. I make him another mug full to take with him. “Here, take this one with you. It sounds like you’re going to be outside a lot today. Maybe this will help keep you a little warm.”

He smiles. “Thanks.” He starts walking toward the door.

When I look over, I see his duffle lying on the floor. I grab it up and run after him. “Zack! You forgot-.” I run right into a wall of chest as I round the corner. I look up into his eyes. “Your bag.”

His arms are still wrapped around my waist and I’m sure he can feel my nipples hardening under this thin top. Those feelings start stirring again between my thighs. Suddenly, I’m back up against the wall and his mouth is on mine. Somehow, out of instinct or something I’ve never had before, I pick one leg up and wrap it around his hip.

This kiss is hard and fevered, unlike anything I’ve had before. Finally, he pulls away and we are both panting.

“Whoa.” That’s all I can come up with after almost seventeen years of school.

He reaches down and picks up the bag I somehow dropped. “Yeah.” He grins. “Thanks again. I’ll call you later today about your car.”

I nod still trying to catch my breath. “Yeah. Sure.”

After he walks out, I slide down the backside of the door and let out a huge sigh. *“Holy mother of Jesus, that was hot.”*

I gotta call Jules.

Zack

What in the hell was I thinking? Kissing her like that was just insane. She is off limits. What could come from this? Nothing but trouble. Damn her mouth, though. Jesus. Yeah, when I get back to the shop, I'll be spending a few minutes in the bathroom with the latest magazine I got in the mail.

I'm imagining sliding those silky pajamas off of her. I felt the hardness of her nipples through her top. *Fuuuuck!*

When I pull up to the shop, Jake is sitting in the parking lot. I jump out of the truck obviously in last night's clothes. Good thing I always keep an extra uniform here.

"Hey, Jake. What're you doing up so early this cold ass morning?"

He shrugs. "Well, the office isn't going to be open today, and stuff at the farm is taken care of. I figured since your dad was out of town, and I'm sure a bunch of jackasses put their cars in the ditch last night, I thought I could lend a hand." He chuckles, making notice of my clothes. "So you had a long night, huh?"

I laugh. "Nah, just helped out a friend." I say as I try to shrug it off. "Yeah, from the sounds of things my day is going to be busy. I was already wondering how I was going to get it all done. The first thing I have to do is go pick up Holli's car."

He looks at me confused. "Holli's car?"

"Yeah, she hit a deer last night on her way home. Messed up the front end pretty bad."

"How do you know all this?"

Shit… I hadn't thought about how to explain all of this. "Hang on, let me change and I'll be right out."

I come out and Jake has a smirk on his face. I look at him and shake my head. "Shut up, douche monkey."

Once we are in the truck, he keeps sitting over on his side chuckling. "Jake, I swear to everything that is holy I'm going to not only kick you out of this tow truck, but I may run your ass over."

Once we reach the car and get it hooked up, he looks at me. "Damn, that deer did get her pretty good."

"Yeah, it'll take me a few days to get the parts in to fix it."

"So, tell me again how you knew about this."

"I drove up on the accident last night."

He shakes his head. "And what, prey tell, were you doing in this neighborhood?"

I kick the side of my truck. "I was making sure she made it home. Okay? She had quite a bit to drink and I knew the roads were icy. Thank God I did because she wacked her damn head."

"Did you take her to the ER?" He asks as we climb in my truck.

"No, it wasn't that bad. I got her car off the road, took her home, got her cleaned up and kept an eye on her in case she had a concussion."

He looks at me like I'm crazy and sighs, flopping back against the seat. "Man, tell me you didn't fuck Holli. She's not the kind of girl you do that with."

I don't know why it pisses me off, but it does. "Don't talk about her like that. No, we didn't have sex. What part of head wound didn't you understand?"

He laughs, "Hey, I'm just saying-."

"Well, stop. She's not like that. We just watched a movie and talked. I woke her up every few hours to make sure she didn't have a concussion."

He looks at me shocked. "You two talked and watched a movie?"

"Yeah, we did. I learned a little more about her, apologized for the things I said to her years ago. I understand a little more about how much of her life has been her decision and how most of it hasn't."

He shakes his head. "I told you living life in the spot light in this town isn't easy. Her parents probably put a lot more pressure on her than mine did."

I think about Jake and all the shit he went through a few years ago. This entire damn town talking about him like he was some sort of crazed killer or psycho boyfriend. Thank God his parents are the good people they are. They stood behind him and helped him get through the tough times.

I nod in agreement. "You're right. I feel really bad, man. She basically compared her life to being a show dog."

He shakes his head. "Her dad might be a little bit of a pompous ass, but he's at least human and will talk to someone. From what I can remember, her mom can be a hateful bitch."

"It sounded like it. Her mom has a thing about her weight."

"Her weight? Holli has a rockin' body."

I don't like him looking at her body. "I know she does, thank you very much. Her mom is nuts."

"Oh, so you *were* checking out her body."

I flip him off as we get out at my shop. "Look, I just want to get to know her. She'll be going back to school soon enough, so it really doesn't matter. Now, I need to service her mom's car real quick so I can get it back to her this afternoon. That way she'll have something to drive while I'm getting hers fixed."

"Are you going to need me to ride out with you?"

I write down some messages off the system from dispatch. "No man, I'll figure something out. Actually, if you could take my tow truck and go grab these cars and bring them back here so I can figure it all out."

"Yeah, sure man, anything you need. That way you can get caught up here while I grab the tows."

I breathe a sigh of relief. "Thanks, man. I didn't expect it to get this crazy while dad was out of town."

“Anytime, man. Hey, maybe you should take some dinner out there tonight. That might help you get to know her a little better.”

I shrug. “Yeah, that’s an idea. Thanks again, man.”

As soon as he pulls away in my tow truck, I get to work finishing up the cars in the garage already. After a couple of hours, I’m able to get Holli’s beamer pulled in so I can do an assessment on the damage. I need to talk to her and get her insurance information so I can send it in.

I don’t have her fucking number! You’ve got to be kidding me.

I don’t have any other option. I have to ask Simone.

Me: Hey can you give me Holli’s number?

Simone: Why?

Me: I have her car I need to talk to her about it.

Simone: Oh yeah, I forgot. Is she okay?

Me: Yes she’s fine. Just a little bump on the head.

Simone: Good. I’m glad you could help ;)

Me: Can I please get her number?

Simone: Fine. Don’t fuck with her though.

A minute later I get a text with the info attached.

Holli

After a long conversation with Jules, she tells me I should jump Zack and "clear the cobwebs out of my vagina." Yes, that is my super supportive friend.

My phone chirps and I'm fully expecting it to be Jules with possibly a tutorial video.

Unknown: Hey it's Zack. I need your car insurance info.

Me: There should be a card in my glove box. Is it really bad?

Zack: About 4500 right now from what I can tell.

Me: Okay thanks. Just let me know if you need anything else.

Zack: Do you have any food allergies or anything?

What the hell? Is he still talking to me?

Me: Are you still talking to me?

Zack: Yes. Who else would I be talking to?

Me: OK um no I don't have any food allergies.

Zack: Okay good.

That was weird.

Several hours later, I'm in my room going through my bookshelf. I want to take some of my older books back to my apartment. I might actually have time to read this semester.

I smile when I pick up the copy of *Gone with the Wind* my Gran left me. I haven't had the heart to open it since she died. She and I read this book together the summer before I started high school. She always thought Scarlett was a strong woman that family was important to. She wanted me to remember that a family needs to be a strong unit, one that you fight for.

As I flip through the pages, a piece of paper falls out.

My Dear Sweet Holli,
If you are reading this then my time on this Earth is over. You have always been my heart since the day you were born. I know that your life hasn't been easy. Your parents have not always made me very happy with the way they've treated you. You should have had more opportunities to be a child. I'm so glad you're following your dreams about college. I knew you wouldn't need money for college. I'm sure your grades have paid for it, but I thought you might like some start-up money for when you finish. So, I've left a trust in the care of my attorney. Go see Mr. Joshua Greene. The money should be enough to start a business or build a home. Possibly both. Your parents have no idea I've done this and my attorney was told to keep this matter private. I've never trusted your mother. She put her claws in your daddy and she thinks I don't know her secrets but I do. One day she'll have to answer to someone bigger than me for all she's done. I would love to skin your daddy for not standing up for you more and raising you with love like he was. At any rate, I love you sweetheart and if you haven't found this letter by your college graduation, Mr. Greene will be in touch with you. Enjoy your life. Have some fun, be naughty. Ha ha. I know you've never been naughty a day in your life, but it's time. You're a smart girl and I know you won't go too crazy. I've always wanted the best for you, Sugar Plum. I love you always, my little Southern Belle.
Love Always,
Gran
Tears are streaming down my face as I fold the letter back up.

There is a knock at the door, so I make my way down the stairs. I look through the window and see Zack standing there with bags in his hands.

What is he doing?

I open the door and he smiles. "I brought take-out, I hope that's okay. I wasn't able to get your mom's car finished today so I was thinking you might need food."

I smile and look into his eyes. "Thank you, that was sweet, but you didn't have to."

He looks at me concerned. “Why have you been crying? Are you okay?” He sits the bags down on the kitchen counter and puts his hand on my face. “Is it from the accident?”

I shake my head and wipe my eyes again. “No, I just found a letter my Gran left me. I miss her a lot.”

He nods. “Do you wanna talk about it?”

“Maybe after we eat. I’m kinda hungry.” I say smiling. I hop up on a barstool, trying to let everything roll off of me. “What did you bring me?”

“I brought Chinese food. I got a little of everything. I wasn’t sure what you would like.”

I smile and move in between him and the bag, peeking inside of it. “I love Chinese food, I’ll pretty much try anything.”

He grins and moves closer to me. I turn around when I feel his breath on my neck. “Oh, so you’ll try anything.”

I feel the heat creeping up on my face, but I’m trying to appear calm. That’s not working though.

He gives a small chuckle. “You’re cute.”

“Um, let’s just eat.”

He shakes his head. “Yeah, sure.”

We take some plates and dish up some of the food. It tastes awesome. “When did we get a place this good in Richter’s Crossing?”

He puts his finger up while he’s chewing. “About a year ago. It’s great, along with the new Mexican place that opened up over on Sixth Street.”

I laugh. “Wow, Chinese and Mexican food. We’re moving up in the world.”

He laughs. “Yeah. I’m just glad we have some new places to choose from. I love the café but I eat there almost every day for lunch. I eat quite a bit at the Tavern, too, so it’s really nice to have a change up.”

After eating for a few minutes, I don't know why I do but I feel comfortable talking about Gran's letter. I explain about the money and everything.

He sits shocked. "So your Gran left you all of this money and you had no clue?" I shake my head no. "For that matter, neither do your parents?"

"No, they've never said anything. I'm sure my mother would have had something to say about it."

I stand up from the bar and start cleaning up. "Thanks again for dinner. You must've had a crazy day."

"If it hadn't been for Jake helping me tow the cars in, I don't know if I'd have gotten out today when I did."

"It's great that you guys are still close."

"Yeah, he's had a lot happen. It was a rough couple of years."

I nod. "Yeah, I remember. That was crazy and horrible. I never believed what all the people were saying. Jake was never that kind of guy."

He shakes his head. "Which story did you hear?"

I shake my head telling him the rumors I heard. Finally I stop and look at him. "Would you like to watch a movie with me again?"

He nods. "Sure."

Zack

Sitting and talking with her like I have been tonight, I've noticed so many things about her. The way she plays with her hair when she gets nervous. How she giggles when something is inappropriate. How just my being near her makes her blush.

Little by little as we've watched the movie, she has settled closer and closer to me. Once the movie goes off, I turn to her. "So what are your plans for the rest of your break?"

She shrugs. "Nothing really."

"Would you consider hanging out with me? I mean my dad is out of town, your parents are out of town." I shrug. "What do you say to getting to know each other better?"

She smiles and nods. "I like that idea."

"I just want to say, you are nothing like I thought you were. Maybe I've just finally pulled my head from my ass."

She giggles. "I was really stand offish back then. It's okay, my friend Jules has helped me see how that can be misinterpreted."

Her cell phone starts ringing. "It's my dad. I better answer this."

I nod. "Okay, I'll gather up our mess from the movie and pick another one if you're up for it."

She nods as she answers the phone. "Hello." "Yes, sir." "Mom knew." "I talked to her the day before you guys left." "A deer hit me." "Zack picked it up and helped me." "Yes, sir." "He's going to return mom's car soon, so that I'll have something to drive. He was really busy from the ice last night." She gets a funny look on her face. "O-okay, I'll see you then." "Goodnight."

"My dad got a call from the insurance company about my car. As it turns out he wasn't aware that I was even home. I guess my mom forgot to tell him about the long conversation we had. He said they are going to come home a couple of days early. He's glad that you're taking care of the car.

He said to make sure I thanked you." She walks towards me and kisses me on the cheek. "Thanks."

I back her against the counter. "I think I liked that thanks. Maybe I could get another one like the one this morning?"

"You took that thank you this morning." She says, looking up through her heavy eyes.

I claim her mouth. Her hands are on my upper arms. I press my hardening erection against her and she groans. I pull back. "Fuck, you're beautiful."

She nuzzles into my neck. I find the side of her neck, licking and kissing my way down her collar bone. She lets out a soft moan. "Oh God."

I pull back. "We need to stop or I won't be able to."

She looks up at me. "Who says I want to stop?"

"You are not the kind of girl who just hooks up. I know that and I want this to be more, I think, but I don't know if it can."

She leans back against the counter again. "So what should we do?" Looking into her eyes, I realize she's a vixen without even knowing it.

I take a step back and ignore my inner voice who is pissed at me for leaving myself with a painful erection. I see this longing look in her eyes, but I see nervousness clouding in the background. I can feel her.

I pull her behind me to the entertainment den and sit her on my lap. I have to arrange myself. "I say we talk. Ask each other questions."

She nods shyly. "Zack, it's okay if you don't want to do this."

I shake my head and grab her hand, holding it against my erection. "Does this feel like I don't want to do this?"

She shakes her head. "I'm not as experienced as the girls you normally date."

I pull her chin up and speak softly. "Baby, have you ever had sex?"

She overpowers my hand to look down, like she's embarrassed. "Yes, once. But I was really drunk, like I don't remember most of it. Other than that, I didn't like the guy and it hurt like hell."

I'm instantly pissed. "Who did that to you? Who in their right mind would take advantage of a girl like you?"

She shakes her head. "That is a story for another time. Right now I want to be brave, be naughty. I want to do something I've never done before."

I nod. "Okay. What did you-?"

Before I can finish, she's slid down off my lap and is undoing my belt. Next, she's unbuttoning my jeans. "Holli, baby, you don't have to do this."

She looks up at me with a wildness in her eyes I've never seen before. "Yeah I know, but I want to."

Pulling down my jeans and boxers, her warm mouth slips over my throbbing dick. She licks and bobs until I'm about to come and there is no way I want to come in her mouth right now.

I pull her up and she whimpers. "Holli, baby, as much as I would love to finish in your mouth, I don't want to right now."

I lie her back on the couch, pulling her pants down and pushing her shirt up over her breasts. I lick her nipples that hardened as soon as they hit the chilly air. Kissing and licking down her stomach, she tenses as I go near her core.

"No one has ever done this for you, have they?"

She shakes her head and answers, "No."

I massage her inner thighs with my hands, working my way to the bare folds of her body. "You were with a real selfish asshole, sweetie. Have you ever come before?"

She nods. I grin at her. "Did you make yourself or did someone do it for you?"

She's panting as I kiss and nip at her inner thighs. "M-me."

Fuck. That is hot. My little vixen. I smile at her. “Well hang on, honey, you’re in for a treat.”

My head delves between her soft thighs, kissing, licking and sucking. I use my finger to assist. I feel her body tensing and I know she’s about to come. I suck hard on her clit and slip the tip of my pinky into her tight ass.

“OH FUCK! AH AH OH GOD. HOLY SHIT! OH GOD, OH GOD, OH PLEASE! OH GOD ZACK PLEASE FUCK!”

I have to hold in a laugh. Once she comes down from her orgasm, she looks almost high. I wipe her juices from my face and pull her up into my arms. “So, I’m supposing that was good for you? Since you probably said more cuss words in one sentence than you’ve said in your entire life?”

She nods her head, giggling. “Yes, that was awesome.” I have to shake my head at the light blush of her body.

She flops her head back. “Holy crap, that really was, I don’t know. I just…holy crap.”

I chuckle. “You’re welcome.”

Holli

Have you ever had one of those out of body experiences? Yeah, I think that is what happened between Zack and me that first time he went down on me. Never in my life would I have thought I could come that hard without my vibrator, but I think I almost lost consciousness. Not that I have a ton of experience, but holy crap. Until that moment I was repulsed by the idea of anyone or anything going near my rear end. Now I find myself reading about it, daydreaming about it and wondering what everything else would feel like back there.

Zack and I have fallen into somewhat of a routine over the past few days. He gets off work and comes to hang out with me. We eat dinner, and other than heavy petting and making out, we haven't went too far. I did finally get him to let me take him in my mouth until he came.

I don't know what it is about him, but I can let my inhibitions go. I love it, it's so freeing. I feel like this entirely different person. He makes me feel so comfortable, like I'm the only person in the world. Jules has been crazy over the latest updates in my life. She has been blowing up my phone like a proud mother hen.

Zack is at work and I sit here wondering. I've got some decisions to make in my life over the next few months. I never really thought about coming back here. My life wasn't ever that great here, and my parents aren't the kind you want to come home to, but between finding my Gran's letter and Zack mentioning the local pharmacist wanting to retire, the thought keeps popping into my head more frequently.

Yesterday we went out to have dinner with the Callahan's, Jake's family. Jake's mom, Drucilla, called and told Zack that he needed to 'bring his butt and mine over there to eat or she was coming to get us'.

I watched their family interact with each other and I want that life. This was how my grandmother acted, she loved her family with her whole heart. It was a strange comfort to have Mrs. Dru wrap me in her arms for a hug as soon as I walked in the door along with Zack. She and my mother ran in the same social circles, were in the same civic organizations, but where Mrs. Dru keeps her family close and encourages them, my mother treats me like some kind of genius commodity, to be auctioned off to the highest bidder.

Today I picked up the ingredients to make lasagna for dinner tonight. I mix the salad ingredients together. Tonight is Christmas Eve and I know we only have each other. I feel arms wrap around my waist. “Hey girl, what you cookin’?”

I smile, leaning back into Zack’s chest. “Lasagna, garlic bread and salad.”

He nuzzles into my neck. “Mmm, smells amazing. Almost as amazing as your neck.” He kisses my neck and I feel the throbbing between my thighs. I squeeze my legs together.

I turn around in his arms and kiss him, “You are so sweet.”

He runs his hand down my side, cupping my ass and whispering in my ear, “Not as sweet as your-.”

I cut him off by kissing him. He grabs me up under my butt, sitting me on the counter and shoving the salad aside. He starts kissing down my neck, ripping my blouse open. I snatch his t-shirt over his head, rubbing my hands up and down his chest. He slides his hands under my skirt, pulling the lace boy-shorts down my legs. He runs his fingers through my folds. “Damn baby, you’re already so wet.”

He goes to duck his head. “No. I don’t want that. I want to um-.”

“You want to what, baby?”

“I want to-.”

“Say it, baby. Say what you want.”

I’m nervous all of a sudden. I can’t say it. I reach down and unbuckle his pants pushing them down.

He reaches and lifts my face. “Say it, baby.”

“I want you inside of me.”

I see a wildness in his eyes. “Right here?” I nod and he grabs his wallet out of his pants. Pulling out a condom, he rolls it on and thrusts into me.

"Ah!"

He looks me in the eyes. "Are you okay?"

I nod. "Yes, keep going."

He backs up and thrusts into me again. "Shit, baby, you are so fucking tight."

I've never felt so alive. I put my arms around his neck. He hoists me up, carrying me to the den while still inside of me. Once we are on the couch, he pulls out just long enough to kick his pants and shoes off. He thrusts back into me. "Ah fuck, baby."

"Oh God, Zack." The thrill and the excitement of it all is giving me balls I never thought I had. "Fuck me!"

He looks at me with a grin. "Damn, girl."

He keeps going, both of us are moaning and saying things to each other I can't even comprehend.

He slams into me one final time as I scream his name over and over.

After he disposes of the condom, he pulls me on top of him. "Wow girl, you get turned on and turn into a little hellcat."

I start to blush, "Stop."

"No, it's really hot. Trust me. It's like it is all just for me. No one knows this girl except me."

I giggle. "You make it sound like I'm two different people."

"It's like you are." He pulls me in tighter. "Like I said, I like it. It's the side of you that is only for me. No fear, no reservations." He kisses me. "It's just you."

I smile. "You know, you're like two different people, too. With me, here, you're this sweet caring guy. A total different guy from years ago. I really like this guy. Like you said, he's just for me."

We kiss and I look up at him. “Thank God the oven cut itself off.” I reach down, picking up our mess. “Let’s go up to my bedroom. I want you to spend the night with me.”

He follows me up to my room, grabbing our clothes and the used condom on the way. I finish pulling the skirt off my body where it was rolled up around my waist and climb into bed with him.

Sometime during the night I feel his hardness against my rear end. On instinct I rub back into it. He groans. “Mmm baby. Again?”

I crawl on top of him, sinking on to him. “Ooh.”

“Baby, I need a condom.”

I start moving my hips. “I’m on the pill. Are you clean?”

He nods. “Yeah, doc Jack tested me last month.”

I let my inner dirty girl come out while riding him. “Oh God! This is so good.”

“Your little tight pussy loves my cock, doesn’t it?”

He rolls to put me on the bottom. “Yes. Oh God! Zack! Harder, fuck my pussy harder! I love your cock!”

He pulls out all the stops, pounding into me harder and harder. “FUCK!” He roars as he comes inside me.

He rolls on his back. “Holy shit. I’ve never. I mean, I’ve never done that without a condom and holy shit, that was awesome.”

Zack

I'm startled awake by a scream. "Oh dear Lord!"

Followed by, "What in the Hell?"

A scream from Holli's mouth. "Oh my God!"

I'm staring face to face with Marcus Brown and Mrs. Lenora Brown as Holli sits nervously beside me, pulling her sheet and quilt tight against her naked chest.

Her father is in shock and her mother looks angry. "Holli, you get yourself up and get that boy out of my house." Her mother sneers.

Something about her mother's facial expression sparks something in her eyes. She reaches over and grabs my hand. "No. Once you two leave my room, we'll be out after we've showered and gotten dressed." I look at her, just as shocked as her parents. "He's not leaving right now, though. Today is Christmas and we planned to spend it together."

"Young lady, you will not talk to me that way in my home."

"Funny thing is I don't hear dad saying that. Now, I would prefer not to be naked having this conversation. Please, get out and we will be down in a few minutes."

I see her dad take her mother's arm and pull her from the room.

I look at her. "Holli, what in the Hell? They are going to kill me."

"No, they won't. I figured out a few things in the past couple of days. If you notice, my father didn't say a word. Up until the wreck he didn't know I was here. She's hiding something, or she's just that hateful of a person."

"But still, Holli, are you sure you wanna do this?"

"I told you, you make me feel so strong and maybe I am a different person when I'm with you. You make me feel brave, and maybe that's what I've needed this entire time."

"Holli, you go back to school in a week. I don't fit in your world."

She grabs my hands. "You fit in my world because I want you to. You are a successful business owner. I have one semester left of college. One." She stands up and I watch as the sheet falls from her body. "Yesterday while you were at work, I went and talked with Mr. Jenkins. I'm going to work a year at the pharmacy with him, learning the ropes of running a small business, while at the same time merging technology. After the year, I will buy him out and have my own pharmacy. If you don't want to be with me, I get it. I don't like it, but I get it and I'm okay with it. You never meant for this to last further than this holiday."

I shake my head furiously. "No, Holli, I want to be with you. I've been drawn to you since I used to pick on you in school, I see that now. I was a slacker and never put much fight into anything. If it didn't come easy, I didn't want it. I see now that I always wanted you, I was just too chicken to do the work to get you."

"Well, let's get a shower and get dressed. I have to talk with my parents."

~*~*~

Thirty minutes later, we are walking downstairs. Walking into the kitchen, her parents are standing at the island, her father with a cup of coffee. Holli walks over, grabbing two mugs and pouring us coffee.

Once we sit down, her mother glares at us. I'm not sure if this is just her *'BRF' bitch rest face* or if she's really that angry.

Her mother turns to us. "Holli, I understand this may be your little rebellion. I know I've always been tough on you-."

Holli put her hand up to stop her. "This is not some sort of rebellion. I don't take pages from your play book."

Her mother looks shocked. "What is that supposed to mean?"

"That means, *I know.*"

Her dad looks as confused as I am, and he looks at her. "Sweetheart, what are you talking about?"

She clears her throat. "I'm talking about the summer before you and mom got married."

"She was in Florida that summer with her aunt." He looks bewildered.

Holli stands up, taking her mug to the sink. She's cool and calm, it's almost frightening. "Oh yeah, she was in Florida. She was dating a local beach shop worker. She got pregnant, had an abortion and came home to you and Gran's money."

Lenora is white as a sheet and almost looks like she's going pass out. She shakes it off. "How do you think you know any of this?"

Holli looks up at her with a glare. "It's funny the things you can find when you're left alone for yet another Christmas. It's nice that you keep journals, so your child can get to know you better. So what happened, Mom? You have your fun with a wild boy and then realize when you got pregnant that you might have to be part of the working class? You couldn't live off of Gran's money if you had a bastard kid you couldn't explain."

Holli pulls a piece of paper from her pocket. "This is a letter from Gran. I found it in my copy of *Gone with the Wind*. My guess is she knew all of this, too." She hands it to her dad.

He reads over it and I see his eyes glisten. He folds the paper and hands it back to Holli. "So, what decisions have you made? I know you've made a decision or you wouldn't be showing me this."

"I talked to Mr. Jenkins down at the pharmacy. He's wanting to retire. I see this as a business opportunity."

Her mother scoffs. "Really, we paid so much money for your education. Then you decide to throw it all away, and what, move back to this small Podunk town to work at a local pharmacy? All for some mechanic?"

Holli looks at her and glares. "You didn't pay a *damn* dime for my college. My grades paid for that you-." Marcus puts his hand up for her to stop.

He looks at her mother. "First of all, besides her apartment that you were determined that she have and her living expenses since you didn't want her to work, we haven't paid anything for her schooling. Secondly, this isn't some Podunk town, this is our hometown. Furthermore, I think she is making an extremely smart decision. She's going to own a pharmacy, and being that it is the only one in this town, I think it's a great move. Also, she's not dating *some* mechanic. He's the only local mechanic I've ever trusted and he's a business owner himself. He's helped his father rebuild an already solid business in the past four years."

She puts her hands on her hips. "Marcus, are you really going to support this? He's only after her for her money."

I've been sitting here quietly watching all of this play out like a reality show. Now, she doubts why I want to be with Holli. "Now, wait just a minute. My feelings for Holli have nothing to do with any money. If I wanted her for her money, don't you think I would've started going after her in high school?"

She crosses her arms across her chest like a defiant child. "You probably just wised up."

I've never wanted to hit a woman in my life as bad as I want to hit her right now.

Holli

I glare at my mother, but before I can say anything my dad speaks.

“Lenora, that is quite enough. You and I need to talk about several things, but right now in front of our daughter, I want to know why you didn’t tell me Holli was coming home for Christmas?”

“She told me the night before she was coming.”

I shake my head. “No, I had told you weeks before, you just pretended I didn’t tell you. The way you have since Gran died. I’ve just always went home with Jules at the last minute or stayed alone at school.”

My dad looks at Mom with a furious look. “Lenora, is this true? We could’ve stayed home with our daughter. I’ve asked you repeatedly for years why Holli didn’t want to spend Christmas with us. You always said she had plans.”

Finally, I’ve had enough of listening to them. They aren’t going ruin my holiday. “If you guys don’t mind, I need to get the food started. I was planning Christmas dinner for Zack and I. There will be plenty.”

My mom huffs and storms out of the room. My dad looks at us. “Holli, I don’t approve of what I walked in on this morning, but I also understand that you’re an adult. I’m sorry that I haven’t been what you needed me to be in a father.” He pulls me in for a hug, “I’m very proud of you.”

I smile. “Thanks, dad. I really appreciate that.”

He turns to Zack. “Thank you for taking care of her car and all after the accident.”

“Dad, he didn’t just take care of the car, he took care of me. He made sure I didn’t have a concussion and cleaned up my cuts.” I smile, “He was really wonderful.”

He sticks his hand out for Zack to shake. “Thank you again, son.”

“Anything for Holli, sir.”

My dad turns to me. "Well, I'm going to my study to talk with your mother."

"Okay, well, I planned an early dinner so it should be ready by five."

He reaches over and kisses my forehead. "That's wonderful, honey."

After he leaves the room, Zack walks over to me, wrapping me up in his arms. "Baby, you did great. You were so damn tough back there. My little hellcat came out and she wasn't the least bit scared. You even cussed a little bit."

I shake my head. "I was scared to death when I woke up to my parents standing in my room, and then had to confront them with Gran's letter and what all I found." I hug him tighter. "Thank you for not running away this morning."

He pulls my chin up so he can lightly kiss my lips. "I'll never run away from you. You won't ever have to face anything alone again."

I nod. "Zack, I don't know if this is the right time, but I- I love you."

He brushes the side of my cheek and kisses me again. "I love you, too, Holli."

I wipe a stray tear from my eye. "Well, I need to get the turkey ready to go in the oven. Why don't you go in the entertainment den and watch something?"

He nods, leaving the room as I open the oven and find the lasagna we never made it around to eating last night. I smile and laugh at myself.

I'm happy. Truly happy.

~*~*~

I call everyone to the table as I'm placing the last of the food on out.

My dad walks in smiling. "This smells great, honey."

I laugh, "It should, most of them are Gran's recipes."

He points to the table. "So that's-?"

I nod. "Yep, *Italian Cream Cake*. Her famous recipe."

My mother sits quietly at the table. She takes a couple of small pieces of turkey, along with some green beans.

Zack and my dad load up their plates. As I start to do the same, she glares at me the way she used to when she caught the cooks helping me bake or something.

My dad moans as he takes another bite. "Honey, this is wonderful." He turns to my mom. "Lenora, you should try some of the sweet potato pie."

She rolls her eyes. "No, some of us care what we put in our bodies. We can't stay thin forever if we don't work at it." She says, making an obvious dig about my body.

Zack perks his head up. "Holli, make sure you grab a couple of more servings, I like having a real woman with curves to cuddle up to." He gives me that devilish grin, *"I'm all about that bass."*

I almost spit out my sweet tea. I look to my father and he is trying to bite back a smile, too. My mother looks as if she'd like to take a machete to all of us.

She stands up. "Well, don't call me when you're all in the hospital having a heart attack from this artery clogging food." She storms away from the table.

Zack stands up. "Baby, I'm going to step out and call my dad. I'd like to see how he and his friend are doing."

I nod. "Sure."

A few minutes after they've left the table, my dad is polishing off another serving of turkey and dressing.

"Dad, I'm sorry I said all of those things about her in front of you this morning. My plan was to talk to her about it in private. I never meant to throw it in your face."

He puts his hands up. "Sweetheart, I've been in love with your mother for as long as I can remember now. I knew she wasn't perfect, and I knew Gran never liked her. I didn't know about some of the things you said, but she and I will talk more about that after the holidays. What I do know is that I'm sorry. The letter from my mom was right. I should've stood up for you. Parents are supposed to protect their children and I didn't do a very good job."

I put my hand on his. "Dad, it's okay. I should've spoken up sooner about how I was feeling. As for the holidays, I should've tried talking to you instead of just mom. It's just since you were always so quiet, I thought you agreed with her."

"No, sweetie. Growing up with your Gran and Pop, my dad was the strong silent type. Gran always took care of raising me, dad was just there as a backup and support. Gran ran our house. I guess I thought that was how it was supposed to go, but your mom and Gran are nothing alike."

I laugh. "You got that right."

He shakes his head. "Zack is a great kid. I see a lot of promise and honor in him. I'm happy you've found him. I could never see you with a suit type like your mom wanted."

I smile. "I'm happy, too." I know I have one more thing to tell him. "Dad, I need to tell you somethings about Scott."

Zack

"I'm glad you guys are having a good time, Dad."

"So, Jack called me. Are you really dating Holli Brown?"

"Yes, sir. I just finished eating Christmas dinner with her and her parents."

"Son, please tell me this isn't one of your games? Marcus is one of our best customers."

I shake my head as if he can see me. "No, sir. I really like her. I'm in love with her. I know it's crazy, we've just started getting to know each other."

"No son, it's not. When you know, you know. Plus, you and Holli grew up together. I know you were mean and a bully to her, but they always say you pull the pigtails of the girl you like."

I chuckle. "Well dad, I don't think Holli ever wore pigtails."

"You get what I'm saying."

"Yes, sir. Well, I'm going to go back inside and help her clean up from dinner."

"Okay, see you in a few days."

I walk back in the house. "Holli?"

"Back here in the den."

"What are we watching tonight?"

Her eyes light up. "*National Lampoon's Christmas Vacation,* then *Die Hard.*"

I laugh at her. "You kill me with your movie choices." I pull her into my chest. "But I love that about you."

A little bit later her dad comes in. "Holli, we are going to bed for the evening."

Holli smiles. "Goodnight, Dad."

"Goodnight, and Zack, I don't expect that I'll find you in the same situation I found this morning."

Holli giggles and I nod. "Yes, sir."

We snuggle into our little cocoon on the couch and watch movies for the rest of the night. Until I say goodnight and head home.

I hug her at her front door. "See you tomorrow?" She says.

"Your parts are coming tomorrow so I'm going to try and finish your car. Would you like to go on an actual date tomorrow night? We can go to the Steak House. What do you think?"

She smiles, "Sounds good."

I give her one last kiss goodnight. She rubs against me. "Babe, you can't do that. I'm trying to be good with your parents inside. Otherwise I'm going to take you right up against my truck."

She cocks her eye. "Would that be so bad?"

I push her up against my truck. "My little dirty vixen." I lift her skirt enough to get her panties off and stuff them in my pocket. She fumbles with my zipper, sliding my jeans and boxers down. Lifting her under her ass, I slide into her.

"Ah fuck. Zack." It doesn't matter how many times I hear her call out my name or cuss, it turns me into some animal.

"You like that, my dirty girl? Your tight pussy swallowing my cock?" She nods

I knead her ass with my hands, sliding my pinky into her tiny rear entrance. She comes and I cover her mouth with mine to keep her from waking up the neighborhood.

"Baby, that was awesome."

I let her down and she grins. "Yeah, it was. Now give me my panties back."

I chuckle. "Nope, I'm keeping them. Best holiday ever."

~*~*~

All too soon, her vacation from school is coming to a close. We've talked about how the next few months are going to go. She's going back down to school and she will be interning, kind of, at a local pharmacy down there for her last semester before she takes her boards. She'll graduate at the end of May and then return home.

I'm going to be staying here and working. I'm going to try to visit her as many weekends as I can while she's in school. Then she's coming home during her Spring Break. She wants to look for a house to buy while she's here. We've been talking about ideas for her pharmacy, she wants to keep it really old school. She's talked about maybe even adding an old fashioned soda fountain with a malt shop.

I've talked with some of my friends that are contractors about helping to make her dreams come true. They are sure that it is entirely possible. They are going to get some sketches and all drawn up. Mr. Jenkins is excited about his upcoming retirement and the new things coming to the pharmacy.

I'm on my way to her house now to see her off. I see her loading her bags in her trunk when I pull up. Climbing out of my truck, she turns around and smiles at me. "Well if it isn't my hottie boyfriend."

I wrap my arms around her. "And if it isn't my little sexy, hellcat, vixen girlfriend."

She giggles. "You know you like it."

I kiss her neck. "Yep, I sure do, especially last night when you did that thing with-." She puts up her hand to stop me, turning red and giggling. "I'm going to miss you while you're gone."

I see her eyes glisten. "Yeah, I'm gonna miss you, too." She leans back. "Well, maybe a little."

I walk her around to the driver's door. "Drive safe, baby. Call me when you get there."

She nods with tears in her eyes. “Okay, I will.”

“Hey, we’ll be together soon. I’m coming down in a couple of weeks, then you’ll be here for Spring Break. We’re going to make this work.”

I kiss her lips and she smiles. “I love you, Zack.”

“I love you, too, baby.”

I watch her little white beamer drive down her long drive way.

Just 150 days until she moves back home for good.

Holli

Graduation day June 1st…

Staring at myself in the mirror and looking at my Crimson gown, I smile. Tomorrow I get to pack up this condo and move to the small house I bought in Richter's Crossing. My mom turns her nose up at it, but my dad thinks it's cute. It's just down the street from Zack's garage. He's been helping me get it set up so I can move in as soon as I graduate. He's moving in with me. Well, after *a lot* of persuasion on my part. I can't believe how much my life has changed in six months.

There is a knock on my bedroom door. "Hey, hooch, you ready to bounce?"

I shake my head and laugh at Jules. "When did you turn into a gangster, with the lingo?"

"It goes with the hot Cuban guy I'm seeing."

"How did that go with your brothers?"

She laughs, "Not well. You know they were expecting a nice Puerto Rican boy." She turns around and flops on my chaise. "So, you look all packed up. Zack's ready to get you taken home tomorrow, I'm guessing."

"Oh yeah. I'm ready, too."

"How are your parents doing with all of this?"

I smile. "Dad is great. Mom is, well, Mom. She and Dad are doing the counseling thing, trying to work on their marital issues, and also trying to get her to be human to me."

She nods, checking her makeup in the mirror. "That's good."

After Christmas, Dad talked her into going to counseling about all the lies. She's still trying to form some sort of relationship with me.

As it turns out, her mom pushed her really hard to marry rich. Some of the same things she did to me, but she came from fake money. Therefore her family had to find a way to make it real. Where my dad's money was real with green stuff to back it up, her family had a lot of debt and owed a lot of people. Eventually, her father died in an *accident* and left her mother with money.

Pushing me and distancing herself from me was her way of coping, I guess.

"Let's go girls." Hearing Zack breaks me from my thoughts.

I smile and run out of my room. He smiles, "Hey, sexy."

He reaches around and grabs my ass. "Hey yourself, vixen."

"Hey, no grab ass while I'm in the room." Jules says.

"You're just jealous, all women want me to grab their ass." Zack and Jules have found a fun, witty relationship with each other over the past few months.

She winks at Zack. "You wish, hot stuff, but you're a little pasty for my taste. I've got a hot Cubano on the burner right now. You white boys don't have the rhythm the Latin Lovers do."

He barks out a laugh. "Whatever, I hear no complaints from my little vixen."

She laughs, "The girl was practically a nun six months ago and you brought out her inner vixen. I have to say, I'm one proud mama bear."

Shaking our heads, we leave to go to graduation. I'm meeting my parents at the auditorium. Zack grabs my hand and leads me out to his truck.

I don't think today could get any better.

~*~*~

Zack

Watching my girl walk across the stage, I'm so damn proud. My dad came down with me, she didn't know that. He's staying at the same hotel as her parents.

After the ceremony is over, we are headed to the restaurant her dad has reservations at. Her dad and mine know my plan. Her mom, well, I left that up to her dad. Lenora and Holli are still working on their relationship, well actually Lenora is working on her relationship with everyone.

Once we are parked and inside, we spend our time eating and talking. When dessert comes, I stand up and take Holli's hand.

"Holli Brown, I don't know what you see in me. Whatever it is, I'm glad you do. I want to tell you what I see in you, though. You are the most wonderful, sweet, caring, intelligent, sexy woman I know. I might not have wanted to fight for you when we were younger, but I want you to know I'll always fight for you now. Will you do me the honor of being my wife?"

She jumps up from her chair and screams, "Yes!"

The people in the restaurant cheer. My father hugs us both, then her parents hug us both. I actually didn't even catch frost bite from her mother.

A little later, we are back at her condo for the last night she'll ever be there. As soon as we walk in the door, she starts a slow strip tease.

Once she's down to her panties, bra and heels, she pushes me into a chair. In a sultry seductive voice, she speaks as she straddles me. "So, would you want to know what I like about you?"

I nod as I feel my dick hardening.

"You are very kind and caring. You show me more love than I could ever imagine. You brought me out of my shell so I could live life. You treat me like a lady in public and a freak in the bedroom. I love that I never get tired of screaming your name when I come. You brought out my inner sex goddess. You help me be brave, you help me see who I am. For all of those things and more that I've forgotten to mention, I love you." She whispers, "I love you," in my ear as she nips at it.

I can't control it, I stand up from the chair and take her to the bedroom, tearing off her bra and panties. She rips my dress shirt open and I hear buttons hitting all over the room. I kick my dress shoes off as she undoes my belt, shoving my pants down. I quickly sink my cock into her wet pussy. “Fuck baby, you are so warm and tight.”

“Oh Zack. I love it when you fuck my tight pussy. Fuck me harder.”

That does it, I pound away into her tight core. “I love it when you talk like a filthy vixen to me.” Soon we are both screaming and rambling incoherent words.

Once we finish, I lie in bed holding her. “I’m so glad you said yes to me.”

“Yep, that would have been pretty embarrassing if I’d said no, wouldn’t it?”

I roll over, tickling her sides. “You wouldn’t have said no to me. You like my dick too much.”

I start hardening. She giggles, “Again, already?”

“Forever.” I say as I slip back into her.

She looks up at me. “Forever.”

Camellia In Bloom

A Richter's Crossing Seasons of Change Novella

By: S.M. Donaldson

For anyone who needed a do-over in life.

Camellia In Bloom

A Richter's Crossing Seasons of Change Novella

Cover by SM Donaldson

Images from shutterstock.com

Editing by Chelly Peeler

Introduction

• Due to mature subject matter this book is for readers 17+.
•This book is written in a true southern dialect, from a true southern person. Therefore, it is NOT going to have proper grammar.

Let me start by saying I hope you enjoy this novella. This is the first in a series. Each Novella in this series will center around a season of the year. Also, it will release during the coordinating season. They will all be based in the town of Richter's Crossing, but they will be able to be read in any order.
This is a new adventure for me and I'm excited.

This Spring Novella is shorter than all of the rest. It is somewhat of an introduction and has a preview from each other season. I hope you enjoy.

XOXO
S.M. Donaldson

Camellia

Spring Break Two Years Ago…

Standing on the white sandy beach of Panama City, Florida behind Spinnaker, I have to laugh at the way some of these people are acting. Dumb girls acting like they're practicing for work at the strip club, guys looking like they're just dying to give them dollar bills or an STD.

My freshly dyed bright red hair is pulled up in a ball cap to shield my face a little from the sun. Shaking my head, I think about how in the world I let Nikki and her roommates talk me into coming down here. I have no idea. I hear the announcer and it reminds me why she did to talk me into it.

Are you guys ready for Luke Bryan?! Well, let's hear some noise!

The drums start thumping. Luke steps out in front of us. *We have a special guest with us for a couple of songs. Everyone put your hands together for COLT FORD! Let's do a little "Dirt Road Anthem!"*

Yeah I'm chillin' on a dirt road
Laid back swervin' like I'm George Jones
Smoke rollin' out the window
An ice cold beer sittin' in the console
Memory lane up in the headlights

I sway to the music on the outskirts of the crowd.

"You look a little lost," I hear in a slow southern drawl.

I spin around to see a guy with bleach blonde hair, a small fraternity tattoo on the left side of his lightly tanned chest and wearing a pair of bright orange board shorts. I shake my head. "No, not lost. Just waiting for my friends to quit making complete asses out of themselves." I point toward Nikki and her friends desperately trying to get Luke's attention.

"Well, can I at least offer you a beer while you're waiting?" He grins.

“No, thanks. I don’t take drinks from strangers.” I give him a polite smile.

He opens a cooler. “Here, I’ll let you get it out and open it yourself. Not much of a chance I can slip you a roofie or anything that way.”

Finally shrugging, I say, “Okay, thanks.” I take one from the cooler, opening it and taking a sip. I’m not much for beer but it’s hot as hell out here.

“So you don’t seem like the spring break type,” he says with a side grin.

I shake my head. “No, my friend Nikki talked me into coming with her and her roommates. This kind of crowd isn’t really my scene, but she promised Luke Bryan. So here I am.” I hold my palms up, motioning around me.

He nods. “Yeah, my frat brothers kinda dragged me here, too.” I give him a look like he’s full of shit. He puts his hands up. “I know, don’t get me wrong, I appreciate the female form in a bikini, but all the crowd and drama is a little much. I mean seriously, look at that girl over there.” He points to a girl whose bikini is barely hanging on and she’s grinding all over anyone standing next to her. “That just seems, I don’t know, desperate. If I ever found out my sister was acting like that, I’d lock her in her damn bedroom.” He starts mimicking the drunk amateur stripper/porn star in front of us. I can’t help but laugh and drink my beer.

Hanging out with him seems easy so we just hang out and drink beer, cheering through the concert.

Finally, he sticks his hand out. “Hi, my friends call me R.J. I guess after a few hours we should introduce ourselves, right?”

I laugh. “Yeah, I guess so. My friends call me Mellie.”

“Nice to meet you, Mellie, I like that little sweet southern voice you have,” he says with a sideways grin.

I chuckle, almost spilling my beer. “My southern voice? What about that deep southern drawl you have going?”

He steps closer to me. "Well, I'm a real live cowboy, Miss Mellie. That's why I have the drawl."

I step closer to him, challenging him. "Oh, you're a real live cowboy? Well, where's your hat?" I say, licking my lower lip.

"Oh, if I broke out the hat, women around here wouldn't be able to resist me." He dips his head so close to my ear, I can hear the vibration throughout my body. "But trust me, I could tie you up, or you could ride me all night long."

I practically snort beer out of my nose. "Really? Does that line work out in Oklahoma or wherever you're from?"

"Texas, baby. I said I'm a real cowboy. As far as the line, I don't know, I've never tried it." He starts laughing.

"Well, I'm gonna say you shouldn't use that line again. It kinda sounds weird." I put my hands up. "Just puttin' that out there for you."

~*~*~

I hear my phone buzzing. I start digging around in the darkness of a hotel room, stubbing my toe on the foot of a bed. Pulling my shorts and top on, sans swimsuit, I look at the text on my phone.

9:30p.m. NIKKI: Where the fuck are you?

10:30p.m. NIKKI: You are seriously scaring the crap out of me. Where are you?

11:45p.m. NIKKI: I'm freaking out here. You need to call me.

12:15p.m. NIKKI: CALL ME NOW! OR I'M CALLING THE POLICE. WE'RE BUSTED ANYWAY MY MOM CALLED AN HOUR AGO OUR PARENTS KNOW.

ME: I'm on my way. I'll explain when I get there. I'm in the same hotel.

Once I get up to my room, bikini in hand, my traveling partners look at me and die laughing. Nikki falls on the bed. "Holy shit. Mellie, I can't believe you went all slut girl on us!" She's trying to catch her breath. "I'm serious. I'm glad you broke out of the shell, I just really wasn't expecting it. So we're leaving or our parents are sending your brother and his friends after us. You can fill us in on the details on the way home."

Once we're in the car, they hit me with questions. "What's his name?"

"R.J."

"That's it? That's all you got?"

"Yep. We hung out all day drinking together through the concert and people watching. It just happened."

"Holy shit. Please tell me you used a condom?"

I shake my head, rolling my eyes. "Yes. We did."

"So are you going to call him?"

"Nope. Didn't get a phone number."

"What did he look like?"

I start to describe him and one of them stop me. "You didn't take a pic with your phone?"

I shake my head. "No. Now enough questions, I'm going to sleep. I have to deal with Drucilla and my dad when I wake up."

River

Two Years Ago…

Rolling over, I throw my arm over a body. A hard body. I open my eyes to see my buddy, Frank. "What in the fuck are you doing in my bed?"

He grunts. "I'm sleeping, fucker, or I was trying to. We didn't fucking get in until three this morning. Your ass must've slept all fucking night."

I sit up. "Where is Mellie?"

He opens one eye. "Mellie? Who the fuck is that?"

"The girl I hung out with yesterday. We hooked up last night and then passed out, I guess."

He closes his eye back. "No one was in here but you when we came in. She must've woken up and did the damn walk of shame. You got her number?"

I cover my face with both hands. "Fuck no. I was gonna get it later."

"You take a picture with your phone? We could look for her today."

I shake my head. "Fuck no."

"Did you make her up and stay in here jacking off all night to Porn Hub? I'll totally understand if you did."

"Fuck you. No, I didn't make her up." I sit up and see her little pink ball cap. "See, this is her hat."

He waves me off with his hand. "Sure, man. Whatever. We'll look for your mystery girl later, I'm sleeping right now. We only have one more day here, let's enjoy it. Well, later, after I'm a little more sober."

I flop back on the bed. *Fuck!*

All I can think about are her amazing tits and that lil' flower tat she has on her ankle. She also has a small infinity freedom tattoo on her lower hip. Really sexy…and I'll probably never see it again.

Camellia

It's spring time once again in North Georgia. Since it's not quite spring break yet, this means all of my friends are hanging out at the lake having cookouts and bonfires. I'm working the Inn, like I do pretty much every. Single. Night. Here it is, another Saturday night and it's just me, a frozen pizza and my latest steamy romance. Don't get me wrong, the Inn is nice and quiet. I get a lot of studying done while I'm working. I read and sometimes it's like I have a great big house all to myself. It's just the fact that staying in Richter's Crossing for the rest of my life isn't really in my plans. Honestly, I don't know what my plans are.

My parents keep telling me that this will all be mine to run one day. I don't want it though, or do I? I just don't have clue. They never have really given me the opportunity to decide for myself. The only person who can halfway understand is my big brother, Jake. My parents are great people and I hate to sound like a spoiled ungrateful brat, but I need some space. They set expectations for Jake and me both. Jake didn't follow those, so it's up to me to make them happy.

How can I make them happy if I'm not making myself happy?

Hearing the door chime brings me out of my pity party. I walk out of the kitchen, making my way to the front desk. "Hello. Can I help you?"

A guy who looks to be about my age turns around and my breath catches. He's every bit of six foot eight, dark hair and eyes. He's wearing a cowboy hat and a short sleeved, snap button shirt. You can tell he works outside a lot. He nods in my direction, glancing down at my chest and back up. "Yes. Do you have any rooms available?" There is something familiar about him. I've met him somewhere before.

"You're in luck, we happen to have a few." Oh my God, I totally suck at flirting. Maybe I would be better at it if I did it more often. Hell, maybe I'd be better at it if there was someone in this godforsaken hell hole that was worth flirting with.

"Ma'am?" he says, trying to get my attention.

I shake loose from my thoughts. "Oh, I'm sorry. So you need a room?" Yes, I'm stinking this up like a freakin' skunk.

"Yes, ma'am, just for a couple of nights." That draw in his voice is sexy.

I grin. "Sure." I push the registration card across the desk. "Can you just fill this out?"

"Yes, ma'am." He starts writing and I glance over. *Hmm. Texas. Damn, I guess everything is bigger in Texas.*

He hands me the registration card and I look down at it. "So, River Sewel, what brings you to our little hole in the wall all the way from Texas?" *River Sewel...not ringing any bells. Maybe he just has one of those faces. One of those absolutely smoking hot faces.*

He shrugs, "Just a little road trip."

I pass him his key. "Well, here is your key. You are just down the hall in room 3. Breakfast is served in the dining room from 6 to 9 in the morning. Supper was finished a few hours ago, but I can warm you something up if you'd like."

He gives me a one sided grin. "Naw, I'm good. I ate a little bit ago." He turns to walk down the hall, but stops. "So, what do people do for fun in this town?"

I shake my head. "Some go to a little bar in town called the Tavern Inn." I shrug. "I'm pretty much here most of the time."

He tips his hat up a little. "Your guy doesn't mind you working out here all alone? All the time?"

I shake my head slightly. "No guy."

He gives me that one sided grin again, making my panties grow wet. Shaking his head, he turns to walk down the hallway. "Damn shame." He stops again. "So you know my name, what's yours?"

I smile. "Camellia. Camellia Callahan."

He nods. "Nice," and then turns away again.

After he continues to his room, I sit down and sigh. Of course the hottest guy I run into lives over 15 hours away from me. I pull back out my e-reader and go back to reading about people who have a way better romance life than mine.

My cell phone ringing brings me away from my fantasy again. It's my mom, crap, I really don't feel like talking to her. All she cares about is this damn Inn. I understand that it's her legacy, but I don't really know if I want it to be mine.

"Hey, Mom."

"Hey, honey. How are things going tonight?"

"Fine," I reply.

"Oh, well did we have any more people check in?"

"Yeah. One," I say kind of shorter than I mean to.

"Okay." I hear her sigh. "Is everything all right?"

"Yeah, it's fine. Just another night here at the Inn."

"Honey, are you sure everything is okay? You've been so distant lately."

"Yes, I'm fine. Look, one of the guests just came up to the desk, I'll talk to you later."

"Okay."

I hang up, feeling a little guilty about lying to get off the phone with her. I just can't sit here and talk about life. The fact that mine is as stagnant as a holding pond in the process of a draught makes me a little depressed.

River

Waking up to the smell of bacon frying makes me think of home. I do miss home and my mom calls me every day to ask when I'm coming back. The truth is I don't know.

I think I just need some time. My father doesn't think I do, but I do.

Walking out to the dining room, I see the sexy little temptress from the front desk last night. Something about being in the same room with that girl makes my dick go crazy. She's talking with an older lady that I can tell is related to her. I grab a plate and start fixing it when the older lady makes her way over to me. "Hello, I'm Drucilla Callahan. Welcome to Twin Oaks. I hope you had a pleasant stay last night. You met my daughter, Camellia, last night when you checked in."

I nod and shake her hand. "River Sewell, a pleasure to meet you. Yes, ma'am, I did. It was great waking up to the smell of bacon frying. That's not something you get in just any ole' hotel."

I take a seat and just like a mother, she sits across from me. "You're right. That's the reason I love this old Inn. I feel like I can get to know our guests better. So how long are you in town for?"

"I'm not sure. I'm just taking some time."

"My daughter said you're from Texas. What do you do out there?"

I take a sip of my coffee. "Well, I mostly work on a ranch. I'm just taking some time off to figure some things out before school starts back up in the fall."

She nods. "School is important. What kind of ranch did you work on?"

"We had a few thousand head of cattle. We also dealt in some horses and hogs," I say as I bite into my toast.

She sits there and I can see wheels turning in her head. "Hmm. Well, it was nice meeting you. I guess I better get to work. I just like stopping by to meet each of our guests."

"Thank you, ma'am."

She stands back up and touches my shoulder, tilting her head a little, "Oh, please call me Dru."

I stand partially up and nod my head. "It was nice meeting you, Dru."

"You too, sweetheart."

She walks through the dining room greeting people and smiling. Her daughter leaves as soon as she makes her way back to the front desk.

After finishing breakfast, I make my way out to the grounds. This is really a beautiful place. There is still a light crispness to the air here in the spring. Mrs. Callahan seems like she really loves this place. You can see she's put her touches all around - the flower beds, the small herb garden and a fence line that runs down the drive.

Walking around the corner of the house, I see her. Camera in hand, she's taking pictures of everything she sees. I saunter over to her and lean down to her shoulder. "Nice camera."

She jumps and almost drops it. I grab the camera as she yelps, "Shit."

I steady my hands on her. "Sorry, I didn't mean to startle you. I just noticed you taking the pictures."

She backs away a little. "It's okay. I didn't mean to yell at you."

I motion to the camera. "So do you take pictures professionally along with working at the Inn?"

She gives me a sarcastic laugh and shakes her head. "No, I just go to school and run the Inn, *my legacy.*"

"Legacy, huh?"

She starts to walk further away from the Inn. "Yep. It's what I'm destined to do." I hear more of the sarcasm. I can pick up on it because I sound that way about my dad's oil company.

I nod. "I understand."

She stops and turns to look at me, "Oh, really?" she blurts out with a snarky tone in her voice.

I nod. "Yeah, princess. I may look like a simple farm boy, but my family thinks they have my destiny and legacies planned out, too."

She shakes her head and turns to walk away. "Whatever."

I catch up to her. "Are you running the place tonight?"

"Yes. I run it pretty much every night. I get a night off here or there when either my parents decide to stay or my brother stays. He's got some heavy classes this semester so that doesn't happen often."

I shrug. "Damn, I was going to see if you could show me some of the sights."

She kicks her foot around. "There's not much to see here."

I give her a one sided grin and look her up and down. "Oh, I beg to differ."

She laughs and turns to walk away, but stops. "Look, I think you're the only guest on the books tonight. If no one else shows up by seven, I'll go show you around town."

I nod. "Deal."

With that she turns, walking away and I watch her ass as she goes, her long brunette hair swishing as she does. As I walk back in the foyer of the Inn, I see a small posting on the bulletin board I'm sure I didn't see yesterday.

Farm hand needed for temporary work, inquire at the front desk.

I walk to the front desk. "Ms. Dru, I saw the posting over there about a farm hand?"

She gives me a soft smile. "Yes. Our full time hand has to have some surgery. He'll need to be off for about three to four weeks. We just need someone experienced to help out with the cows and horses. It comes with a room in the barn. It's not much, but it's private." She shrugs. "You seemed to have a little experience a little bit ago, but I figured you were headed back to Texas."

"I was just on a road trip, but maybe staying somewhere for a few weeks and making a little money would be good."

"All right then. I'll write the address down and you can come out to the farm first thing tomorrow morning. I'll introduce you to my husband and son then."

I take the piece of paper she scribbles on and nod. "Thank you, ma'am."

Camellia

What is it about that guy? He gets under my skin. Trying to shake it loose, I continue my walk around, snapping pictures of the landscape. Then I see him leaning over the rail fence staring off into the distance. I snap a few shots of him. I can't help it, he looks so at peace, like it's where he belongs. My thoughts are interrupted when I hear a truck coming down the two trail drive leading to the Inn. Looking down the drive, I see my brother's truck. I jog over to where he's parking.

He steps out of the truck looking exhausted. "Hey, Jake-off, what's got you looking so glum?"

He shakes his head. "I'm just tired. Classes are kicking my ass. I had to ask Dad to cut my hours a little at the office."

"Damn, and here I was going to ask you to cover for me." I shove at his chest softly.

"I know, little sister, but I just can't right now. You do need to get out of here though."

I blow out a long breath. "Yeah, tell me about it."

He leans back against his truck, crossing his ankles. "So, you still haven't talked to them?"

I shrug, "Why would I? It's not like I have any other plans right now."

He sighs. "If you could be anything you want to be, could do anything you want to do, what would it be?"

I kick the dirt around at my feet. "Well, I've always liked taking pictures, but I do like being here sometimes, as well as traveling."

He laughs. “Well, that is a mouthful. Have you thought about photo journalism or something?”

“Maybe. I don’t know. I just don’t want to piss them off.”

“Trust me, it’ll be easier the earlier you do it,” he says, pushing off the truck and walking toward the Inn.

I think about hanging out with River tonight and decide it’s a good idea. I mean my friend, Nikki, always says I need to keep the cobwebs cleaned out and he’d be the perfect guy, he’s leaving in a couple of days.

~*~*~

Later, I grab the basket I’ve packed with our supper. Since no one else came in, we decided to take our supper to go tonight. Kind of our take on a picnic.

He holds the front screen door open for me. “You ready?”

I nod, “Sure.”

Once he backs out of his parking spot, he looks over at me. “So where to?”

“Well, first we’ll go down by the Old Mill. They have a cool little water fall, we can eat our supper there. Then we’ll head over to one of the local field parties for a bit. I can’t stay out late though, I have to be back at a decent hour. I’m not supposed to leave the Inn.”

He grins. “Sure thing.”

Once we make our way down beside the river to the Old Mill, he parks. “Wow, this is pretty.”

As we sit on his tailgate, I separate our food. “Yeah. I love it out here. I take a lot of pictures of this place.”

He sits back in the bed of the truck a little. “So, what’s your story?”

I shrug as I hand him a sub. "Not much. I go to college here at State. I work at the Inn, so that takes up most of my nights. Pretty much sums it up. What about you?"

He takes a sip of his sweet tea. "Well, I'm from Texas. I went, or I go to school out there. My father wants me to go into one side of the family business when I graduate, but I'd much rather go into the other side. Running our ranch. We had a difference of opinion big time, so I left to clear my head for a little bit."

I nod, chewing my food and swallowing. "Sounds like we have a little in common."

He sticks a chip in his mouth. "So have you ever just left and went crazy for a little bit?"

I chuckle thinking about it. "Yeah. Once."

He shakes his head. "Funny."

I hear a song coming on the radio that I like. "Can you turn it up? I like this song."

He laughs and jumps off the tailgate. After he turns it up a little more, he comes back. "What is it with girls and Luke Bryan?"

I laugh. "I just like him. I don't know why. He's just seems sweet and fun. Plus, this song just brings back memories for me."

"So what? You've had a night that you didn't want to end before?"

I nod and smile. "Yep. It was actually the first time I saw him in concert."

"I've been to a couple of his concerts. They were a lot of fun and I guess I actually had one like that, too. So do you only like country music?" he asks.

"No, I kinda like all music. No boy band stuff though. My favorite is classic rock and old school country." I grin.

"When you say old school country, what exactly are you calling 'old school'?"

I smile. "Good old belly rubbing music. Alabama, Conway, George, Strait and Jones, Charlie Rich, Waylon, Willie, Hank Jr. and Merle." I shrug. "Good stuff."

He grins. "Hang on just a minute." He jumps down and runs to the cab, messing with the radio. He comes back grinning and takes my hand to pull me down. "I think you'll like this."

Some old Alabama comes through the speakers. I step into him and we start moving slowly together. Pretty soon, his head dips in and he takes my lips with his.

He quickly puts his hands around the backs of my thighs and lifts me back on to the tailgate, running his hands down to my ankle. I reach and unsnap his shirt. In the moonlight, I catch a glimpse of something. "Wait." There is something about him, something about his kiss. It's familiar.

He pulls back and I see the tattoo on his chest.

River

Why is she stopping? What freaked her out? "What's wrong? Did I misread or are we moving too quickly?"

She looks scared. "Um, I'm going to show you something."

She starts to pull her waist band down. Hey, this is going right where I wanted. Until she stops. "Do you have a flashlight?"

I nod and grab it out of the cab of the truck. Shining it on her, she pulls the waist down a little further. *That tattoo.* I look up at her, lost. "Mellie?"

She nods and readjusts her clothing. "Um. I think we should go."

I grab her upper arm. "Why? What's wrong?"

"I just…this is…this is all weird. Can you please take me home?"

I nod. "Okay." We gather everything up and climb in the truck. Once we're on our way back to the Inn, I look over at her. "Can you answer me one thing?"

"Yeah," she says softly.

"Where did you go?" I sigh. "I woke up the next morning panicking and I didn't have a number for you."

"We weren't supposed to be there. We were supposed to be camping, our parents found out and since we were only college freshmen, we hightailed our asses back home." She shrugs. "Sorry, didn't mean to make you worry."

"I can't believe this. You look so different." I motion down to her long flowy skirt and boots. "You dress so different, so conservative."

She laughs. "I had on a bikini, with shorts and a tank top." She rolls her shoulders. "I dyed my hair bright red for spring break, last minute crazy idea. Plus, you had blonde hair back then."

I nod my head and groan thinking about it. "Yeah, life of the frat. You do stupid shit, including planning to get a girl's number the next morning."

Once we pull into the Inn parking lot, she looks over. "I'm sorry. This is crazy. I can't believe of all people, it's you. I mean, I've thought about you over the years."

I smile. "Yeah, me, too. The guys swore I made you up or something, just to get out of club hopping."

"Well, since you're one of the craziest things I ever did in my life, my friends were thinking about having me committed." She shakes her head, laughing.

As we walk up to the porch, I grab her hand. "So the night you didn't want to end was that night, I'm guessing."

"Yes. It was. Then my phone woke me up and my friends were screaming that we were busted and in trouble." She shrugs. "It kinda burst the bubble. You know?"

I stop her, pulling her close and talking in her ear. "So let's not let *this* night end. Let's make up for that night a couple of years ago."

She smiles and steps back. "I suppose you're leaving town day after tomorrow, so what could a little fun hurt?"

I can't tell her I'm not leaving town for a bit, she'll freak out.

She unlocks the door and I grab her up, stumbling into the Inn. She stops me, reaching behind me to lock the door, then she leads me to her room.

She shoves me on the bed and I roll her over on her back. "I've been thinking about that little tattoo you showed me for two years now." I pull her skirt and panties down. I lean down and kiss that little infinity tattoo. "Ah, no landing strip now. All bare." I lean down and run my tongue through her soaking wet slit. Sliding my hands up her top and tugging it off, she stops me to shed her bra. I see those amazing tits again. "Damn, girl, your body has haunted my dreams and been my favorite fantasy."

Standing up, I quickly shed my clothes, grabbing a condom from my wallet. "You ready for this, baby? We're both sober this time."

"Yes," she pants out. "Fuck me."

Sliding into her feels like home. Sure, I've been with a few girls since her, but no one compares.

Camellia

I spent a day and a half basking in the glow of River. Dear sweet baby Jesus, that man knows how to deliver. He was gone when I woke up yesterday morning. I guess he took a page from my book. It's different this time though. I have his contact information, but I don't think I should use it. It's best to leave the past in the past and move on.

My brother is right. I need to make a plan for myself before I try to tell my parents I don't want this Inn.

My mom steps in my room. "Honey, why don't you do something fun today? You're always out here. Your dad is in Birmingham at a medical conference for a few days, I can handle the Inn. You need to get out. Go do something. I'll stay here tonight, you stay at your apartment or maybe at the farm."

Mom doesn't know, actually no one knows, that I turned over my apartment to Nikki a few months ago. There wasn't really a point to me having it. *I'm always here.* I didn't want to give it up. It was a small space, but it was mine. What's the point though, right? I'm at the Inn, I'll always be at the Inn. *It's my legacy!*

Maybe I'll hit up the Tavern tonight. A few drinks should get me out of my funk, maybe some fun karaoke. At the very least I can make fun of a few others. Some guy singing David Allan Coe or some old lady singing Loretta Lynn. Deciding it's a great idea, I grab my bag and throw some clothes in it. I'll go to my old apartment and get ready. Nikki will be up for going out, she's always up for going out.

A few hours later, Nikki and I are looking in the mirror and finishing our make-up.

Well, I'm finishing up and she's staring at me. "So let me get this straight. The guy from the beach two years ago shows up and neither of you recognize each other until you're about to get freaky, then you have a couple of days of great sex and he just leaves?"

"Pretty much. In our defense, we both had a different hair color back then, we both looked a little different and we were both intoxicated." I hold up my eyeliner pencil, pointing it in the air. "However, the sex didn't change, it only got better. Now my snatch is cleaned out and I want more. Thanks for your friendly advice, Nikki."

"Hell, I didn't tell you to sleep with that guy!"

"No, but you're always telling me to just have something casual, keep the cobwebs cleaned out." I toss my make-up back in my case.

"Yeah, but I would've never said that guy. Your emotions were all over the place after that." She fluffs her hair and then shakes her head a little. "You know what? Forget it. It's done, it's over. Let's go get drunk and make an ass out of ourselves at karaoke."

My old apartment is just down the street from the Tavern so we're in walking distance.

I've been going to this little bar since before we were old enough to drink. Our parents never minded. I guess they thought if we were going to be out misbehaving, at least here the owner would call someone if we got stupid. Most of the time we always came just to have fun, but tonight warranted a few drinks.

Once we're inside, we make our way to the table near the corner that my brother and his friends always sit at, and I see that bitch Claire, the town slut, is here and already in rare form. She likes to remember that she was a cheerleader in high school and can't seem to get past it. She was popular and easy, and my brother and his friends were stupid enough to hook up with her at one point or another. She was evil and she spread lies about any girls that seemed to show an interest in the guys. For some reason she thinks this is still high school. She walks over to the table before I can even take a sip of my Jack and Coke.

"So it's the little sister. Is that brother of yours coming tonight? He would be if he was with me."

Nikki makes a gagging noise and I look at Claire like she's disgusting. "Not that it's any of your business, but Jake is busy studying and even if he did 'come' tonight, as you say, it wouldn't be with you."

She rolls her eyes. "Oh, please. He's been there already."

I stand up, I'm not in the mood for her tonight. "Once. Let me spell this out for you. In H-I-G-H-S-C-H-O-O-L. You're kind of a disgusting regret among his friends."

Nikki slams her shot. "Didn't you get a cease and desist order from the health department?"

"Did you know that Weight Watchers works?" she sneers at Nikki.

That's it, I've had enough. Nikki was always super skinny until a year ago. She found out she has a thyroid condition, so her weight has fluctuated and changed a lot over the past year. It's been hard for her and I'm not going to put up with this bitch putting her down.

I bolt up out of my chair. "You need to get the fuck away from us."

"Really, little sister? What are you going to do? Threaten me some more?"

I put my finger on the tip of her nose. "No, I'm gonna promise to knock your fucking teeth down your throat!"

Suddenly, I'm being pulled away. Familiar arms are wrapped around me. His smell. What is he doing here? I look in front of me to see my brother's friend, Zack, and over my shoulder to see River.

I wriggle out of his grip and storm over to the bartender, Tuck. "I need another drink and you need to keep her ass on a leash if you're going to let her in here."

Tuck chuckles, filling my order and I storm back over to where River and Nikki are.

I stop in front of him. “What are you doing here? You left.”

His shifts around and stuffs his hands in his pockets. “Funny thing about that, I’m working for your parents for a couple of weeks on their farm.”

Nikki’s watching back and forth between us like a ping pong match. “Why didn’t you tell me?”

He grimaces. “Well, I kinda thought I’d surprise you.” He motions to the table he was sitting at with some of my parents’ farm hands. “The guys wanted to take me out tonight. I was going to swing by and surprise you tomorrow. Didn’t know I’d have to tame a hellcat in you tonight.”

Nikki stands up. “So, I’m taking it you’re River?”

“Yes. Are you Nikki?”

She shakes his hand. “Yes, nice to finally meet the man responsible.”

“Responsible for what?” He looks confused.

I jump in front of Nikki. “Shut up, Nikki. We are NOT talking about this tonight. I’m drinking.”

River

Responsible. What in the hell was I responsible for? I just need to shake it off.

"Let's get some more drinks. I'm gonna go hang out with the guys, you ladies have a good girl's night." I kiss Mellie on the head. "I'll talk to you tomorrow. We'll sort all of this out later."

Two hours later, she's trashed. She's up there singing "Goodbye Earl."

Once she and Nikki finish, they stumble from the stage. Josh, one of the guys from the farm, looks over to me. "Man, we should make sure they make it home. I know Camellia's apartment, well Nikki's apartment now, is close by."

"I thought Dru said Mellie's apartment was here in town?" I look at him confused.

He sighs and scratches his head. "Look, Mellie doesn't know I know that she gave it up to Nikki. She doesn't want her parents to know. She just felt like it was a waste to have her own apartment since she never got to be there. I'm sure she's staying there tonight though." He looks pained.

"Wait, are you and Nikki?"

He shrugs his shoulder. "Yes and no. She doesn't think I should be in a relationship with her."

"Why? She seems like a fun, great girl. She's loyal, I can tell you that much. I thought she was gonna kick my ass a little bit ago."

"Nikki found out about a year ago that she has a thyroid problem. She used to be super skinny, so she's kind of having some kind of identity crisis or something. She thinks there's no way I want more from her than sex, since she thinks she's a cow. I think her curves look sexy as hell.

Actually, I wasn't interested in her until she put a little weight on. So what's the story with you and Doc's daughter?"

"We actually met a couple of years ago in Panama City Beach at spring break. This is completely random that I ended up here. We didn't put it together until a couple of nights ago." I shrug.

"Oh, so you're the boy from the infamous Spring Break. Those girls got in so much damn trouble."

Josh and I make conversation until we see the girls getting up to leave, well, more like trying to get up.

We walk over and Josh takes Nikki's hand. "Come on, feisty girl, we'll get you back to the apartment."

Nikki starts saying something in his ear. His eyes get big. As I get Mellie pulled into my arms, she starts running her hands over my abs. "Babe, you gotta stop that."

"Just take me back to the farm. Nikki looks like she needs servicing and Josh looks like his eyes are gonna blow out of his head."

Josh gives me that pleading look as Nikki practically starts rubbing his crotch in front of us.

I nod. "Okay. Yeah, come on, I have my truck. Josh, can you bring her jeep to the farm tomorrow?"

He nods and asks about the keys. Nikki tells him they're at her apartment.

Once we are back at the farm and standing beside the truck, she looks at me. "So why did you decide to stay?"

"I actually decided to stay the first morning. Your mom had a post-up on the board about needing a temporary farm hand while one of theirs was out for surgery. I figured I could do that for a couple of weeks and make a little cash before I headed home. At that time, I didn't know," I motion between us, "about us."

She lets out a huge breath. "I just wish you'd have told me afterward. You know?'

I nod. "Yeah, I'm sorry. I really did want to surprise you. I mean we've had a great time, and I'm not just talking about the sex either."

"Yeah, so which room are you staying in?"

"The small one in the barn loft."

She winks. "Well, let's go."

Once we're inside, she makes quick work of my shirt and pants, dropping to her knees in front of me and taking me into her mouth. Minutes later, I'm pulling her up and ridding her of her clothes. Picking her up, I slam into her and against the wall. She lets out a moan and I slam into her harder.

She belts out, "Fuck!"

By the time morning breaks, we've had sex in every part of this loft.

Rolling over to face her, she's beautiful. Her eyes pop open. "Why are you staring at me?"

I laugh. "You're doing the same. Can you tell me something?"

"I can try," she says nervously.

"Why was Nikki ready to kick my ass last night?"

She lets out a deep breath. "This is weird since I never thought I'd see you again. What you didn't know was that the night at the beach was my first time. I was never as carefree as my friend, so you were my one wild night. When we got back home, we got into major trouble. A few weeks later, I discovered I was pregnant." To say those words stun me is a little less than accurate. She puts her hands up. “It didn’t happen, I had a miscarriage. I know we used condoms, but I guess one of them failed. I don’t want to try to figure it out now, I just had a difficult time through all of it. Especially since I had to go out of town to be treated. My parents were still pissed enough about the trip to Spring Break, there was no way I was telling them I got knocked up. Nikki kind of took care of me for a few weeks, I went through a little depression. That’s when I pretty much started taking care of the Inn all the time and my mom decided it was my future.”

I pull her into my chest. “How did I not know it was your first time? Damn, I’m sorry you went through all of that without me.”

She pulls away. “We were both kinda drunk and it’s not like I was advertising it. As far as the other, I didn’t even get your phone number before I ran out of your room, so it’s not like I could really hold you responsible. So I’ve told you something. Well, a lot of somethings. How about you tell me something? Why are you running away from home?”

Camellia

He lets out a huge breath. “Well, kinda the same as yours. My family is wealthy. Like stupid wealthy. They own an oil company and a ranch. While I love working on the ranch with animals, my father wants me to get ready to take over Sewel Industries, because it’s my legacy.” He gives me a weird chuckle. “You get that one, right? Well, my sister is the one who loves it, I would rather work with my hands. My dad wants to give her some dumb office job and put me in charge. She’d be so much better than me.”

“Wow, it’s the same all over, I guess.” I look at the time. “Shit, I better get out of here before my brother shows up out here. Josh would cover for us, but he can’t for long.”

I get up and snatch my clothes on. “I’m gonna go in the house to shower and change. I need to get to the Inn.”

Making my way across the yard, I see my brother in the distance. I duck into my parents’ house and get ready.

A little while later, I pull up at the Inn. My mom is sitting in the dining room. I grab a plate, filling it up and sit down. She smiles, “How was your night?

I nod. “Fun,” I say, taking a bite of toast.

“You know, I got a great look at your photos last night. You’re very talented. I didn’t realize how much you’ve gotten into it. Have you thought about doing it for a living?”

I snort. “What, taking family photos for the townspeople while I work at the Inn? Have a little studio out of the back of the Inn?”

She looks like I’ve slapped her. “Sweetheart, what is wrong? Why do you say it like I’m punishing you?”

I stand up quickly. "Because, Mom, as you guys keep telling me and showing me," I throw my hands in the air and wave them around. "This. This is my legacy. I will stay out here all the time, have no sort of social life and snap scenic pictures when I get the chance. I finally gave up on having my own apartment, I turned it over to Nikki a few months ago. Months, Mom. I haven't left this Inn in months and no one even noticed." I slam the side of my fist into the door facing. "I go to school getting a degree in business. A degree I hate. I shop for the Inn. I come home to the Inn and stay here pretty much all alone, because we don't have that many guests. You're busy at the farm, Dad is busy at his practice and Jake is busting his ass in school to make up for some shit he shouldn't have to. You're here during the day and I'm here at night. Nikki comes to visit me and keeps me updated on the events happening around town while I sit here and become the damn crazy cat lady without fucking cats. That is my life, I'm trapped. Sorry, it does kind of feel like a punishment." I storm out of the dining room, down the hall to my room and slam the door.

A little while later, my mom knocks on the door. "Honey, can I please come in?"

I wipe the tears from my face. "Sure."

She sits down on the bed with me. "What do you want out of life? Just tell me."

I blow out a large breath. "Honestly, I don't know. I've never really been able to have my own ideas."

"What makes you happy?'

"Taking pictures. Traveling. Seeing new and exciting places. I do love the Inn, but I hate being here all the time."

"Sweetheart, I never meant to make you feel trapped here. You should've told me sooner, I would've understood. Both of you kids feel like you can only do the things we want you to do."

I shrug. "You guys were such great parents. It's what would make you happy."

She pulls me to her chest. "No, what makes us happy is for you to be who you wanna be. Yes, we'd love for you guys to follow in our footsteps, but if that's not what you want then don't do it."

She laughs. "You know one of the best moments I've had being your parent?"

"When?"

"The time you snuck off to spring break. I actually got to be a parent to you. Your brother at least gave us the opportunity to do a little parenting, but you never gave us the chance." She crosses her legs. "You came home and we actually got to ground you. That was a monumental occasion."

"I met River that trip."

"Huh?" My mom is confused.

"We met and um, well, we kind of hooked up." I duck my head. "I had to run out on him when we got busted. We both looked different then, but we figured it out the other night."

She sits back and rests on her hands. "Wow, and you were brought back together. It's fate."

I bark out a laugh. "You been sneaking peeks at my romance novels, Mom?"

"Well, considering your father and I were just supposed to be each other's booty call, I believe in fate."

I know my eyes must look like a cartoon character's bulging out of my head. "Mom!"

“Look, you kids seem to think your dad and I were never young. Never had to make decisions? We did. Your daddy and I knew each other forever, but we never thought of each other like that. That is until he was trying to make a girl jealous and I was mending a broken heart. One drunken night led to two, two led to several. The girl in question decided to come around and then my ex came back into the picture. We went our separate ways and parted on good terms. Until your dad saw him grab me by my throat one night outside of a bar, then everything changed. We were together from then forward. I believe in fate. We were each other’s ‘friend’ before so he could rescue me outside of that bar. That man’s next girlfriend was killed by him. Your father saved me, so yes, I believe in fate.” She grabs my hand. “So what are you going to do now?”

I shrug, “What do you mean?”

“Are you going with him? Look, I saw your face light up that first morning. That’s the reason I put the posting out there. I was so happy to see a genuine smile on your face for the first time in months.”

“Mom!” I flop back on the bed. “I don’t know.”

She lies back beside me. “You’ll figure it out.”

~*~*~

Two weeks seem to fly by. River and I planned to spend more time together getting to know each other but just as soon as he started at the farm, one of the guy’s wives had to be rushed in for an emergency C-section a month early. So it’s lucky Mom did hire him. The farm has been crazy busy with cows giving birth and other things, so our time together has been limited. Now, he’s leaving and I still have no clue what I’m doing. I’ve thought about all of my options. I’ve thought about so many scenarios and ways that things could play out. I know I want my photography and I really want River, but I have to let him go home and decide what he wants for himself.

So now I'm standing at my family's farm. He pulls me into a hug. "I'm gonna miss you. You're going to call me, right? No running this time?"

"No. No running. Yes, I will call you and I'm going to miss you, too. We'll visit though. It seems I'll have a little more time on my hands. My mother is demanding that I get my apartment back and says I can work a couple of nights a week at the Inn, but no more," I say, smiling into his eyes.

We share a long, slow kiss before he gets in his truck and drives away.

Acknowledgements

This is always the hardest part. Well, besides the blurb. I hate the blurb. LOL

Thank You to my readers. Without you I would not be having this awesome adventure. You have helped make my dreams come true and for that I'm truly blessed and grateful.

I need to give a big **Thank You to Chelly Peeler**. She's not only my editor but my friend. She has listened to my craziness for months now. She loves my characters and understands my craziness. Thank you again.

To my husband thank you for standing behind me for all of years and always pushing me in your own way. To my son Bailey, thank you for trying to understand why mom is on her computer so much.

To my Mom for listening to my random story ideas and telling me to go for it. To my sisters' thank you for always supporting me. You guys always have my back. Daddy I miss you every day and I know you're watching over me.

To my BETA readers Candice, Ashley and Jessika thank you. You are awesome.

Thanks to my Blog Tour Queens Casey D. Peeler and Chelly Peeler @ Hardcover Therapy.

Thanks to all of the book bloggers out there who spend so much time helping us promote books and everyone who leaves a review you are all awesome.

To my Author friends thank you for being supportive and inspirational all at the same time.

I mention the song *Backroad* in the book it is by the very talented Georgia boy Corey Smith. I love his music and the way he sings about growing up in the South. Go check him out!

http://www.coreysmith.com

About the Author

Photo by: Shelly Sale

S.M. Donaldson is a born and raised Southern girl. She grew up in a small rural town on Florida's Gulf Coast, the kind of place where everyone knows your business before you do, especially when your Daddy is a cop and your Mom works for the school system. She married one of her best friends at the age of 20 and has one son. She is a proud military wife, has always had a soft spot for a good story, and is known to have a potty mouth. At the age of 31, she decided there was no time like the present to attempt her first book. Sam's Choice was born and she hasn't stopped since. If you are looking for a good, steamy, Southern set romance with true Southern dialect, she's your girl.

My Links:
www.smdonaldson.com
www.facebook.com/s.m.donaldson.author
www.goodreads.com/AuthorSMDonaldson
Twitter: @SMDonaldson1
Instagram: SMDONALDSON1981

Other Titles by S.M. Donaldson

The Sam Series

Sam's Choice
Sam's Fight for Freedom

The Temptation Series

Lying with Temptation
Acting on Temptation
Fighting Temptation

The Secrets of Savannah Series

Secrets Behind Those Eyes
Secrets in The Lyrics
Secrets in Battle

Novellas

Just the Other Sister Series
(E-book only)

Seasons of Change Novella Series

Summer of Forgiveness
Falling for Autumn
Holiday with Holli
Camilla In Bloom

Marco's MMA Boys

Letting Lox In
In sly's Eyes
Holding Huck's Heart (COMING SOON)

Made in the USA
Middletown, DE
08 September 2021

47911281R00152